THE ADVENTURES OF JACK BRENIN

BOOK ONE

THE
GOLDEN
ACORN

D1151483

About the author

Catherine Cooper was a primary school teacher for 29 years before deciding she'd love to write for children. She is the author of five books, including *Glasruhen Gate* and *Silver Hill*, the sequels to *The Golden Acorn*. Catherine's love of history, myths and legends and the Shropshire countryside around where lives shine through her charming stories.

THE ADVENTURES OF JACK BRENIN

BOOK ONE

THE GOLDEN ACORN

CATHERINE COOPER

ILLUSTRATIONS BY
RON COOPER and CATHERINE COOPER

infiniteideas

First published in 2009 by Pengridion Books
This edition 2010
Infinite Ideas Limited
36 St Giles
Oxford
OX1 3LD
United Kingdom
www.infideas.com

Reprinted 2011

LONDON BOROUGH OF WANDSWORTH		
9030 00004 7957 4		
Askews & Holts	19-Nov-2015	
JF	£9.99	
	WW15014781	

ISBN 978–1–906821–65–4

Cover designed by D.R.ink
Text designed and typeset by Chandler Book Design,
www.chandlerbookdesign.co.uk
Printed and bound in India by Gopsons Papers Ltd., Noida

For Ron

for being there

THE MAP
OF
GLASRUHEN VILLAGE

NEWTON GILL FOREST

← TO NEWTON GILL

THE BRENINS' HOUSE

THE BACK LANE

GROVE FARM'S PASTURE

THE PLAYING FIELD

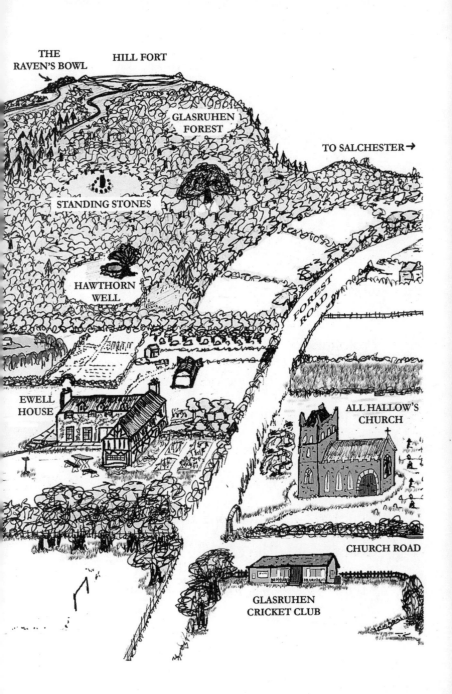

CONTENTS

Prologue	'The One'	1
Chapter 1	The Golden Acorn	5
Chapter 2	Introductions	20
Chapter 3	Glasruhen	36
Chapter 4	Book of Shadows	52
Chapter 5	Questions and Answers	70
Chapter 6	The Gnori	86
Chapter 7	Addergoole Peabody	102

Chapter 8	Camelin's Tale	119
Chapter 9	Preparations	137
Chapter 10	The Raven's Bowl	150
Chapter 11	Flying Lessons	168
Chapter 12	Into The Tunnel	186
Chapter 13	Meetings	205
Chapter 14	Flight	224
Chapter 15	Bad News	240
Chapter 16	The Westwood Roost	256
Chapter 17	The Search	273
Chapter 18	Into The Past	293
Chapter 19	Revelation	312
Chapter 20	Thief	328
Chapter 21	That Which Was Lost	345

A BRENIN BOY YOU NEED TO FIND

The ONE

BORN AT SAMHAIN OF HUMANKIND

PROLOGUE

Nora tapped her wand impatiently on the kitchen table before speaking to Camelin.

'I'm sure I'm right. Jack Brenin is *The One*.'

'He can't be, he's so small and weedy; he's supposed to be strong and brave.'

Nora thought for a while before she spoke again. 'He's a Brenin.'

'Well, there has to be a better Brenin than this one.'

'The prophecy's quite clear and this Brenin was born on the right night, in the right place and at the right time. The trees have been watching him since he arrived, they seem satisfied he's *The One*.'

'The trees could be wrong,' Camelin mumbled in case he was overheard. He knew how fast word could travel from one tree to another. If Arrana, the ancient Hamadryad, heard him he'd be in big trouble. She lived in the oldest oak tree in the heart of Glasruhen Forest and was always *very* well informed.

'I'm sure he'll help us. If he doesn't all will be lost. He's our last hope and we're running out of time.'

'If he's our last hope we're doomed.'

As Nora paced up and down the kitchen, the end of her wand began to splutter; red sparks erupted from the tip.

'We need help. I'm going to write to Elan; she needs to be here.'

As Nora wrote Camelin hung his head. He knew she was right. Time was running out; Arrana was slowly dying. She was the only Hamadryad left on Earth and without her protection the tree spirits of the forest would eventually fade away and only hollow trees would remain. Unless they found someone willing to help them find a way to open the portal into the Otherworld and bring back new Hamadryad acorns, their own time on Earth would end too. As each year passed Arrana grew weaker. It would need a very special person to accept the challenges which lay ahead. Camelin continued to sulk. Jack Brenin had not impressed him.

'He's not the kind of boy who's going to care if the spirit of an ancient oak tree lives or dies.'

'If he passes the test he will.'

There was a long silence. Eventually Nora fished in her pocket and produced a beautiful golden acorn and placed it carefully on the table.

'Put this where the boy will see it, it's the only way to be sure.'

'I bet he kicks it. I was watching him yesterday kicking cans and stones about. What kind of help could he possibly be? The journey we've got to make might be dangerous, too dangerous for the likes of Jack Brenin.'

'Take the acorn. If he sees it and picks it up we'll know he's *The One*.'

Camelin scowled. He picked up the golden acorn and reluctantly left the kitchen to find a good place to hide and watch. He might have a long wait. He wasn't happy: Nora was probably right but Jack Brenin was the furthest thing from a hero he'd ever seen.

THE GOLDEN ACORN

'Oi, Pimple! Leave it!' one of the boys from the middle of the field yelled as Jack went to kick the ball, 'Don't even think about it.'

Jack had been watching them play football for the past half hour. No one had asked him to join in. No one had taken any notice of him, until now. The size of the goalie running towards him should have made him think twice, but it was too late, his foot had already made contact with the ball.

'What you do that for?' snarled the keeper.

'Only trying to help. Any chance of a game?'

'No, clear off, you don't belong here.'

'I live here.'

'Since when?'

'Since yesterday.'

'Well if I see you here again you're gonna wish you didn't.'

As the goalkeeper turned to rejoin the game he pushed Jack hard on the shoulder sending him to the ground. Tears welled up in Jack's eyes; he wished he'd never come to the field. He thumped the grass with his fists. It wasn't fair; he hadn't asked to come and live with Grandad. He didn't know *anyone* here.

Jack watched the boys from where he lay. He knew he ought to go. The game hadn't restarted yet. There was a lot of shouting as everyone ran over to a tall boy who had blood gushing from his nose. Jack began to feel uncomfortable; the boys turned and looked in his direction. Someone pointed, another yelled, *get him*, then they all started yelling. The ball he'd kicked must have hit the tall boy in the face. For a moment Jack froze as they ran towards him. He managed to scramble to his feet and run as fast as he could towards the gate. Hot tears burned his cheeks. Half stumbling, half running he skidded into the back lane behind the field. He wished he'd got his bike but he'd not been able to bring it with him to Grandad's. The boys were gaining on him, their voices growing louder and louder. He didn't want to think about what might happen if they caught him. Jack knew he didn't have enough time to make it back to the safety of Grandad's house. As he rounded the corner he looked for somewhere to hide. In desperation he saw a gap in the hedge. Sometimes being small had its advantages. He flung himself into the undergrowth, wriggled through the long grass and squeezed under the bushes. He hoped they hadn't seen him. He sat very still on the other side of the hedge. His heart pounded so loudly that he was sure they'd be able to hear it.

'He's got to be here somewhere.'

Jack recognised the keeper's voice. The boys began searching the undergrowth. He could hear their footsteps getting closer and closer. They were nearly at the place where Jack had dived through the hedge.

'Do you think he's gone through there?'

Jack made himself as small as he could and held his breath.

'He's mad if he has. No one goes into Nutty Nora's. She'll have him if she finds him in her garden!'

Jack didn't like the sound of Nutty Nora but he wasn't going to leave his hiding place. They were so close now. One of them tried parting the branches but instead of exposing Jack he yelled and jumped back clutching his hands.

'Ow! Now me hands are bleeding as well as me nose; them thorns are lethal.'

'Come on, leave him for Nora. We'll get him another time, let's get on with the game.'

The others started agreeing with the goalkeeper but none of them moved. The tall boy with the bleeding nose and hands was still trying to peer through the leaves.

'If he's got through there he'll be cut up good and proper. Maybe he'll bleed to death.'

'Serve him right too.'

The boys began to laugh and the goalkeeper yelled through the hedge.

'Can you hear me pixie boy? Nutty Nora's going to get you, don't stay in there too long or you might not come out again.'

Jack put his hands over his ears but he could still hear the keeper's voice.

'The old witch turns people into stone.'

Jack held his breath; he didn't dare move. The sooner he could go home the better. The boys walked away and the shouting eventually stopped. Jack strained to listen. He was scrunched up, uncomfortable and frightened. Jack didn't want to meet Nutty Nora but he didn't want to go back into the lane just yet either. He wasn't sure if the boys had really gone. He decided to wait a while, at least until his heart stopped pounding. He looked back at the hedge he'd wriggled under; it was covered in long, sharp thorns. He made a quick check of his hands and legs. There wasn't any blood, only a prickling sensation on his palms. As he scratched them small red spots began to appear; he must have nettled himself.

He looked around cautiously from his hiding place. He was at the bottom of a very large garden. There was an old house in the distance, a bit like Grandad's, but the sun was in his eyes and he couldn't see it too well. A sudden movement gave Jack a fright; someone was coming towards him. He backed further into the undergrowth and held his breath again. He wished his heart would stop pounding. He was desperate to scratch his hands. They wouldn't stop itching but he didn't dare move. Was this Nutty Nora? If he were found he'd be in trouble; he was obviously trespassing. Jack looked around for a means of escape. It was then he noticed the statues, lots of them, more than most people had in their gardens. His knees began to tremble as he remembered the keeper's last words. The tall figure was definitely a woman. She was so close now that he could have reached out and touched the bottom of her long flowing dress. He shut his eyes and hoped she wouldn't see him.

'Come out Jack Brenin; I know you're hiding underneath my blackthorn hedge.'

The woman's voice was stern but she didn't sound annoyed. He wondered how she knew his name. There wasn't any point in trying to hide. He crawled out and tried to look sorry as he stood up. In front of him was a very tall lady. She looked a lot older than his Grandad. She had a lot of wispy silvery hairs interspersed amongst the brown. As Jack hung his head he could see she had beautiful hands with long tapering fingers. He hoped the tall woman looking down at him would know he was sorry for being in her garden.

'Have you hurt yourself?'

'Only my hands.'

'Let me look.'

Jack showed her his palms.

'I'm sorry...' he began, but the woman interrupted him.

'Follow me. I've got just the thing for nettle rash.'

Jack wasn't sure what to do. He didn't want to be impolite but he had no idea who this woman was. He wasn't sure if he should follow her. What if she was a witch?

'I'm not going to hurt you and despite what those boys were shouting I can assure you these statues are not made from people.'

She smiled at Jack.

'I'm Eleanor Ewell but everyone calls me Nora. Your Grandad won't mind you being here.'

'You know my Grandad?'

'Of course I do, and your Dad. We've lived next door to each other all our lives.'

'But you know my name?'

'I know all about you Jack Brenin. Now follow me and let me see to your hands.'

Jack obediently followed her. As they made their way towards the house he had time to look around. The garden was immense. They were on a path which led them around vast flowerbeds. Jack could hear birds singing. They passed a pedestal birdbath in the shape of a large leaf, a small lawn, a picnic bench and a large bird table. The thick, prickly hedge appeared to surround the whole garden. Near the house was a white cylindrical dovecote; it was perched on top of a thick pole, with a tall thatched roof. Under the trees were carpets of bluebells and occasionally patches of white flowers. There was the distinct smell of garlic as they walked under a shady archway of trees.

Jack wondered what kind of things Nora knew about him. If she knew his Dad she'd know he was an archaeologist working in Athens; they'd lived in Greece since he was five. He didn't remember Nora. He was sure that if he'd met her before he wouldn't have forgotten her. He didn't remember much about Grandad either. How could his Dad have sent him to England? He'd had to leave the school he loved and the little white house on the top of the hill. He'd probably never see his friends again. He didn't want to live in Grandad's creaky old house. He wasn't sure Grandad really wanted him to be there either. His thoughts were interrupted when Nora stopped in front of a huge wooden door with an arched top.

'This is my herborium.'

'Herborium?'

The door creaked loudly as Nora pushed it open.

'It's where I prepare my lotions and medicines.'

The sunlit room smelt strange. There were shelves, filled with bottles and jars, which went from the uneven stone floor to the low-beamed ceiling. Everything had been labelled neatly in small flowing writing. Bunches of dried flowers and herbs hung down from hooks. By the door was a bookshelf filled with leather-bound books of all shapes and sizes. A large umbrella and broom stood in a huge plant pot on the other side of the door. Jack felt as if he'd stepped back in time. There wasn't anything modern in the room at all, not even an electric light. Candleholders with half-burnt candles of all shapes and sizes were dotted around the room. Nora pointed to the long wooden table with four high-backed chairs on either side. It was covered in bowls and bottles.

'Sit yourself down. I'll have those hands sorted out in no time.'

In front of Jack, lying on the table was a large square book. It looked heavy. The edges of the pages were ragged, as if they'd been torn to size instead of being cut. On the outside, in between two moonlit trees, he could see the words *Book of Shadows* written in beautiful silver writing. Nora hurriedly picked it up and returned it to one of the bookshelves before taking a dark brown jar down from the top shelf. She spooned out two blobs of green goo onto two pieces of lint and brought them over to where Jack was sitting.

'Hands out.'

Jack held out both palms and Nora strapped the pieces of lint onto them. The green goo felt wonderfully cool. Within seconds the prickling and burning sensation had stopped.

'Is that any better?'

'Yes, thanks.'

'A compound of dock and rosemary leaves works every time.'

'I didn't know that,' Jack replied politely, trying to sound interested.

Nora laughed and smiled at Jack.

'I'd be surprised if you did. Now, tell me, why were those boys chasing you?'

Jack explained and ended by apologising for coming through the hedge. Nora nodded and smiled when he'd finished.

'You are always welcome here Jack. The hedge knows that, otherwise it wouldn't have let you in.'

Jack had no idea what Nora was talking about. Maybe the boys were right and she *was* nutty after all.

'I was sorry to hear about your mum,' she continued.

A lot of people had said this to Jack since his mum had died. If she'd still been alive his life wouldn't have changed so drastically. It wasn't fair. He should have been spending his half term holiday in Greece with his friends. Instead it had been decided he was to live in England with Grandad. His Dad thought it would be a good idea for Jack to spend the last few weeks of term at the local school. It would give him chance to make some new friends before starting at the secondary school in September. He'd only arrived the day before and so far none of the boys he'd met had been very friendly. He hoped they weren't going to be in the same class.

Nora was looking at Jack intently, as if she was reading his thoughts. He wasn't quite sure what to say.

'I think I'd better be going now.'

'Yes, that's probably quite enough for one day. The rash will go completely if you can manage to keep those bandages on for about an hour.'

Jack smiled gratefully.

'Come on. I'll show you a short cut home.'

Once more he followed Nora through the vast garden. They didn't speak until they were opposite the statues.

'Do you like them?' Nora asked.

Jack didn't know what to say. The statues were pure white. They were all of women in flowing robes. He looked harder at the one nearest the path. She had a lovely face and slightly pointed ears.

'They look sad,' he replied.

'They're nymphs,' explained Nora.

'Like Echo and Daphne?'

'You know about nymphs?'

'My mum told me about Echo and Narcissus and how Daphne got transformed into a Laurel tree. They were two of her favourite stories.'

Jack swallowed hard and fought back the tears. Nora gave him a kindly smile.

'We'll talk about nymphs another day. Come on, not far now.'

Eventually they stopped in front of a large overgrown hedge. He thought he heard Nora whisper something before she bent down and pointed towards the thick branches. A small gap had appeared. Jack wasn't sure it had been there before.

She turned and whispered in Jack's ear.

'Follow the pathway through the yew trees and you'll arrive at your Grandad's garden. Whenever you want to visit, come back the same way. I'll look forward to seeing you again.'

Jack stepped through the arched gap into a tunnel. The narrow pathway snaked away into the distance through the dense trees. The yews' fine needle-like leaves seemed to quiver as he brushed them with his arm. He turned round to say goodbye but Nora had gone. He couldn't even see the hole anymore. There was nothing else to do but follow the path.

It wasn't long before he came to another gap. He stepped out into the sunshine at the bottom of his Grandad's garden. Jack wasn't sure he'd be going back through the trees again to Nora's in a hurry. Even if he wanted to he'd probably never find the way in again. The yew trees were so tightly packed together that as if by magic the path he'd come along seemed to have completely disappeared.

Jack sighed as he made his way towards the house. He wasn't looking forward to spending the rest of his life living here. He'd gone out to try and have a game of football and ended up spending the afternoon with an old woman. She'd been kind but there was something strange about her. He'd never met anyone like her before.

After his narrow escape from the boys, he was reluctant to go back to the field. His Grandad wasn't expecting him back for a while. It would be better if he didn't have to explain why his hands were bandaged. He decided to go back to the lane and try the other direction.

The hedgerows were thick and high on either side of the single track. It was impossible to see through them. The earthy smell of newly turned soil meant his Grandad's vegetable plot was on the other side of the hedge. He could hear him whistling somewhere in the distance. It was hot and stuffy in the lane and Jack wished he'd brought a drink with him. A slight rustling from behind made him turn quickly. He thought he saw someone duck back behind one of the trees. Was it one of the boys from the field? Jack felt uneasy. The air was still. He got ready to run. Maybe this hadn't been such a good idea after all. Perhaps all the boys were behind the trees waiting to jump out at him. He stood still, undecided what to do. Should he carry on or go back to the safety of the garden? Was his imagination playing a trick on him? There might not be anything behind the tree at all. The only way to find out would be to go and have a look but Jack didn't feel brave enough to do that. He decided to go back to the house. As he turned he felt a sharp blow on the back of his head.

'Ow!'

Something hard had hit him and bounced off into the grass. Jack rubbed his head. He span around expecting to see the jeering faces of the boys from the field but the lane was empty. What could have hit him so hard, and who could have thrown it? There were lots of pebbles and stones on the path; it could have been any of them. Jack stood very still and listened. There wasn't a sound apart from a slight rustling of leaves. For the third time today he could hear his own heart pounding. He didn't like being alone in the lane. He got the feeling he was being watched. Next time he went for a walk he'd go with Grandad.

He was about to turn and run when he saw a gleam of light. Something underneath the hedge glinted in the sunlight. He bent down and pulled the grass apart. A small shiny object lay on the ground. Where had it come from? Jack looked around before he picked it up and examined it more closely. It was a golden acorn, not quite like any acorn he'd ever seen before. It was beautifully carved, big and heavy and warm in his hand. Jack put it in his pocket then searched around to see if he could find any more.

INTRODUCTIONS

Jack wasn't a morning person. He lay in the strange bed hoping the last few weeks of his life had been a bad dream. He desperately wished he were back in Greece in his own bedroom. His hopes faded when he heard Grandad making breakfast downstairs.

The first thing he saw when he eventually opened his eyes were the contents of his pockets on the bedside table. Two bandages with their middles stained green lay in a crumpled heap and there on top was the shiny object he'd found. He groaned. So the events of the previous afternoon *had* really happened. Whatever Nora had put on his palms had worked.

Would today be better than yesterday? He turned

over and pulled the sheet back over his head. His meeting with Nora was still on his mind. He hadn't told Grandad about it, he hadn't wanted to. He decided she was just a batty old woman and best avoided. He could see why the boys from the field called her *Nutty Nora*.

His thoughts were interrupted when Grandad called from downstairs.

'Hurry up Jack. Breakfast's ready and you've got a visitor.'

He groaned again and reluctantly got out of bed. He wasn't sure he liked the sound of *a visitor* and would rather have known who it was before he went downstairs. He'd no idea who it could be or how long they would want to stay. He went over to the window and pulled the curtain open a fraction. Sunlight streamed in through the crack making him squint. Trees surrounded Grandad's garden, Nora's trees. The chimneys he could see beyond them belonged to her house too. Avoiding Nora wasn't going to be easy. Before going down he looked in the mirror and tried to comb his dark unruly hair but it just sprang back into its own chosen style. He sighed as he put the bandages in the bin and stuffed the acorn in his pocket.

When he entered the kitchen he saw a girl with long chestnut hair sitting at the table chatting with

Grandad. She had an olive complexion like his own and freckles on her nose and cheeks. She looked towards Jack and smiled.

'Jack, this is Elan, Nora's niece.'

'Oh… er… hello,' was all he could manage.

He could feel his cheeks burning. He had no idea what to say to her.

'I'm staying with my aunt for a while and she wondered if you'd like to come round and have tea with us this afternoon?'

Jack gave his Grandad a pleading look. This wasn't the sort of thing he was used to. Girls didn't invite him for tea, especially not the kind of tea he imagined this was going to be, with real china cups and small neatly cut sandwiches. The thought of going back into Nora's house again sent a shiver down his spine.

'I won't be able to come. I'm going to the Cricket Club with Grandad this afternoon.'

Jack felt pleased he had a good excuse.

'Nonsense!' Grandad exclaimed, 'we've only got to set out a few chairs for the match. We'll be finished in no time.'

Jack felt his cheeks burning again.

'When do you want him to come round?'

'As soon as you've finished,' Elan replied giving

Jack an especially big smile, 'Nora has something she wants you to see.'

'I... I... I... er...don't...er...' but before he had time to think of another excuse Elan was already out of the kitchen door. She turned when she reached the bottom of the garden and waved before disappearing through the hedge.

'Elan tells me you met Nora yesterday.'

Jack nodded.

'Do I have to go?'

'It would be rude not to. You must have made a good impression. Not everyone gets invited to Ewell House.'

'Couldn't you come with me?'

'When we've finished at the Club I'll walk with you as far as the front gate but then you're on your own.'

After lunch Jack walked back down the lane, only this time with Grandad. As they passed the field the same boys were playing football again. Jack kept well hidden behind Grandad so they wouldn't see him. He took the opportunity to look around as they made their way towards the Cricket Club. A large hill loomed above the hedge in the direction they were travelling. In places the trees had grown together to form a kind of archway, a green tunnel, which gave some shade from the afternoon sun. It wasn't long before they reached the gate to the Club.

Once inside the ground Jack noticed a large black bird sitting on top of the pavilion clock. It cocked its head on one side and cawed loudly.

'Is that a crow?'

'Too big for a crow, more like a raven,' replied Grandad as he unlocked the shed where the chairs were stored.

For the next half hour Jack helped take the flat chairs over to the pavilion and arrange them in rows for the afternoon's game. He could only manage one at a time. He was hot and thirsty by the time they'd finished.

'Get yourself down to the kitchen, tell the ladies who you are and they'll give you a drink. You might even get a piece of cake. I'm going to make sure the changing rooms are clean.'

Jack went inside the pavilion. He could hear the chinking of cups and saucers coming from a room at the end. He'd only taken a couple of steps when a heavy hand came down on his shoulder.

'Got you!' the man holding Jack exclaimed. 'Down 'ere with you. Let's see what you've got in your pockets.'

Jack was marched down to the end of the corridor and thrust into the kitchen. He didn't dare look around and wasn't sure what he was supposed to have done. He tried to tell the man who he was but his voice only came out in a high-pitched squeak. By now the man was speaking to the ladies in the kitchen.

'I've got him, caught him red handed, sneaking in he was. Here's your thief.'

The two ladies turned and stared at Jack.

'OK laddie, empty your pockets,' ordered the man as he released his hand from Jack's shoulder.

'I haven't stolen anything. I've been helping my Grandad.'

'A likely story.'

Suddenly Jack felt very guilty. He remembered the shiny acorn in his pocket. Was it stolen? How would he convince the man he'd found it?

'I'm still waiting,' growled the man who now stood with his hands out in front of Jack.

If he ran they'd think he was guilty. There was nothing else to do but empty his pockets. Jack placed a crumpled tissue, a piece of string, half a packet of mints and the heavy acorn in the man's hands.

'And the rest.'

'I haven't got anything else.'

Jack hung his head. Tears were welling up in his eyes.

'Perhaps there's been a mistake,' one of the ladies began. 'Are you sure he's the thief? He hasn't got anything valuable here.'

'He's small enough to have come through the window,' the man continued as he pointed up to an open skylight. 'He was lurking about in the pavilion. What's he doing here anyway? Up to no good if you ask me.'

'I've been helping my Grandad, Sam Brenin.'

'Sam Brenin!' exclaimed the man.

'Did I hear my name?' asked Grandad as he entered the kitchen.

Jack rushed over to him.

'They think I'm a thief but I haven't taken anything. I found the acorn yesterday.'

'What's missing?' asked Grandad.

'All the small change from the tea money,' replied the older woman. 'We thought it was probably a youngster because nothing else was taken.'

'And when is Jack supposed to have stolen this money?'

'Sometime last Saturday night. It was there in the

afternoon; by Sunday morning it was gone,' replied the man grumpily.

'Jack's not your thief,' Grandad assured them. 'He only arrived here on Friday. Give him his things back Don and go and do something useful.'

Don reluctantly handed back Jack's belongings but he didn't apologize as he left the kitchen. Jack didn't understand why no one had questioned him about the golden acorn.

'Here you are Jack,' said the younger woman kindly as she poured out a glass of orange, 'and help yourself to some cake.'

Grandad sat down at the table.

'After I've had my cuppa we'll get over to Ewell House.'

'Can I wait outside?'

'That's fine. I won't be long.'

Jack wasn't worried how long his Grandad took. He wasn't in any hurry to get to Nora's house. He went over to the trees opposite the pavilion and sat in the shade. It really was a hot afternoon. As he looked around he saw a cricket ball half hidden by a clump of dandelions. He was just about to go over and pick it up when a sudden movement, a flutter of wings, distracted him. From the corner of his eye he saw the big black bird he'd seen earlier. It landed on top of a dustbin which was underneath the open kitchen window of the Club House. He watched in fascination as it leaned in and helped itself to a rather large sandwich. Once it was securely in its beak it dropped back down onto the grass. With a hop, skip and a couple of jumps the bird made its way towards Jack with its prize. The snatch hadn't gone unnoticed and the alarm had been raised from inside the kitchen.

'Shoo him off Jack!' shouted the older woman as she leaned out of the window. 'Shoo that thieving crow away!'

Jack stood up and started flapping his arms as he ran towards the bird. It didn't fly off or look in the least bit frightened.

'You'll never fly like that,' it said through a beakful of sandwich, 'and I'm not a crow.'

It skipped unhurriedly across the field, finally taking off and landing in one of the large trees opposite the cricket ground.

Jack stood rooted to the spot. He hadn't taken his eyes off the bird. He was stunned. Had he imagined the whole thing? Birds don't talk. Maybe the odd word and a few squawks but not proper sentences. Perhaps he was coming down with a bug, he did feel a bit hot;

maybe he'd got a temperature. From the pavilion he could still hear the women complaining.

'Put his head right inside the window, if you please! Bold as brass! Took that sandwich right off the plate.'

'Never seen anything like it,' the other replied. 'Better close the window. He might try it again.'

As the window slammed shut Grandad appeared in the doorway.

'He was a cheeky chappy,' he laughed.

Jack was still worried.

'Can ravens talk, you know, like parrots?'

'I'm not sure,' Grandad replied. 'Why don't you ask Nora? She knows a lot about birds. She knows a lot about everything.'

The front garden of Ewell House was a blaze of colour. There were flowers everywhere. Grandad opened the gate and gave him an encouraging smile.

'I'll be off now. See you later, have a good time.'

Jack hesitated, took a deep breath, then closed

the gate and set off down the path. On the wall by the front door was a green circular plaque with a large tree embossed on it. Ewell House was spelled out above it in capital letters. Jack looked for a bell to ring but could only find a knocker. It was decorated with three oak leaves and two large acorns. Apart from the colour, the similarity between the two acorns and the one in his pocket was unmistakable. His heart began to beat rapidly; his hand trembled as he lifted the knocker.

Elan opened the door. Jack felt a bit better knowing he wasn't going to be alone with Nora.

'Come in, it's this way to the kitchen.'

He followed Elan down a dark passage. It was an old house like Grandad's. The floors, walls and ceilings were all uneven. At the end of the hallway they entered a large kitchen. The smell of freshly baked bread was still in the air. Nora stood by a large range, stirring the contents of a pot. Sunlight streamed in through the windows lighting the whole room. He liked it better than the strange place he'd sat in yesterday afternoon. There were more bookshelves full of the same kind of leather-bound books he'd seen in the herborium. Two large patio doors were open and Jack could see the garden beyond.

'Before we have tea,' Nora began, 'there's someone I'd like you to meet.'

Jack looked around the kitchen expecting to see another person.

'No, not here,' laughed Elan.

'We're going to have to go into Glasruhen. It's not too far.'

Jack looked puzzled as Nora continued.

'Glasruhen begins just beyond the hedge you went through yesterday. It's a very old forest. You might see and hear some strange things this afternoon but I don't want you to be frightened. Nothing will hurt you.'

Jack wasn't sure he liked the sound of *strange things* but before he had time to worry about anything Nora continued.

'Now, I believe you have something which belongs to me.'

Jack shook his head. He'd put the bandages in the bin; what else could he possibly have that belonged to Nora?

'If you haven't brought it, you'll have to run along home and collect it because you'll need it once we get to the middle of Glasruhen forest.'

'I don't know what you mean,' replied Jack.

'Something you might have found yesterday afternoon? It's probably in your pocket?'

Jack felt uncomfortable.

'The acorn?'

'Yes, the acorn. You do still have it don't you?'

Nora and Elan looked expectantly at Jack. He brought the acorn out of his pocket and offered it to Nora.

'No, I want you to have it for now but you must keep it safe. It's the only one we've got.'

'What do you see Jack?' Elan asked.

It seemed like a stupid question but Jack answered politely.

'A golden acorn.'

'I knew it!' Nora said as she took Jack's other hand and shook it vigorously. 'I knew you were *The One*.'

'Er…. I don't understand.'

'There's a prophecy, which was given to us. It tells of a mortal boy who can see the Druid's Acorn,' explained Nora.

'That's you Jack,' continued Elan. 'No other mortal can see it's made of gold.'

'You're *The One*. I knew I was right. You've been *chosen*,' continued Nora.

'Chosen to do what?'

'Help me,' said a voice from the doorway that Jack thought he recognised.

As he turned around his mouth dropped open. There in the doorway was the raven from the Cricket

Club. He looked at Nora, then Elan. Could they see and hear the talking bird too?

'Is it real?' he asked nervously.

'Of course I'm real,' the bird croaked.

'I believe you two have already met,' said Nora.

The raven gave a rather loud *caw* as it made its way across the stone floor. There was a lot of wing flapping as it passed Jack but his head never moved and he watched Jack with a jet black eye.

'Let me introduce you to Camelin.'

'Don't see the point of introductions,' muttered Camelin. 'He's not going to stick around long enough to help. Look at his legs. They're trembling!'

'Camelin, that's enough,' Nora chided. 'I'm sorry Jack. Camelin forgets himself sometimes and can sound quite rude. He's not used to visitors but I'm certain you two are going to get along just fine.'

A grumpy sound came from Camelin's direction and Jack tried a smile but without any conviction.

'Nora sent Camelin to put the acorn where we hoped you'd see it,' explained Elan. 'You passed the test when you picked it up.'

Jack frowned and looked directly at Camelin. 'I bet Nora doesn't know the acorn was bounced off my head,' he thought to himself. He suspected the talking bird had done it deliberately.

'We can talk when we get back from Glasruhen, when Jack's been introduced to Arrana.'

'If you think I'm rude wait till you meet her,' Camelin grumbled.

'Oh!' exclaimed Jack, looking worried, 'who is she?'

Nora gave Camelin a reproachful look then turned to Jack.

'Arrana is a Hamadryad. She lives in the oldest oak tree at the heart of Glasruhen forest. She's very old now and doesn't always appreciate being disturbed by visitors, especially not ravens with sharp claws, but I'm sure she's going to like a polite boy like you Jack.'

Camelin began muttering to himself again.

Jack stared at Nora in disbelief. His mum used to tell him stories about nymphs and dryads, but they were only myths, not real life. He wished he could go back to Grandad's but he wasn't going to be able to excuse himself, not so soon after arriving. He wasn't sure he ought to go into the forest. Grandad said it was all right for him to visit Nora and Elan but he didn't know anything about the talking raven. He should have told Grandad. If he had, he wouldn't be in this mess.

'Shall we go?' Nora asked, and without waiting for

anyone to reply she strode off towards the bottom of the garden. Jack walked with Elan a few steps behind.

'Some of us don't need to walk through bushes,' croaked Camelin loudly. He flapped his wings noisily before taking off towards the forest.

'Just ignore him,' said Elan. 'He's always grumpy.'

When they reached the hedge Jack wondered how they were going to get through. There was no sign of a gate or gap in the thick prickly Blackthorn. Nora stood very still. She brought her hands together then raised them in a circular motion. There was a faint rustling, then a louder scrunching kind of noise. To Jack's amazement the hedge parted, creating a dense tunnel as far as the eye could see. Jack's knees began to wobble; his heart pounded wildly in his chest. He felt very sick. He could hear the raven above the trees; he knew it was laughing at him.

'It's OK,' whispered Elan as she gave Jack's hand a squeeze.

It was anything but OK, only Jack couldn't find his voice to protest. He obediently followed Nora onto the path. He heard the rustling and scrunching as the gap in the hedge sealed again behind them. He was trapped in the tunnel and had no other choice but to follow Nora into the depths of Glasruhen.

GLASRUHEN FOREST

The tunnel felt airless and gloomy. No one spoke as they made their way along the path. Even though there wasn't any breeze each tree they passed swayed and rustled its leaves. The next tree did the same, then the next.

'They're sending a message to Arrana,' explained Elan. 'She'll know we're on our way soon.'

Jack watched the message being passed from tree to tree. It quickly disappeared deep into the forest. Once it was gone the trees became still.

'Can they hear what we say?' whispered Jack.

'Oh yes, trees see and hear everything, which is why Nora is so well informed. Poor Camelin can't do anything without her knowing.'

Jack wanted to ask Elan if Nora was a witch but didn't want to appear rude. He hadn't realised she could speak to trees as well as birds.

'Nora's a Seanchai,' explained Elan, lowering her voice.

Jack had never heard of a *Shawna-key* before. He plucked up courage to ask Elan the question that had been bothering him.

'Is that a kind of a witch?'

'Oh no!' she laughed. 'Nora's a Druid. She's the guardian of the sacred grove, the keeper of secrets, and she knows the history of every tree in the forest. It's too complicated to try and explain everything now. Wait until you've spoken to Arrana.'

Jack was relieved Nora wasn't a witch, but was being a Druid any better? Elan didn't seem to mind. He began to worry again. He hadn't realised he was expected to speak to Arrana. What would he say? How could he even be contemplating talking to a tree? It was ridiculous but then, until today, he'd never met a talking raven before either. He must be having a bad dream. He'd wake up soon and find himself in bed at Grandad's.

'Not far to go now,' announced Nora.

For the last ten minutes they'd been walking uphill and the end of the tunnel was in sight. It stopped abruptly at the edge of a dense forest of massive oak trees. Their branches were laden with leaves; their trunks gnarled and twisted. Jack felt as though he was being watched by hundreds of eyes. Trees appeared to be swaying of their own accord and he thought he could see faces peering down at him through the leaves. He could definitely hear whispering. It grew louder as they began to snake their way through the gaps in the trees.

Nora came to a sudden halt and everything went quiet. Jack looked ahead. There in the centre of a circular clearing was the largest oak tree he had ever seen. Its canopy spread out to touch each of the other trees that surrounded it. The tree was magnificent. As they walked underneath the branches and moved closer towards the base of the trunk, Jack felt more curious than afraid. He had an overpowering urge to put his hands on the rough bark but before they got any closer Nora stopped again. She raised her head and began speaking in a loud voice.

'Arrana The Wise, Protector and Most Sacred of All, we have come to speak with you.'

'When you address a Hamadryad you have to use their full name or they don't realise you're talking to them,' explained Elan in a soft whisper. 'Nora has to shout; Arrana's so old now she spends a lot of her time sleeping.'

'I've never heard a name as long as that before,' replied Jack.

'Names are very important and powerful things, you can learn a lot from them. Arrana was given hers in Annwn before she came to Glasruhen.'

'*An-noon*. Where's that?'

'It's sometimes known as the Otherworld.'

Jack shook his head. He'd not heard of this place either.

'Annwn is a land in another world, a place of peace and happiness, where it's always summer. There used to be portals on Earth, secret gateways which could only be opened in certain ways at special times of the year. Only Druids had the knowledge and skill needed to perform the rituals that opened the gates. They each possessed a golden acorn. Without it they couldn't pass between the two worlds. The one in your pocket is very special: it's the only one left.'

All the time Elan had been whispering Nora had waited patiently before the great oak. Nothing happened and Jack began to wonder if they were playing a joke on him after all. He put his hand in his pocket and felt the warm heavy acorn. What was he supposed to do with it? If all this was real how could he possibly be *The One*? He wasn't special; he had no powers.

There was a sudden movement. A gasp seemed to echo around the forest. Jack watched in fascination as the trunk of the massive oak began to waver and shimmer. It was a small movement at first but gathered momentum quickly until the whole tree was in motion and eventually became a blur. When it stopped the gnarled trunk of the oak had transformed itself into the most beautiful woman Jack had ever seen. She was also the tallest. He had to tilt his head right back to see her face. Her copper coloured hair flowed down in beautifully groomed tresses. Her skin was nut brown and smooth. He knew he should be frightened, it wasn't every day you came across a woman as tall as this, but instead he was fascinated. Jack wasn't sure what he'd expected Arrana to look like. Maybe small and wrinkled, especially since he'd been told she was very old. Camelin described her as bad tempered but she looked kind and gentle. This wasn't a trick, it was really happening. How was he supposed to speak to her, he couldn't even remember all her names, and what should he say? He realised he was staring and managed to close his mouth but his feet were rooted to the spot. He wasn't able to break free from the Hamadryad's gaze.

'I've been expecting you,' began Arrana.

She spoke slowly in a deep, striking voice that sounded more like singing than speaking.

'Step forward Jack Brenin and show me the sign.'

Jack's rigid body went limp and he suddenly felt afraid. Nora hadn't prepared him for this. What should he do? He looked at Elan, then Nora, but they both nodded their heads encouragingly and smiled. He took a couple of hesitant steps towards the gigantic Hamadryad and felt compelled to bow. As he stood up he held the golden acorn out on the palm of his trembling hand. He raised it as high as he could so Arrana could see it.

A long willowy arm reached forward but Arrana didn't take the acorn. Instead she gently placed a slender finger in the centre of Jack's forehead. He immediately felt her presence. He knew she could read his thoughts and sense how he was feeling.

Arrana gasped.

'It's true! This is the mortal boy the prophecy speaks of. There's hope for us all now.'

Jack wasn't sure if she'd spoken aloud or not. He should have protested. He wasn't who they thought he was; they'd got the wrong person. He didn't want to believe what he could see and hear but Arrana's touch had taken away any fear or doubt he'd ever felt.

'If you speak with your heart I can hear you Jack,' Arrana's voice told him. 'Don't be afraid.'

'I'm not,' replied Jack truthfully, although no words left his mouth.

'We need your help,' Arrana continued. 'You are our last hope.'

'I'm not *The One*. I just found an acorn in the grass.'

'If you hadn't picked it up we wouldn't be speaking now. The other signs cannot be wrong. You were born at sunset on the first day of the New Year in the shadow of Glasruhen Hill.'

Jack felt a sudden relief. His birthday was in October not January.

'Our new year begins at Samhain,' Arrana's voice continued, 'as the sun sets on the last day in October. In other words the day of your birth.'

Jack couldn't speak. He was trembling again.

'We need your help. The time for my eternal sleep approaches. Unlike other nymphs I'm not immortal. I need another to take my place before it is too late and I fade away into nothingness. Without a Hamadryad's protection this forest will not survive. The dryads will disperse and leave behind them hollow trees. Glasruhen is the only refuge left on Earth where the old ways exist.

We are eternally grateful to Eleanor, Keeper of Secrets, Custodian of the Book of Shadows, Guardian of the Sacred Grove and friend to us all.'

From behind the trees Dryads stepped into the clearing, their anxious faces watching Jack expectantly. He could feel the sorrow in Arrana's heart and see the looks of sadness in every pair of eyes.

'How can I help? I'm just an ordinary boy.'

'Journey through the window in time with Camelin into the past and find what was lost. Eleanor needs it so she can re-open the portal and return to Annwn. Only the Mother Oak there bears the Hamadryad acorns she must collect.'

'It's impossible to go back in time.'

'There is a way. Eleanor has the knowledge and power, but without your help she too will soon die. Each year a Druid must drink a potion brewed from the leaves of the Crochan tree which grows only in Annwn. All Eleanor's leaves are gone. She must return. Her cauldron has to be re-made before the ritual can be performed. We only have until Samhain. Time is running out for us all. If the portal remains sealed we are all doomed.'

Jack looked at Nora. She smiled and nodded again. Could she hear what Arrana said? He didn't think so.

'You won't be alone Jack. Eleanor and Elan will guide you and Camelin will teach you all you need to know. You are the Brenin we've been waiting for. What other proof do you need? You have the Druid's token. How many other mortals do you suppose can see or hear the spirits of the trees?'

Jack didn't answer. He knew if he told anyone what he'd seen or heard in the last few hours no one would believe him.

'Before you decide, you ought to know that there may be danger. You'll need courage and strength...'

'There isn't much of that around here,' Camelin muttered as he swooped down and landed by Nora's feet.

Jack felt his face redden. He was angry with the talking bird. How long had he been listening? It was obvious he could hear Arrana. A sudden determination filled Jack's heart. He might not be very big and he certainly wasn't very strong but there were other things he could do. He always kept his promises and tried to do his best; they had to count for something.

'I'll help you,' said Jack loudly so everyone would hear his decision.

Camelin choked back a *caw*, Nora and Elan hugged each other and Arrana smiled. The forest filled with song, the most beautiful music Jack had ever heard. He wished he could join in. Singing was something he did well, something he doubted Camelin could do at all.

Arrana addressed everyone when the singing stopped.

'This is our only chance to succeed. Everyone must help.'

She bent over and presented Jack with a gnarled twig. It wasn't very long or impressive but he accepted it with a bow.

'This will help you. Use it wisely Jack Brenin. Carry it always and a part of Annwn will be with you. Keep it close.'

'Thank you,' he said solemnly.

'We will meet again,' Arrana said sleepily inside Jack's head before she began to shimmer and fade back into the trunk of the oak.

The whispering began again; one by one the Dryads disappeared back into the trees.

Camelin hopped around Nora's feet and cawed loudly.

'Why should he get a *lath*? Only the Druid's acolyte gets a *lath*.'

'I don't understand,' replied Jack. 'It's only a twig.'

'Only a twig! Only a twig!' spluttered Camelin. 'Just you wait till you see what that twig can do.'

'Camelin,' snapped Nora, 'you heard Arrana. She said everyone must help Jack and that includes you.'

Camelin turned abruptly and waddled off before he could be chided again. Jack could still hear him muttering to himself as he flew away.

'I'm sorry Camelin is so rude,' said Elan. 'He feels responsible for a lot of our problems and helpless to do anything about them.'

'Once he starts to teach you to fly he'll feel important and won't be so grumpy,' explained Nora.

'Fly!' exclaimed Jack.

'All in good time,' said Nora. 'I think we should be making our way back now for tea; it's been quite an afternoon.'

Jack felt light-headed after his experience with Arrana. Nora had started talking in riddles again. Why did he need to fly? Camelin would never be able to teach him. He was terrified of heights. Even if Nora wasn't a witch, if she thought he was going to sit on a broomstick she was mistaken. He would have to ask her later what she'd meant. Right now he needed to know more about the lath. It was obviously very special. His head filled up with questions.

'What's a *lath*?' he asked Elan as they walked back through the forest.

'*Lath* means wand, but once you've empowered it with your symbol it will become a *hudlath*, a magic wand. That's why Camelin is so upset. A mortal can only be given a lath by a dryad. Your wand is very special. It's from the Hamadryad Oak and contains all the magic of Annwn.'

Jack's mouth was open again, only this time he didn't close it. He was too busy trying to think about the ordinary looking twig in his hand. It was only when they came to a clearing and he felt the sunshine on his back that he realised they'd taken a different route. They entered a large meadow full of knee-length grass and tall buttercups. It looked like a golden carpet in the sunlight. Nora stopped in front of an open well. A crystal clear stream ran down from the hillside and trickled into it. Pieces of rock, covered in moss and strange carvings, surrounded the well. The clearing was almost circular and looked as if some ancient building had once stood there. Nora knelt down and put her lips to the water. At first Jack thought she was drinking but then he realised she was speaking.

A multitude of bubbles broke the surface and a mass of long dishevelled green hair, entwined with waterweed, old twigs and some dead leaves, rose from the water. Underneath the tangle was a pale green face with strange slanting eyes. The creature shook its head and sent a spray of water everywhere. Jack could see its ears were pointed and it had unusually long arms. The foaming water clung to its body like a gown. When Nora said he might see some strange things in the forest she'd not been wrong. This was the strangest creature Jack had ever seen.

'What is it?' he whispered to Elan.

'A water nymph.'

'A water nymph!' exclaimed Jack. 'But aren't they supposed to be beautiful?'

'She thinks she is!' explained Elan, but before she could say any more the creature began to speak to Nora.

'I hope it's important?' she wheezed. 'I was very busy and you've disturbed me.'

'Jennet,' said Nora, addressing the water nymph, 'Elan is here and we've brought Jack Brenin to meet you.'

She stepped aside so that the water nymph could get a better view of Elan and Jack.

'Well that's quite a different matter. Why didn't you say they were coming today?' She looked at Elan first and nodded her head, then turned towards Jack and spoke to him directly.

'Come here Jack Brenin so I can get a good look at you.'

Jack stepped forward rather reluctantly and stood in front of the nymph whilst she inspected him. He felt uncomfortable as Jennet not only looked but also sniffed the air around him. When she'd finished she turned back and addressed Nora.

'He's not much to look at is he?'

'I agree,' croaked Camelin. 'He's going to be as much use as a chocolate teapot.'

An awful sound came from Jennet and Jack only realised she was laughing when Nora looked crossly at her.

'I'm going to do my best,' Jack announced loudly.

This must have satisfied Jennet because she turned her attention back to Nora.

'Does he know what he's got to do then?'

'Not yet, but he's spoken to Arrana and she's explained our problem to him.'

'Is that all you wanted to tell me? I'm very busy you know.'

'No,' said Nora sternly. 'I want you to promise to help Jack should he ever need it and tell the other water nymphs they must promise too. You can start by working out which symbol Jack needs for the lath Arrana gave him.'

Jennet screwed up her face and narrowed her eyes.

'What do I get in exchange for this?'

The water began to bubble around Jennet again as she waited eagerly for her gift. Elan stepped forward and produced a large black shiny marble from her pocket. The bubbles were now turning into what looked like a mini-whirlpool. Jennet stretched out a long arm and wrapped her spindly green fingers around the offering.

'This is very acceptable,' she crooned and pointed towards one of the rocks in front of the well. 'This will be your mark. Come and touch it.'

Jack approached the well, taking care to stay out of Jennet's reach. He put his right hand upon the cool mossy rock. There was a flash of light. The rock became burning hot. He pulled his hand away. Glowing in the rock was a strange symbol. His finger was throbbing and when he examined it, the same symbol was glowing there too.

'Make sure you succeed Jack Brenin. We're all counting on you.'

Jennet's words were almost lost as a final surge of bubbles engulfed her. Then she was gone.

'Take the lath,' said Nora. 'See what happens.'

Jack held Arrana's twig in his right hand. He felt a strange hot burning sensation in his fingertips. The gnarled twig glowed too. It almost shone. To Jack's astonishment it was now perfectly smooth.

'Don't you point that wand at me,' shouted Camelin as he hopped out of Jack's way. 'Somebody show him how to put it away before he does any damage.'

Before Nora could give Jack any instructions the wand grew even brighter. Sparks flew. One caught the tip of Camelin's tail and slightly singed his sleek black feathers.

Jack dropped the wand. Before it hit the floor it turned back into the same gnarled twig Arrana had given him.

'I told you he'd be useless but I didn't realise he was going to be dangerous. Look what he's done to my feathers!'

Jack hung his head. He didn't want Camelin to see his smile. It had been an accident, unlike the acorn Camelin had aimed at his head, so in a way it served him right. Now they were even, but it wasn't a good start if they were going to have to get along.

BOOK OF SHADOWS

'Pick up your wand Jack,' said Nora kindly. 'You'll soon get used to it when you've had a few lessons. It's quite safe as long as you don't hold it in your right hand.'

Jack's mouth was open again, which seemed to amuse Elan.

'Wouldn't it be better if he didn't hold it at all?' Camelin grumbled as he twisted and turned to try and see the damage to his tail.

'If you haven't got anything good to say, don't say anything at all,' Nora snapped.

Camelin gave a loud *humph* and flew into the nearest tree.

'We'd better be getting back for tea,' said Nora and set off along the path. Jack and Elan followed a little way behind.

'Do all water nymphs look like Jennet?'

'Oh no!' Elan laughed. 'She's good looking compared to the others!'

Jack wasn't sure he needed to meet any more water nymphs.

'Why was she so excited about the marble?'

'It could have been anything shiny. Nymphs like sparkly things too. It really doesn't matter as long as it's not reflective.'

'Why?'

'They've no idea that they aren't beautiful. If Jennet saw her reflection she wouldn't be very happy. Nymphs can do quite a lot of damage when they get upset.'

The last thing Jack wanted to do was annoy Jennet. She didn't look very pleased, even when she was laughing.

'If you ever need help call her name through the water but make sure you've something to give to her in return.'

'Would she get upset if she didn't like what I offered her?'

'It's possible but she'd be more likely to disappear and refuse to come up again. It's best to carry something at all times. You never know when you might need help. Camelin's got a lot in common with water nymphs. He hoards anything in his loft if it sparkles or shines. The only difference is he likes mirrors. He's very proud of his appearance.'

Jack thought Camelin and Jennet had something else in common too. They both seemed grumpy and bad tempered.

'Did you say Camelin has a loft?'

'Yes, up there. Can you see it?'

Elan pointed to the roof of Ewell House which was just visible through a gap in the trees.

'That round window is Camelin's 'front door'. He has the whole attic to himself. I'm sure he'd give you something to keep in your pocket if you asked him.'

Jack didn't want to ask Camelin for anything. He decided to go through his things later. He was sure he'd have something a water nymph might like, just in case.

It wasn't long before they reached the hedge. Nora stood and raised her arms. Jack heard the rustling and scrunching as the hedge parted again. Even though he'd seen it happen earlier, it still made his legs tremble.

Camelin was already in the garden. He was prancing up and down on the lawn with a small twig in his beak. He stopped when he saw them and made a great flourish in the air. Jack looked at his own wand and wondered what would happen if he did the same. Somehow, he didn't think he'd be allowed to use it without supervision for a while, although he was desperate to find out what it could do. His thoughts were interrupted when a large white goose waddled around the corner and cackled loudly. She stopped abruptly and stared at Jack.

'This is Gerda,' said Nora, as the goose stretched her neck to get a better look. She nodded her head several times then started cackling at Nora.

'She's pleased to meet you.'

Jack nodded back to Gerda.

'Can she speak too?'

'Only to Camelin and Nora,' explained Elan, 'but she understands everything we say.'

Jack was relieved that not all the birds in Nora's garden could talk.

'Gerda's our watch-goose. She helps to keep unwanted visitors out,' explained Elan.

The large goose snapped her beak and raised her wings. She shook her feathers, flicked her tail and cackled loudly again before waddling over to the pile of food Nora was sprinkling on the patio.

'Perhaps after we've eaten you could try and get to know Camelin a bit better,' urged Nora.

At the mention of his name Camelin swooped down and landed in front of the patio doors. He hurried past everyone.

'I'm afraid there's nothing for you,' said Nora. 'I believe you ate earlier.'

Camelin turned around and glowered at her.

'That's not fair. I knew I should have gone somewhere else to eat my sandwich. I'd forgotten what a blabbermouth that ash tree is.'

'It's a beautiful tree,' replied Nora, 'very reliable and always quick to inform me of anything which happens on the other side of the lane.'

'Too quick!' added Camelin sulkily. 'It's not easy being a raven when everyone pokes their nose into your business.'

'Don't you go taking any of Gerda's food either,' said Nora sternly when Camelin began shuffling towards the patio.

Afternoon tea didn't turn out to be tiny sandwiches or tea in china cups, as Jack had feared. Instead he enjoyed freshly baked bread rolls stuffed with cheese and a glass of Nora's homemade ginger beer. Afterwards she sent him out into the garden to see Camelin.

'Did you save me any cheese?'

Jack shook his head.

Camelin sighed and gave Jack a pathetic look.

'They make really good sandwiches at the Cricket Club you know; big ones too, not like those tiny little triangular ones they have at the Village Hall.'

'Do you steal food often?'

'Well, I don't consider it stealing. I like to think I'm doing them a favour, you know, like a tasting service. If the food isn't any good I don't eat it; they know there's something wrong with it then.'

Jack tried not to smile; food was obviously very important to Camelin.

'How often do you leave anything?'

'It's only happened once. Last summer there was a Mexican night on at the Village Hall. I heard someone talking about a chilli and I fancied something cool, only when I tried a beakful it was red hot. Took me two days to stop my beak burning. Won't be having any more of that in a hurry.'

Jack had to laugh, especially when Camelin shook his head and made a disgusted kind of noise.

'I've not been back to the Village Hall since then.'

Jack thought that was probably a good thing.

Elan came out carrying a small square book, which she offered to Jack.

'This is for you.'

'Thanks,' he said, looking puzzled.

It was handmade like all the other books he'd seen on Nora's bookshelves. It was decorated with two trees. Their entwined knotted roots were made from twisted copper wire. In the middle, written in silver letters, were the words, *Book of Shadows*. It was like the one he'd seen in Nora's herborium, only smaller, and at the bottom was his own name.

'Wow! What's it for?'

'It's for you to write in, not with a pen, with your wand.'

Jack's eyes became wide; he was going to be able to use his wand after all.

'The first page is blank,' explained Elan. 'If you write my name or Nora's at the top your message will appear in our books. We can write back to you the same way.'

'But I don't know how to use the wand.'

'When you're ready,' said Nora, 'take it in your right hand, wait until it transforms then instruct it to become your pen.'

'What do I say?'

'When your wand gets used to you, no words will be necessary. It will instinctively know what you want it to do, but for now try *scriptum*. Don't get excited or you'll have sparks flying again.'

Jack had no idea how he was going to keep calm. To have a magic wand and be taught how to use it was incredible. He gave the book to Nora and took the wand in his right hand. The tip of his finger felt hot and soon the whole twig started to glow. It wasn't long before the gnarled bark became smooth again.

'Wow!' exclaimed Jack.

There was a crackle as sizzling lights erupted from the tip of the wand.

'Not again!' shouted Camelin and hurriedly skipped out of the way.

'Take a deep breath,' instructed Nora.

Jack watched in fascination as he managed to bring the wand under control. His hand was shaking and the wand wobbled about but the sparks had stopped.

'Imagine it's a pen,' urged Elan.

Jack concentrated hard. He visualized his pen and

prepared to say *scriptum*, but before the words left his lips his wand transformed itself.

'You've done it!' squealed Elan as she jumped up and down.

'Brilliant,' said Nora.

'Beginner's luck,' Camelin croaked.

'I can't believe I just did that. Was it me or the wand?'

'It was you,' replied Nora. 'The wand only works to your command.'

'Try writing something to me,' said Elan as she ran into the kitchen. 'I'll write back and you can see how it works.'

Nora passed Jack the open book. He didn't know what to write. He put Elan's name at the top of the page and underneath wrote...

...Am I doing this right?

He watched the words sink into the page and disappear. Seconds later Elan's reply appeared...

...Yes... we'll try it again tonight when you get home.

'I think that's probably enough for today,' said Nora.

Jack put his wand into his left hand. The smoothness vanished immediately. He knew without looking that he was holding the twig again; he could feel the rough bark under his fingertips.

'If you have any questions about the task you have agreed to undertake just ask your book,' explained Nora. 'It also contains the history of the Otherworld in the section about *The Annals of Annwn*.'

Jack flicked through the pages; they were all blank.

'But...' he began.

'It's magic Jack,' laughed Nora. 'You have to know what to do before it will reveal any secrets.'

'Do I have to use the wand?' asked Jack nervously. He didn't want any accidents in Grandad's house.

'No, it couldn't be easier,' continued Nora. 'Touch your name with your finger and the book will recognise you; ask a question and it will reveal the answer.'

'If you want to write any secrets down, use the back pages. It will be invisible to anyone who might pick it up,' added Elan.

'It's amazing!' exclaimed Jack. 'Thanks!'

He couldn't wait to try it out. It was going to be better than a laptop. He'd have an email, notebook and search engine, only he was going to be the power source. It still sounded incredible but he'd seen it work. It had really happened and he felt confident he'd be able to do it again when he was back at Grandad's.

'Camelin will take you down to the hedge,' announced Nora.

Jack would rather have gone out of the front door and he suspected Camelin didn't really want go with him through the garden.

'Come back tomorrow,' Nora continued, 'we've got a lot of things to do before you're going to be ready for the ritual.'

'Ritual?'

'We'll talk about it tomorrow.'

Before Jack could ask anything else Nora and Elan went back into the kitchen leaving him alone in the garden with Camelin.

'This way,' Camelin grumped.

Jack's mind was working overtime as they made their way to the hedge. He was too busy with his own thoughts to worry about speaking to Camelin. He wondered what other surprises were in store for him. Could he be getting himself into something dangerous? Maybe Camelin was right and he wasn't going to be worthy, or it could all be a dreadful mistake and this prophecy didn't mean him after all. Perhaps he'd find out more from his Book of Shadows.

'Here you are,' croaked Camelin.

'I'll see you tomorrow.'

'Can you bring some cheese with you?'

'I don't know if Grandad's got any cheese.'

Camelin looked disappointed.

'I'll see what I can find,' said Jack kindly.

'You won't tell Nora?'

'No, I promise, but she might find out.'

'Not if I meet you here tomorrow. I've got a safe eating place. It can be our secret.'

Camelin didn't seem to be as grumpy now he was talking about food.

'If you haven't got cheese anything will do, except banana. I don't like banana.'

'I won't forget,' laughed Jack. 'Bye.'

Jack wasn't alone until after dinner. He excused himself, went up to his room and took out his Book of Shadows. He couldn't decide what to do first, write to Elan or try to find out more information about Annwn. He touched his name with his finger and watched as the silver writing glowed brightly. Without warning the book opened and pages began to flip over, slowly at first, then quicker until the book lay still. Beautiful flowing writing began to appear.

The Law and Annals of Annwn.

Jack plucked up courage to ask about the Otherworld.

'Where is Annwn?'

Beyond the four Portals of the mortal world.

'What is my task?'

Jack's hands trembled. He was scared and fascinated at the same time. The book didn't answer straight away so he repeated his question.

'What is my task?'

You must return to the past and find the three missing cauldron plates which were lost. Once the cauldron is remade the ritual can be performed and the Western Portal on Glasruhen Hill can be opened again.

This must be the ritual Nora spoke about.

'How can I return to the past?'

The answer came straight away.

You must fly.

'Fly!'

This was the second time he'd heard that word today but before he could ask the book anything else it snapped shut with a resounding thud. Try as he might, Jack couldn't get the book to open again beyond the first page. He decided to write to Elan.

…I've got some answers but I think I've broken the book.

I can't get it to open again.

It wasn't long before Elan's reply appeared.

…It won't be broken. Bring it tomorrow and Nora will answer your question.

Jack lay awake. He kept replaying everything he'd seen and heard again and again. He didn't know if he wanted the responsibility Arrana had given him. He was worried he would fail. The word *fly* filled him with fear. He hated the flight from Greece to England and he really didn't like heights. There must be a mistake; he'd have to talk to Nora about it.

Eventually he fell asleep.

A tapping on the window woke Jack. His head hurt and his eyes didn't want to open. Reluctantly he got out of bed to investigate. When he drew back the curtain there was Camelin perched on the window ledge about to tap the window again with his beak.

'Rise and shine!'

It was obvious Jack had been asleep. He was sure Camelin was pleased he'd woken him.

'What do you want at this time in the morning?' grumbled Jack as he opened the window.

'I've got a message from Nora. You're invited for lunch so you can come round straight after breakfast. She's already asked your Grandad and he said it would be fine.'

Jack stifled a yawn.

'Don't forget to bring something with you,' added Camelin.

Without waiting for a reply he flew off in the direction of Ewell House.

It was still early but Jack decided to get up instead of going back to bed. Last night he'd found two loops on the spine of his Book of Shadows where his wand could be stored. He made sure it was securely in place before putting it into his backpack.

He could tell Grandad was impressed when he walked into the kitchen.

'I'm glad you're up and dressed early,' he began. 'You've been invited over to Ewell House for the day.'

Jack was about to say he already knew and only just managed to stop himself in time. Explaining to Grandad that he'd been told by a talking raven was probably not a good idea.

'I'm glad you've made a friend already,' Grandad said as he started breakfast. 'If you're going to be out I can crack on in the garden. There's a lot to do.'

Before Jack left he went back into the kitchen. There wasn't any cheese in the fridge and he hoped Camelin wouldn't be too disappointed. He searched around the pantry and found a piece of fruitcake, which he wrapped up and put in his backpack.

'I'll see you later,' he called to Grandad, who was already working in his vegetable plot.

The shortcut through the hedge didn't seem as bad as it had the first time and it hadn't been difficult to find. It wasn't long before he was standing at the bottom of Nora's garden.

Before Jack took another step he heard a muffled but familiar croaky voice.

'This way.'

He looked around but he couldn't see Camelin.

'In here.'

Jack caught a glimpse of Camelin's head from behind Nora's rockery.

'You took your time, I've been waiting ages. You didn't forget did you?'

'No.'

'Come inside.'

It was like a small cave and perfectly dry. Jack crawled in. He could see why he'd been invited. Neither of them would be seen from the house.

'This is great!' exclaimed Jack.

'It's safe in here. What the trees can't see or hear can't get reported back. What have you brought me?'

'There wasn't any cheese but I got you some cake.'

Camelin's eyes grew wide when he saw the size of the package Jack produced from out of his backpack. Once it was unwrapped, Camelin began to attack the cake and gobble it down greedily. Then he delicately and slowly picked up every last crumb until nothing was left.

'You can bring me something every day in return for your flying lessons,' he announced.

'You're not really going to teach me to fly are you?'

'How else do you think you're going to get through the window in time? We've got to fly.'

'But I'm a boy. It's not possible.'

Camelin began to laugh.

'You won't be a boy when you fly, stupid. Nora's got to turn you into a raven first, just like me.'

Jack's mouth fell open.

'How?'

'She'll take you up Glasruhen Hill and do a special ritual at the Raven's Bowl. You've heard of the Raven's Bowl haven't you?'

Jack shook his head. He'd only heard of Glasruhen yesterday.

'Of course you'll have to be naked.'

'Naked!'

'You won't need your clothes when you're a raven!'

Camelin laughed as he hopped out of the cave and flew off.

Jack needed time to think. Why hadn't he been told yesterday about the ritual? He didn't mind helping but there was no way he was being turned into a raven, especially a naked one. He went over and over everything he'd seen and heard. He needed his questions answered. He'd have to talk to Nora. He wriggled out of the cave, picked up his backpack and set off towards the house.

QUESTIONS AND ANSWERS

Jack didn't know what he was going to say to Nora. He'd promised Arrana his help and he knew they were depending on him but he wasn't sure he wanted to be changed into a raven. He was certain he didn't want to fly. There had to be another way for him to get through the window in time. He didn't even know where it was. He'd been too excited and eager to leave the house this morning. If he'd been thinking straight he could have tried asking the book some more questions. Now he felt apprehensive.

'Are you ok?' Elan asked. 'Nora asked me to come and look for you. When Camelin eventually came back he said you were on your way but you didn't arrive and she wondered if you'd got lost or changed your mind.'

He must have been in the cave quite a while and he'd no idea how long he'd been standing in the garden lost in thought. Jack felt embarrassed. He didn't want to tell Elan where he'd been or why he was worried. He looked around.

'I... er... I thought I heard water. Has Nora got a fountain?'

'No, it's a lake.'

'A lake!'

Elan led Jack around the back of the kitchen garden down to the water's edge. They stood in the sunshine by a group of willow trees. Their long tapering branches were draped in the water. It was breathtakingly beautiful. The water reflected the bright blue sky and sunlight danced across the ripples that lapped the shore by their feet.

'Wow! You've got a boat too.'

'Nora uses it to row out to Gerda's island when she takes fresh straw for her shelter. Poor Gerda's on her own now. She lost her mate a long time ago and never quite got over it. Nora says she gets very sad some days.'

There was a loud cackling as Gerda waddled by. Jack wondered if she'd overheard Elan. Her beak was full of long green stalks. She seemed to nod her head several times in a kind of greeting.

'Nora sent her to get some chives from the herb garden. She likes to help and she's very good at grabbing them with her beak.'

'How does she know which ones to pick?'

'Nora's taught her about all the different plants in the garden.'

It seemed incredible for a goose to be able to understand and follow instructions but Jack had to accept it was true. Not long ago he'd been talking to a raven which could not only understand him but talk back too.

'Where's Camelin?' he asked.

'He's in his loft. You'll be able to see him later. I think Nora wants to talk to you first.'

Jack and Elan made their way back to the house. As they entered the kitchen Nora was chopping the chives and talking to Gerda who cackled happily back. She sprinkled the herbs into a large steaming saucepan that bubbled on the range at the far end of the kitchen. The smell of freshly baked bread again filled the room. He felt so at home in this kitchen. It was like Grandad's but much more interesting. The large dresser behind the table didn't have china plates or ornaments on its shelves. Instead it was covered in rocks and fossils. On the work surface two huge pieces of amethyst were being used as book-ends. Gerda waddled out of the open doors and settled down on the patio in the warm sunshine. Jack looked around but there still wasn't any sign of Camelin.

'I'll go and collect the eggs,' announced Elan as she picked up a basket and headed into the garden.

Jack thought it was probably a good time to talk to Nora now they were on their own.

'I think Camelin's probably right. I'm not going to be much help.'

'Nonsense, you're going to be just fine. He'll change his mind, you'll see.'

Jack hung his head.

'You said you'd try your best. What more could we ask? You listened to Arrana and agreed to help. Not many boys of your age would have done that.'

Jack shuffled his feet. Nora was waiting for him to reply but he couldn't find the right words.

'Now, there are things you need to know. Our first and most important task is to prepare you for the ritual.'

'I'm afraid.'

'That's only natural. You've seen a lot of unusual things in the last few days. You're bound to feel different.'

'Do I have to be turned into a raven?'

'You didn't find that out from your Book of Shadows.'

Jack felt worried when Nora scowled.

'What has Camelin been telling you?'

'Not much, but he did say you were going to transform me into a raven and I'd have to be naked.'

'Yes, he'd take great delight in telling you that. We wouldn't do anything to hurt you. The ritual is very quick. It involves a walk to the Raven's Bowl at sunrise on a very special day of the year.'

'Where's the Raven's Bowl?'

'I'll show you.'

Nora selected one of the books from the dresser and carefully opened it at the middle page. She unfolded a hand drawn map and spread it out on the table. It was different from any map Jack had seen before. It wasn't drawn to scale and there were strange words and symbols around the edge. Nora pointed to the top of Glasruhen Hill and then let her finger move slightly lower down.

'Here,' she said, and pointed to a craggy rock on the map which was labelled the Raven's Bowl. 'There's a natural hollow in the rock. That's where we have to perform the ritual.'

'Will a lot of people be there?' Jack asked with renewed concern.

'Please don't worry. No one will see us and you can have my cloak. I doubt Camelin told you that.'

'He didn't.'

'The ritual is quite easy. You'll have a few words to learn but I'll do the rest. All you'll have to do is lie on the rock and look into the water inside the Raven's Bowl. When you see the reflection of the sunrise recite the words and touch the water with your forehead.'

Nora paused.

'The hardest part will be down to you Jack. You'll have to want to become a raven with all your heart or it won't happen.'

Nora was right. It would be hard. The last thing on earth he wanted was to be a raven. Even if he agreed to the ritual he'd never be able to leave the house so early in the morning and climb up to the Raven's Bowl. What would he say to Grandad? How could he explain where he was going?

'Don't worry,' said Nora as if she could read his mind. 'We'll invite you to stay here for a couple of days. You'll see, everything will be fine.'

'Will I have to go back to the Raven's Bowl and do the ritual again to change back?' enquired Jack, and then as a worrying afterthought he asked, 'I *will* be able to change back won't I?'

'Of course you will. Once the ritual is complete you'll be able to change into a raven and back again whenever you want just by putting your forehead on Camelin's.'

'When's it going to happen?'

'This Saturday.'

Jack felt sick.

Nora returned the book and picked up a piece of paper from the dresser and handed it to Jack.

'I've written out a list of the things you'll need to know before the ritual. You'll be able to ask your Book of Shadows when you get home. You've put my golden acorn in a safe place haven't you? We'll need it for the ritual.'

Jack nodded and checked his pocket. The acorn was there. He looked at the paper. It was going to take him ages to ask all the questions Nora had given him.

'The book wouldn't answer one of my questions last night and then I couldn't get it to open again.'

'That was my fault. I didn't want you to know about the transformation ritual until I'd spoken to you but I can remove the block now.'

Jack got his Book of Shadows out of his backpack and gave it to Nora. She held it between both hands.

'*Cardea,*' she whispered.

A blue light glowed from the closed book.

'There you are, all done. Now you can ask anything you want and you'll get the answers.'

'Thanks,' said Jack nervously. He wasn't sure how answers would help him feel better about what lay ahead. He was glad Nora was convinced he'd succeed. He wished Camelin felt the same.

Elan came in with the basket full of eggs.

'Will Camelin come down soon?' asked Jack.

'No, not until after lunch,' replied Nora. 'I've forbidden him to eat with us. He's been sent upstairs to think about his bad behaviour. He's in his loft sulking.'

'Could I go and see him?' asked Jack.

'I think that would be alright,' replied Nora. 'Elan will show you the way.'

Jack followed Elan along the passageway. At the end she turned right and started to climb up a steep creaky staircase.

'What did he do to make Nora so cross?'

Elan stopped, turned to face Jack and started to laugh.

'Early this morning Nora made an apple pie and left it on the windowsill to cool. Camelin must have seen it when he went out to give you Nora's message.

He sampled the insides. Unfortunately he sucked out all the filling!'

Jack laughed at the thought of Camelin using his beak as a very efficient straw.

'How did Nora find out?'

'The lid collapsed. She realised there was nothing left inside and knew straight away where it had gone. The beak-shaped hole in the top rather gave it away. He got well and truly told off when he came back; even more so when he asked if he could have the rest of the pastry since it wouldn't be any good for lunch. He was sent up to his loft and much to his disgust Nora put the rest of the pie out for the birds in the garden. Camelin's had to watch them finishing it off. He wouldn't dare go down and steal anything else.'

'I thought it would be something to do with food,' chuckled Jack.

'It's his big weakness. In fact that was another reason why Nora was so cross. Instead of saying he was sorry he said he'd wished he eaten it all and giving it to the other birds was a waste of good pastry. He doesn't like starlings, mainly because they can clear the bird-table of scraps before he gets there. He shouldn't get annoyed. He's not allowed on the bird table. It's a bit of a sore point.'

Elan opened a door at the top of the stairs.

'When you get to the ladder give him a shout.'

'I don't think he likes me much.'

'You could always try tempting him with some food. He's not so crabby when his stomach's full!'

The only thing Jack had in his pocket was a half-eaten packet of mints he'd bought at the airport in Athens.

Jack crossed the attic floor. He looked around but there didn't seem to be any sign of Camelin. He heard a faint cough from somewhere above his head. At the far end of the attic was a rung ladder leaning against an opening in the roof.

'Hello,' shouted Jack.

'What do you want?' snapped Camelin. 'If I'm not allowed downstairs I don't see why you should be allowed up here.'

'I thought we could talk.'

'Well you thought wrong. I'm too hungry to talk.'

'I've got some mints.'

'I'm not usually allowed sweets but this is an emergency. Hand them over.'

Jack fished in his pocket and brought out the mints. Camelin's face appeared in the opening.

'They smell good.'

'I'm not sure you'll like them. They're extra strong.'

Camelin started chuckling.

'Always willing to sample anything new. You'd better come up.'

Jack climbed up the small ladder and was impressed by the sight, which greeted him. Camelin's room wasn't the dark, dusty place the word 'loft' suggested. It was light and airy. Sunshine streamed in through a large round window creating a pool of light on the floor. In its centre was a furry cat basket with a beanbag bottom. The rafters were covered in shiny objects which glinted in the sunlight. The low roof meant that Jack had to shuffle through the opening and crouch down. He was grateful he wasn't any taller. As he pulled himself into the loft his hand touched something sticky. It was then that Jack noticed the floor. He'd never seen such a mess. Empty sweet wrappers, crisp packets and ripped bags were strewn everywhere. What looked like an empty pizza box had been stuffed into the far corner.

'You can have that if you want,' said Camelin as he nodded towards the half-eaten yellow chew which was stuck to Jack's hand. 'It's banana flavour.'

'Thank you, but no,' said Jack as he looked around for some means of getting rid of the sweet. He pulled over an empty paper bag and wiped it onto that.

'Where's the mints then?' Camelin enquired as he hopped around Jack.

Jack offered one to Camelin. Instead of taking it the raven grabbed the pack and skipped off to the cat basket. He ripped the paper off and scooped up the mints. Within seconds he shot out of the basket and hopped wildly around the loft. He stretched his wings out and flapped them towards his beak.

'I'm on fire!' he croaked.

'I said they were extra strong,' replied Jack trying not to laugh. 'Spit them out.'

The mints shot out of Camelin's beak like rapid fire from a machine gun. They whizzed past Jack's head and hit the back wall. For a moment Jack wondered if he'd been Camelin's intended target.

'I don't need any more of them. They're worse than chilli,' gasped Camelin. 'I'm going to need something nice after that.'

'I haven't got anything else.'

'Well I'll just have to break into my emergency rations,' Camelin grumbled as he poked his beak inside a large wicker basket and began rummaging around.

When he found what he was searching for he waddled over to the cat basket and settled down inside. Jack watched as he tossed a small bar of milk chocolate into the air and caught it on the way down in his beak. He thought he ought to change the subject.

'I like your room. Your cat basket looks really comfortable.'

'Its not a cat basket,' replied Camelin indignantly. 'It's a raven basket and it was made to measure. Look.'

He stood up, turned around twice and settled down again, only this time on his back with his legs sticking up in the air.

'It's a perfect fit.'

Jack had to stop himself from laughing. He didn't want to offend Camelin but the sight of him in the raven basket was very funny.

'Was there anything else? Because I'd rather not have to get up again.'

'I need to know about the window in time. Why can't I climb through it?'

Camelin shook with laughter.

'You'd have to be very tall to do that, taller than the tallest giant. We've got to fly through because it's up in the clouds, right over the top of Glasruhen Hill.'

Jack felt shaken. This wasn't good news.

'Scared are you?'

'Yes,' Jack admitted. 'I don't like heights.'

'Oh, that's brilliant!' exclaimed Camelin sarcastically.

'The only one who can help and he's scared of heights. Have you told Nora?'

'No. Perhaps it could be our secret?'

Camelin gave Jack a long look.

'Ok,' he said eventually. 'We can trade. I'll keep your secret if you do something for me, but you mustn't tell anyone.'

'I've said I'll bring you food and I've already promised I won't tell.'

'No this is extra. The food's for the lessons. This is for your secret; you mustn't laugh. Agreed?'

Jack wondered what he was agreeing to but, whatever it was, Camelin wasn't laughing any more so it had to be important.

'Agreed.'

'I want to learn to read.'

'You can't read?'

'No, nor write.'

'Why didn't you ask Nora?'

'Because she'd want to know why and if she knew she'd say no.'

Jack thought it might be rude to ask Camelin the reason but the raven continued.

'I want a wand. If I can't read and write I'm never going to get one.'

'It's not a problem. I'll teach you. We can do a bit each day.'

'And you won't tell Nora?'

'I promise. It will be our secret.'

Camelin gave a dismissive flick of his wing and Jack presumed he wanted him to leave. As he was making his way down the ladder Camelin called to Jack.

'You can tell Nora my empty stomach's made me realise how sorry I am for eating her pie.'

'OK. Will I see you later?'

'I expect so.'

When Jack got back to the kitchen he gave Camelin's message to Nora. She laughed.

'I doubt he's sorry at all and he certainly isn't joining us for lunch. He can sit up there and starve for a bit longer.'

Jack was certain Camelin wasn't going to starve. Nora obviously hadn't seen inside the wicker basket where Camelin stored his emergency rations.

Nora began to ladle steaming soup into three bowls which she had ready on the table.

'After we've eaten I'd like you to go to Newton Gill Forest to meet the Gnori. It's important you go on your own. It will help you understand what's going to happen to Arrana and the whole of Glasruhen Forest if we don't succeed. You'll be able to get home from Newton Gill so take your things with you. Elan will show you the way and tell you how to get home.'

Jack ate his soup slowly. He wasn't in any hurry to meet the Gnori whatever it might be.

THE GNORI

After lunch Jack checked that his wand was securely in place before putting the Book of Shadows into his backpack. He said goodbye to Nora and followed Elan to the gap in the hedge at the bottom of the garden. She stood aside to let Jack go through.

'Go right instead of left but don't leave the path. After you've been to Newton Gill Forest and you're ready to come back just turn around and the path will lead you home.'

'Can't you come with me?'

'No, this is something you need to see and do for yourself.'

'How will I know where to find the Gnori and

what am I looking for?'

'The path will lead you. When you can't go any further you have arrived.'

Jack wanted to ask Elan what he would say to the Gnori but she'd already disappeared.

'Bye,' she called from the other side of the hedge. 'See you tomorrow.'

Jack looked around. He'd hoped Camelin might have been flying overhead but he couldn't hear him. He took a deep breath and set off to find Newton Gill Forest. Sunlight filtered through the gaps in the canopy as Jack walked along the path. He could see the trees whispering to one another. Unlike Camelin Jack didn't mind Arrana and Nora knowing where he was. He didn't feel alone with the trees for company.

The changes were so gradual that Jack didn't notice them until a sudden shiver went up and down his spine. The light was fading even though it was still early afternoon. The leaves had disappeared. Thick bare branches lined each side of the path and none of the trees swayed or whispered. He didn't like the deepening gloom. It was different from Glasruhen; here nothing moved. There were no nymphs peeping out from behind the trees. As Jack peered through the shadows he thought he could see gnarled, sad-looking faces on every trunk. Jack's heart felt heavy. He didn't want to go any further.

'Hello,' he whispered.

He held his breath. There wasn't a sound.

'Hello,' he called more loudly. 'Is anyone here?'

A cracking branch made Jack swivel round. He wasn't sure but the face on the tree next to him seemed to move. Jack reached out and touched its twisted misshapen nose with his finger. Immediately a pair of eyes opened. Jack jumped backwards.

'I'm sorry,' he gasped. 'I didn't realise you were alive.'

'I wouldn't call this being alive,' the tree replied. 'There aren't many mortals who come here and even fewer who talk to me. Who are you?'

'I'm Jack Brenin. Nora sent me to look for the Gnori of Newton Gill Forest. Is that you?'

'Goodness no! You're in the forest but to find the Gnori you'll have to go further in. If I'm not mistaken you're the Brenin we've been expecting.'

Jack shouldn't have been surprised. Everyone and everything seemed to know who he was.

'Do you have a name?'

'Not any more. We're all the same. We're Gnarles. Dead wood. This is what happens to trees when the Hamadryad dies. The Gnori you're looking for is a hollow tree now. Dead wood. It used to be Allana the Beautiful.

'I'm so sorry,' Jack replied. 'I've met Arrana so I understand.'

Without Allana we are nothing. Once Arrana is no more the Gnarles will disappear too. All the Dryads left Newton Gill a long time ago. We're all alone now.'

Jack felt sad as he watched a tear trickling down the gnarled face.

'Is there anything I can do to help?'

'I doubt it. There isn't much life left in any of us now. For a while the Dryads used to come back and sing but that was a long time ago. I can't remember the last time we heard any singing.'

'I can sing something for you.'

More eyes had opened and were staring hopefully at Jack. This really was something he could easily do. He'd been in the school choir since he was six. He thought about the beautiful music he'd heard in Glasruhen and he knew some hymns that were similar. The Gnarles might like one of them. He closed his eyes to concentrate and sang the tune without the words. His voice rang through the forest pure and clear. When he'd finished he heard a great sigh from the Gnarles.

Each wore a strange crooked smile and tears were in all their eyes.

'That was beautiful. You sing as well as any Dryad.'

Jack didn't think this was true but he was pleased the Gnarles liked his song.

'I ought to go and find the Gnori now.'

'You will come back and sing to us again sometime, won't you?'

'I will. I promise.'

'If we can help you in any way just let us know.'

The Gnarles gave a great collective sigh and one by one their eyelids closed. Jack continued along the path. It wasn't long before he stood before what had once been a great oak, just like Arrana. It was still, tall and proud. Its branches touched each of the other dead trees around it but all of them were strangely still. Jack bowed as he had done to Arrana. He went over and touched the bark. He could feel the hollowness, the emptiness, and knew the whole tree was dead. He was overcome with sadness. If he didn't succeed Arrana would become a Gnori too and the whole of Glasruhen Forest would die. He now knew why Nora had sent him into Newton Gill Forest. He couldn't let this happen again. The bottom of the great oak had already begun to decay. He looked inside. It was hollow as far as he could see. He needed to go home; he'd seen enough. As he stood he caught a glimpse of something red behind the Gnori. Then it moved.

'Hello. Is anyone there?'

'Who wants to know?' came the reply.

Jack stepped back in surprise. On a rock sat a small man in a dark green suit. A bent black feather had been tucked under the headband of his bright red hat. A pair of glasses were perched on the end of his long pointed nose. He glowered at Jack then leapt up and blocked his exit with his knobbly walking stick.

Jack tried a smile, which didn't help.

'I didn't think anyone lived here.'

'You're trespassing. This is my tree now.'

The little man looked angry. He raised his stick in the air and waved it about.

'I've got permission to be here,' replied Jack.

'Well, if you want to pass you'll have to give me something. If you don't I'll beat you. There's no escape and there's no one here to help you.'

The stick came very close to Jack's head. He took another step backwards. Was this strange little man like Jennet? Did he want something shiny? Jack felt relieved he'd put a small silver dolphin in his pocket. It used to be on a key ring. He'd thought it might appeal to a water nymph if he ever needed help.

'Something shiny would be most acceptable,' the old man crooned as if he'd read Jack's thoughts. 'I'm sure you'll have something I'd like.'

Jack produced the dolphin.

'Silver, bah! I need gold. Give me your gold.'

Jack had no intention of handing the only golden object he possessed to this angry little man. What could he do? He seemed very confident he could prevent Jack from getting past. Did he have some special kind of power or did he just rely on his own strength? He wasn't like any man Jack had ever seen before. He was sure he could outrun him if he got past the man's knobbly stick. Jack felt worried but then had an idea.

'I've got something in my backpack you can have.'

The little man's face crinkled. His eyes became slits as he stepped eagerly towards Jack.

'Take that!' exclaimed Jack as he whipped his wand out of his backpack.

Sparks erupted in an uncontrollable shower. Each one made the little man jump and shout as it singed his skin. Jack didn't waste any time. He dodged sideways to avoid the stick and ran as fast as he could down the path. To his surprise the little man was faster than he'd imagined and Jack could hear his footsteps not far behind. The fallen twigs and branches crunched noisily as they ran along the path. Jack saw the Gnarles blinking their eyes as the light from his wand lit the murky grove. There was a loud crash. Jack looked back. The little man lay face down on the path. His pointed nose was stuck in the ground and he was beating his fists wildly. A large branch pinned him to the ground.

'Stinking Gnarles,' the man cried. 'I'll beat you sore for this.'

Jack looked at the trees. He didn't want them to suffer on his behalf.

'Don't worry, he can't hurt dead wood,' the Gnarle next to Jack explained. 'We'll keep him here for a while. He won't be bothering you again in a hurry.'

'Thank you,' said Jack and gently touched the Gnarle's face. He replaced his wand, fastened his backpack and set off briskly. He sang for the Gnarles until he came to the end of Newton Gill Forest.

Jack had an uncomfortable feeling that the strange little man knew about the golden acorn. Maybe it wasn't just by chance they'd met in the forest. He ought to tell Nora. He hesitated when he reached the gap in Nora's hedge, but instead of going back to Ewell House he decided to write to Elan as soon as was back in his room.

Jack got quite a shock when he eventually opened the door of his bedroom. He'd got a visitor. Camelin was waiting for him.

'You took your time,' he grumbled. 'Got any more cake in the bag?'

'No, only my Book of Shadows and my wand.'

Camelin looked disappointed.

'You had the last piece this morning. There isn't any more. Anyway, what are you doing here and how did you get in?'

'You left the window open, which is like leaving the front door open, so I hopped in.'

'Has Nora sent you?'

'She thinks I'm still in the loft.'

Jack doubted that. Nora would probably know where they both were by now.

'I thought we might start my lessons. No time like the present.'

'I've got to write to Elan first. It's important.'

While Jack got out his book and wand Camelin rummaged around the room. He poked his beak into drawers, looked under the bed and peeked inside the wardrobe.

'Where's your basket?'

'Basket?'

'For your emergency supplies.'

'I don't have one.'

'Don't have one!'

Camelin looked genuinely shocked.

'What do you do if you're hungry between meals?'

'I don't usually get hungry.'

'You will when you start flying. I keep telling Nora it's hungry work being a raven but she doesn't believe me.'

Jack watched as his message to Elan faded into the page. Her answer came back straight away.

... We'll investigate.

Nora thinks she knows who it might be.

She says to keep your window closed.

'Can we start now?'

There wasn't any paper in Jack's room. There weren't many of his belongings here at all. He'd only brought one suitcase with him. The sensible thing would be to use his wand in the book.

'OK, let's start with your name.'

Jack wrote Camelin's name out in big letters. Under the capital 'C' he drew a cat.

'C is for Camelin and cat.'

'I don't like cats. Can't you draw something else?'

'What do you like that begins with the letter C?'

'Cake.'

Jack laughed as he drew a cake with icing and a cherry on top underneath the C.

'*a* is for apple pie.'

Camelin nodded in approval.

'*m*?'

'Macaroni. I just love macaroni. It's much easier to eat than spaghetti.'

After half an hour Jack had successfully drawn egg foo yung, a lollipop, ice cream and noodles and Camelin was able to sound out his name using the pictures of his favourite foods as clues.

'Does Nora cook egg foo yung for you?'

'Oh no, we don't have any Chinese food at home. I know a really good takeaway though. I'll show you when you can fly. We can go there together.'

'Do you steal the food?'

'Naw, they feed me. They think I'm lucky. I do a bit of a dance for them round the back where the kitchen is and eventually they bring a tray out for me.'

'I hope I learn to fly as quickly as you're learning to read.'

'Oh I doubt it. You don't look the type to be able

to fly and besides you said you don't like heights.'

Jack didn't reply. As he stared down at his book a message from Elan appeared.

'Look!' exclaimed Camelin when he saw Elan's name. 'Egg foo yung, lollipop, apple and noodles... E l a n... it's from Elan.'

Jack was impressed. Camelin really was a fast learner.

'What's it say?'

'It says Nora is looking for you. She's got a job she needs doing and you're to go back to Ewell House straight away.'

Camelin sighed.

'I'll see you tomorrow,' said Jack as Camelin took off from the window-sill but instead of flying over to Nora's he swooped high above the trees and circled back.

'Watch this!'

To Jack's astonishment Camelin flipped over and flew upside down. He circled again then soared higher and higher before plunging back towards Jack's window. He did a triple loop the loop and went straight into a barrel roll. He finished the display by landing neatly on a nearby branch.

'That's amazing! How long did it take you to learn to fly like that?'

'I'm a natural stunt flyer,' Camelin smirked.

Jack watched as Camelin started to preen his feathers. When he was satisfied none were out of place he took off and returned to Ewell House. As Jack watched Camelin he wondered if he'd ever be able to fly like that. It looked great fun.

Grandad was still working in the garden so Jack took the opportunity to look at the piece of paper Nora had given him. For the next hour he asked his Book of Shadows the questions Nora had listed. He learnt more about nymphs. There was more than one type and they inhabited air, earth and water. The Undines lived in wells, springs and rivers; Jennet was obviously one of these. Jack wasn't likely to forget her in a hurry. He read about the wonders of Annwn, about the forests, the Mother Oak, the Crochan tree and the Queen's glass palace. At the bottom of the last page was a list of important people with their full titles.

The Seanchai
Keeper of Secrets and Ancient Rituals,

Guardian of the Sacred Grove,
Healer, Shape Shifter and Wise Woman.

This had to be Nora. Jack recognised some of her names straight away but she'd never said anything about being a shape shifter. He knew he should have been surprised but he wasn't. He was curious to know what shapes Nora could change into. The other name he didn't know.

Coragwenelan
Queen of the Fair Folk,
Guardian of the Gateways of Annwn,
Immortal Nymph and Shape Shifter.

It must be important information or the book wouldn't have shown him. Would he have to meet the *Guardian of the Gateways of Annwn* if he succeeded and the portal was opened? Was the Queen of the Fair Folk as tall as Arrana or as beautiful as Jennet? Now he knew Nora was a Shape Shifter it wouldn't be a shock if it happened. It seemed the more he learnt the more questions he needed answering. He'd only two more questions left on Nora's list when Grandad called him down for supper. As soon as Jack put his wand down the book snapped firmly shut. He left them both on the bed and decided to carry on and finish the questions after he'd eaten.

Grandad told Jack all about his new potatoes and spring onions while they ate.

'Did you have a good day?' he asked.

'Yes thanks,' replied Jack. There wasn't much else he'd be able to tell Grandad, and then he remembered Gerda's island. 'Nora's got a lake and a boat. Elan took me to see it this morning.'

'It's a big place, Ewell House, all right. I did some work on Nora's kitchen garden a few years back. I saw the lake then.'

'Is it all right if I go back again tomorrow? I've been invited.'

Grandad gave him a knowing look. Jack suddenly felt his cheeks burning. Grandad obviously thought Elan was his girlfriend. But maybe it was easier for him to let him think that than for Jack to try and explain what Nora was planning to do.

'That's fine Jack. I'm glad you're having a good time. I was worried you might be bored living here.'

Jack smiled. He hadn't had time to be bored, not since a golden acorn had bounced off his head.

After dinner he went back to his room. As soon as he stepped inside he knew something was different. His things had been moved slightly but his backpack had been ripped open and discarded on the floor.

It had to be Camelin. He'd probably been back looking for food. He only had himself to blame. Elan had told him to close the window and he'd forgotten. He ought to close it now. As he crossed the room he saw a bent black feather on the floor by the window. He'd have to speak to Camelin in the morning but he wouldn't tell Nora. He didn't want to get the raven into any more trouble.

As he lay in bed he thought about the things he'd seen and heard in Newton Gill Forest. He would go back and visit the Gnarles again. They were so sad. He couldn't let that happen to Glasruhen. He'd have to be careful not to let the angry little man see him. He certainly didn't want to bump into *him* again. Suddenly Jack sat bolt upright. He remembered the little man had a bent feather in his hatband, a black feather. He suddenly felt afraid. There was a bump outside the window. He grabbed his wand so he'd have some light and pulled back the curtain. Jack gasped. Two hands clung onto the window ledge. Slowly a red hat without its bent feather, an angry face and the long nose of the little man he'd met in the woods came into view.

ADDERGOOLE PEABODY

Jack was frightened. He was glad he'd closed the window. At least the little man couldn't get in. Should he call Grandad or try to use his wand? He was unable to move or call out. The little man bared his teeth and shouted. Jack heard his muffled snarl through the window.

'I've come for my gold!'

A sudden movement in the sky made Jack look up. A dark shape with its wings tucked in, twisted and spiralled down towards the window. The little man was making too much noise to notice the attack from above. At the last minute before it crashed into the window the bird levelled out, rapped its beak on the little man's head then opened its wings and flew into a nearby tree.

'Camelin!' exclaimed Jack.

'Ow!' the little man screamed and instinctively put his hands on his head to stop the pain.

Jack saw the look of horror in the little man's eyes when he realised he'd let go of the window ledge. He plummeted out of sight. A great wailing began. Jack knew he'd landed in the holly bush. Grandad must have heard the commotion. With his nose pressed flat on the window he craned his neck but he'd lost sight of the man. Everything went quiet. Jack peered into the darkness to try to find Camelin. He waved his wand to get his attention but sparks began to fly everywhere. As Jack raised his wand the little man was tossed out of the bush and somersaulted in the air. Camelin swooped and chased him in a circle around the lawn. The little man stopped running and looked up. His spindly legs started to shake when he saw Jack open the window. He turned in an instant and ran off at a great speed through the vegetable garden. Camelin flew over to Jack.

'Put that down before you do any damage.'

Jack put his wand in his left hand. Everything went dark and it took a few moments for is eyes to adjust. Camelin hopped into Jack's bedroom.

'I think he was after the acorn. Who is he?'

'A Bogie.'

'Ergh, where?' said Jack, checking his nose.

'No, *he's* a Bogie,' explained Camelin, nodding in the direction the man had gone.

'What's a Bogie?'

'Someone you should never talk to. They learn all your secrets then trade them for something they want.'

'I spoke to him in Newton Gill Forest.'

'I hope you didn't tell him anything.'

'I don't think so.'

'That's good,' laughed Camelin, 'because I've just told him you're a great wizard and if he comes here again you'll turn him into a Brownie.'

'But... I'm not a great wizard.'

'He doesn't know that; he didn't like what you did to him with your wand.'

Jack realised his hands were trembling and he was glad his wand was safely in his left hand.

'What's a Brownie?'

'Don't you know anything? A Brownie is about the same size as a Bogie but the complete opposite. They're helpful and kind and have tiny noses.'

'So why was the Bogie afraid?'

'Bogie's are very proud of their long noses. The longer it is, the more important they think they are.'

'Do you know who he is? Does he have a name?'

'Oh yes, he's got a name. Addergoole Peabody. A nasty, mean, sneaky, thieving Bogie.'

Jack took the bent feather off the table.

'I found this in my room earlier. I think he must have been in while I was having dinner. My rucksack was ripped and my things had been moved.'

'That's why Elan told you to keep the window closed.'

Jack didn't mention he'd suspected it had been Camelin who'd been through his things.

'That's one of my feathers you know. Sneaked up on me and pinched it when I wasn't looking. Ripped it right out of my tail. I've been wanting to get my own back on him for ages.'

'There was a break-in at the Cricket Club. Was that him too? They thought *I'd* stolen the tea money.'

'Probably. He's been breaking into lots of places and stealing things.'

'How do you know?'

'Nora's been getting reports from the Night Guard for a while now about things going missing.'

'Night Guard?'

'They're like security guards. Of course they're under my command. I give them their orders.'

Jack wondered who the Night Guard could be. He watched Camelin lean out of the window and give a long, low whistle. It was answered immediately by a short, shrill sound.

'Come up. It's OK,' he whispered into the darkness below.

It wasn't long before a brown, furry face appeared at the window. The creature hopped nimbly into Jack's room and leapt onto the table. It stood on its hind legs balancing gracefully on its large feet. Its long tail trailed behind.

'It's a rat!' exclaimed Jack.

'It's no ordinary rat. This is Motley.'

The rat tipped his head onto one side and bent slightly forwards. His nose and whiskers twitched several times before he began squeaking rapidly. Camelin listened and nodded as he followed Motley's conversation.

'Why can't I understand him?'

'Because you're not a raven. Put your wand back in your other hand. You'll be able to understand him then.'

The room lit up as Jack moved the wand.

'Not so bright... not so bright if you don't mind,'

106

complained Motley. 'Can't you turn it down a bit? Cut the dazzle.'

'I'm sorry, it's new. I haven't got used to it yet.'

'Just think about something dark,' Camelin advised.

Jack remembered the gloom of Newton Gill Forest and immediately his wand dimmed to a pale glow.

'Not bad,' said Motley. 'A natural.'

'Beginner's luck,' Camelin grumped.

Motley didn't take any notice of Camelin and gave Jack an encouraging nod.

'Back to important matters… my report… we've sent Peabody packing or, rather, you did Jack when you tossed him out of the bush with your wand… the Night Guard were following him to see where he'd holed up…'

'I know where he's been,' interrupted Jack.

Camelin and Motley looked surprised.

'He said the Gnori in Newton Gill Forest was his tree now, if that's any help.'

'Nora won't be pleased,' said Camelin.

'Dead wood don't talk,' explained Motley.

'You mean he's in the dead wood so nobody knows he's there?'

'Spot on,' confirmed Motley and Camelin together.

Motley began pacing up and down on the table before he spoke again.

'Camelin... go and stop the Night Guard... that Forest's not a good place to be after dark... I'll report back to Nora... she needs to know what's happened.'

Camelin gave an embarrassed cough. It was obvious to Jack who was *really* in charge.

'Meet you back at headquarters,' announced Motley.

'Yes, OK. See you later,' Camelin agreed before flying off in the direction of Newton Gill Forest.

'Can't stand around talking all night... got responsibilities... rounds to be done.'

Motley leapt nimbly onto the window ledge.

'Thanks,' replied Jack, because he didn't know what else to say.

'Don't forget to close the window,' Motley squeaked as he scampered down the thick ivy that grew everywhere on the walls of Grandad's house.

Jack made doubly sure the latch was down on the window before putting his wand on the table. He felt very tired as he climbed back into bed but he lay awake for ages, too excited to sleep.

It was nearly one o'clock the following afternoon when Jack eventually woke up. He'd heard Grandad shouting upstairs to say he'd left Jack's breakfast on the table but that was hours ago. He drew the curtain a fraction. Grandad was still busy in the vegetable garden. If he hurried up he could get downstairs and clear away the breakfast things before Grandad came back in. He didn't want him to know he'd overslept. He was curious to know if anything else had happened. He checked his Book of Shadows; there were no messages.

As soon as Jack got downstairs he quickly put the breakfast things away. He was closing the pantry door when Grandad came into the kitchen.

'That's a good lad. You've washed up and put everything away.'

'Is it lunch time now?'

'I should say. I've worked up quite an appetite this morning. There must have been a fox in the garden last night. It's bashed all my spring onions down. It's taken me ages to sort them out.'

Jack knew exactly who'd been in Grandad's garden but couldn't tell him.

'Are you off to Ewell House this afternoon?'

'Yes, if that's alright. I've been invited.'

After they'd eaten Grandad got up and took an envelope from the mantelpiece. 'I nearly forgot. This came for you this morning.'

Grandad handed the envelope to Jack. He thought it might have come from his Dad but it didn't have a stamp. There was a card inside.

'It's from Elan. She's having a party on Friday night. There's a note in here for you too.'

Grandad took the note from Jack.

'Nora's inviting you to stay for the weekend. Now you don't have to go if you don't want to.'

'I think I'd like to go,' Jack said after he'd pretended to think about it for a while.

'Will you need a present?'

'It just says a party. It doesn't say it's her birthday.'

'I'll make up a bouquet of flowers for you. I bet she'll like some Lily of the Valley. I've got pink ones as well as white.'

Jack thanked his Grandad and went back upstairs. This time his room was as he'd left it; nothing had been disturbed. Before he was ready to leave he wet his comb and tried to make his hair sit down. It didn't.

Grandad was back in the garden.

'I'm off now,' Jack called as he made his way towards the gap in the hedge.

Nora and Elan were sitting at the kitchen table making cheese sandwiches when Jack arrived.

'Isn't Camelin here?'

'Still in bed. He had rather a late night,' laughed Nora. 'Motley tells me you gave our Bogie quite a fright.'

'I didn't mean to; it just happened.'

'No harm done. It will do him good to have something to think about. As a precaution I've doubled the Night Guard. If anything so much as moves beyond the hedge we'll know about it.'

Jack was still worried about Peabody going through his belongings.

'I think he was looking for the acorn. He said he wanted gold.'

'All Bogies want gold,' laughed Nora. 'He probably thought you were an easy target; he got more than he bargained for.'

'But how did he know I had any gold?'

'He probably didn't, but I don't think he'll be bothering you again in a hurry.'

Jack hoped Nora was right.

'Thanks for the invitation.'

'Are you going to accept?' Nora asked.

Jack nodded.

'How did you get on with the list of questions I gave you?'

'All done.'

'That's good because I've got some words for you to learn for the ritual.'

Jack took the paper and read the words aloud…

> *A feather from a raven's wing,*
> *This is the token I do bring.*
> *As sunrise lights the darkened sky,*
> *Transform me so that I can fly.*

'You'll need to be word perfect,' said Nora.

'I will be,' Jack assured her.

'These sandwiches are for Camelin,' explained Elan.

'All of them?' exclaimed Jack.

'He's very partial to cheese and Nora needs one of his wing feathers for the ritual. We're going to try to persuade him to make the right decision.'

There was a familiar *caw* as Camelin swooped into the kitchen.

'They smell good.'

'They do,' said Nora without looking up. 'They're for Jack.'

'All of them?' exclaimed Camelin.

'He missed his breakfast,' Nora replied.

Camelin gulped and looked longingly at the pile of sandwiches.

'So did I, and I haven't had any lunch either.'

Nora looked at Camelin and Jack.

'You both realise how important this ritual is don't you? We only have the one chance to get everything right.'

They both nodded.

'I can't wait to see Jack as a raven,' chuckled Camelin without taking his eyes off the plate.

'We're going to need one of your feathers.'

'A feather!' he squawked. 'Don't you know how precious feathers are? I'd be naked without any feathers!'

'We only need one,' said Nora persuasively.

'I don't want to pluck out any of my feathers. It hurts and I'd feel very faint. I'd need a great deal of food to help me feel better.'

'Maybe you could have one of Jack's sandwiches.'

'I'd need more than one.'

'It would need to be a wing feather so he'll be able to fly.'

'A wing feather! I'd need a whole plate of sandwiches to help me recover from losing one of those!'

'I'm sure Jack wouldn't mind.'

Jack was trying not to laugh.

'That's fine,' he managed to say in a very wobbly voice.

Camelin didn't waste any more time in negotiations.

'Ouch!' he yelled as he plucked out one of his wing feathers then staggered dramatically around the table. 'Oh! I feel so dizzy!'

Nora put the whole plate of cheese sandwiches next to him and took the feather. 'Thank you,' she said. 'I hope the sandwiches help.'

'They will!'

Nora held the wing feather up and examined it.

'Perfect. This will do nicely,' she said to herself before turning to Jack and Elan. 'We'll leave Camelin to recover and go down to the library.'

She set off clutching the feather; they followed her down the long passage. As she opened one of the doors Jack gasped. He'd never seen a room like this before. It was full of bookshelves, each one filled with hand-made books.

'Nora made all of these,' whispered Elan.

Jack was speechless. He watched Nora open one of the volumes and put the feather safely inside.

'That's the book Nora needs for the ritual.'

'What happened to the cauldron plates? How did they get lost?' asked Jack.

Elan looked at Nora. Jack felt he'd said something wrong.

'Am I allowed to know?'

'You are, but I would rather Camelin told you. It's his story and he's taken responsibility for the loss but it really wasn't his fault,' explained Nora.

'He blames himself for all of our problems,' continued Elan.

'But why, if it wasn't his fault?'

'Camelin will have to answer that question,' replied Nora. 'Once he trusts you he'll tell you. Now, how about a bit of wand practice?'

Jack nodded. It was certainly something he needed.

'I've put a bucket of sand in the garden, just to be on the safe side,' laughed Nora.

They went through the kitchen. Camelin was nowhere to be seen. Neither were any of the cheese sandwiches.

'He'll be sleeping that lot off,' said Elan. 'He'll not be down again until supper time.'

'He knows you're going to be using your wand this afternoon so he definitely won't come down,' chuckled Nora.

Jack saw the bucket by the bird-table once they were in the garden.

'Watch,' said Nora as she took her wand.

The gnarled wood became smooth. Even in the sunlight Jack could see the tip glowing.

'When you take aim try and concentrate. Gather the sparks into a ball then send it towards the bucket... like this.'

There was a blue flash from the end of Nora's wand. A small ball of light sped towards the bucket; as it landed in the sand it went out. Nora turned to Jack and smiled encouragingly.

'Now you try.'

Sparks flew again around the tip of Jack's wand but they weren't as erratic as they had been. He stared at the crackling explosions and brought them together at the tip.

'That's really good. Try to project it,' urged Elan.

There was a splutter of laughter from above. Jack knew Camelin was watching from the loft. He was determined to show him he could control the wand. He took a deep breath, aimed and fired. The ball of light sped towards the bucket. A great flash and a loud crack told Jack he'd missed his target. The bird-table rocked, then creaked before it broke in two.

'A natural,' croaked Camelin sarcastically.

'I'm really sorry.'

'It's not a problem. I'll mend it when you've finished. Camelin will be pleased; he hates the other birds feeding in the garden. Why don't you stay and practice for a while.'

Jack's next few attempts weren't any better than his first. The hardest part was concentrating the sparks into just one ball of light. One spark nearly singed his hair as it escaped from the ball he was trying to make. Another shot high into the air and narrowly missed a starling's tail. The ball of light travelled so fast the poor bird had to flap his wings frantically to escape. Jack could hear Camelin chuckling from the loft.

After half an hour Jack was able to fire a ball of sparks into the bucket... most of the time. He went back to the kitchen to say goodbye to Nora and Elan.

'I don't think I've done any more damage. I'm really sorry about the bird table.'

Nora raised her wand and pointed it in the direction of the garden. Green sparks flew out of the patio door.

'There, that's sorted the bird table out. We'll see you on Friday. Learn your words and remember, you need to be perfect for the ritual.'

'I will. I promise,' said Jack as he waved goodbye.

Jack looked towards Camelin's loft. He couldn't see him but he could still hear him laughing. Learning the words wouldn't be a problem; wanting to be a raven was. By Saturday morning if he didn't want to transform with all his heart it wasn't going to happen.

That night Jack lay awake worrying.

CAMELIN'S TALE

'I've been waiting hours for you,' Camelin grumbled after Jack let him into the bedroom. 'I couldn't get in because the window was shut.'

'I was told to keep it closed.'

'Where've you been?'

'Shopping with Grandad; I've got school next week and I needed some things.'

'I came for my lesson but I'm too hungry to think now.'

Jack laughed. He'd anticipated Camelin might need a snack the next time he appeared. He went over to the wardrobe and brought out an old biscuit tin Grandad said he could have and a bag from his rucksack. Camelin's eyes grew wide as Jack shook the bag over the tin. A packet of biscuits, individually wrapped chocolate cakes and an assortment of chocolate bars tumbled out.

'Help yourself.'

Jack hoped Camelin wasn't going to be too greedy.

'They've got to last. I don't know when I'll be able to get any more.'

'Mmmm, they do smell good.'

Camelin stuck his beak into the tin and rummaged around. As his feathers spread out and parted Jack noticed a scar on the back of his head.

'Help me read this one first before I eat it,' Camelin mumbled when he eventually surfaced with one of the cakes firmly clasped in his beak.

Jack unwrapped the cake and read the writing on the label.

'Knowing what's inside is half the fun,' Camelin explained. 'That's another reason why I'd like to learn to read.'

For the next half hour they made good progress with his letters.

'Is that a scar on your head?' Jack asked when they'd finished.

'Yes, it is.'

'I've got one above my eyebrow. Look!' Jack said as he bent his head so Camelin could see the thin red line on his forehead. 'Got it playing football last year at school. How did you get yours?'

For a while Camelin was silent and Jack wondered if he'd asked the wrong question. He was about to apologise when Camelin gave a great sigh.

'I suppose you're going to have to know sooner or later. You can't go back into the past with me until you know everything, so I might as well tell you now.'

Jack was intrigued. Camelin paced up and down the window ledge a few times before he spoke again.

'I got the scar from a Roman soldier.'

'A Roman... but there haven't been any Roman soldiers here for hundreds of years!'

'That's true, but it *was* a Roman soldier who hit me. It was in AD 61 to be precise. The Emperor wanted to be rid of the Druids. There was a fort nearby and the soldier there were ordered to burn the Sacred Groves, kill the Druids and anyone connected to them.'

'But....' Jack spluttered.

'I'd been sent on an important errand by Nora when a soldier caught me.'

'Nora!' interrupted Jack. 'How can you both be *that old* and why didn't you fly away?'

'If you keep interrupting I'm never going to finish. Nora and I *are* both *that old* and I couldn't fly away because I wasn't a raven; I was a boy.'

Jack was stunned. He'd not considered the possibility that Camelin could ever have been anything other than a raven. He knew Nora was old but according to Camelin they'd both been alive for hundreds of years. How could that be? Why was Camelin still a raven if Nora could perform the transformation ritual? This revelation had thrown up more questions than answers. As Jack tried to make sense of what he'd just been told, Camelin continued with his story.

'I'd been sent to collect the last three cauldron plates, one from each of the sacred wells in Glasruhen Forest. There were thirteen plates altogether; Nora had the other ten. Lots of people, nymphs and dryads were waiting at the portal on the hillside for me to return. Once she had all the plates Nora was going to lace them together and make a large cauldron. It was a very special cauldron; too powerful to be kept in one piece unless it was being used by the Druids for their rituals. This cauldron, with the Druid's golden acorn, could open the portal between Earth and Annwn.'

Some of this was starting to make sense to Jack.

'So what happened to the cauldron plates after

you got hit on the head?'

'I don't know. The soldiers left me for dead and I would have been if Nora hadn't found me. She saw the Sacred Grove burning and knew there was a problem. The only way she could save my life was to transform me into something else, something which could support the little strength I had left. There wasn't time for complicated rituals. She did what she could and transformed me into a raven. I've been like this ever since. So you see, it's my fault the cauldron plates were lost and without them the portal has remained closed.'

Jack didn't know what to say. Nothing could change what had happened but he wanted Camelin to know how sorry he was.

'You know I'll do anything I can to help,' Jack said in a very solemn voice.

'I know that now. I wouldn't have told you any of this if I didn't think you were the only one who could help us. They were bad times when the Romans started killing the Druids. Most of them fled to Mona, you know. It's called Anglesey now. It was a big mistake; they got massacred there.'

'Wasn't there anything Nora could have done?'

'Nora and Gwillam, the High Druid, had a plan. Anyone who wanted to would be sent into Annwn for safety. They could have come back to Earth once the danger was passed. When I got to the shrine Gwillam was already dead. I took the plate from the well and ran as fast as I could towards Glasruhen but that's when the soldiers caught me. I felt the blow on the back of my head and the rest is just a blank.'

Camelin paused for breath.

'That's why you're so important. We need you to go back into the past with me, find out what happened to the plates and recover them. Only then will we be able to remake the cauldron and return to Annwn. We've been waiting all this time to find the right person.'

'Arrana said Nora would die soon if she doesn't get back to Annwn.'

'Nora can only make the elixir she needs from the leaves of the Crochan tree which grows in Annwn. It's why she's lived so long. The elixir extended the Druids' lives so they could tend the trees and live as long as the Hamadryads in the forests. She gave me some of it when she transformed me.'

'Are you going to live forever?'

'Only if I stay as a raven. I can transform back into a boy again in Annwn. Then I'll be just like you, but we're all in trouble if we can't find the cauldron plates in time.'

'Couldn't the trees have told Nora what happened?'

'The Romans set fire to the groves. Fire traumatises trees and the ones that survived didn't remember anything except the flames.'

'Why couldn't you go through the window in time on your own and look for the missing cauldron plates?'

'The window is high above Glasruhen Hill. To break through the thin veil between the present and the past we must travel towards each other at the same speed. We'll only have a split second to fly past each other at the exact place where the window opens. It's not something I could do on my own. For this to work we had to find a boy, born in the right place, at the right time and who is the same age as I was when it happened... and that's you.'

Jack was feeling excited and also a bit scared. Nora was right when she'd said he would see and hear some strange things. He hadn't realised, until now, that so much depended on him.

'If all this works and we get through the window do you know how long we'll be gone?'

'A fraction of a second in real time, I think!'

'So no matter how long we spend in the past we won't be gone long enough for Grandad to miss me?'

Camelin nodded his head. Although he'd been given a lot of information Jack still felt there was something else he hadn't been told.

'Is there anything else I should know?'

'It's about the window. It's only going to be open for a few minutes. If we don't get through it this time we'll have to wait another hundred years. Nora can't perform the ritual if it's not in the right place and by then it will be too late. Arrana will be dead.'

An uneasy silence filled the room.

'I'm scared I might fail.'

'So am I,' whispered Camelin. 'I'm sorry I wasn't very nice to you, only you don't look very strong or brave and I think it's going to be dangerous when we go back into the past. I was there. I know what Romans are like. It's not going to be easy.'

'I promise I'll do my best.'

'I know you will.'

They sat in silence. Jack thought about everything Camelin had said.

'If we find the cauldron plates how are we going to get them back?

'We don't have to bring them back. We hide them somewhere safe and fly back through the window. Once we get back we tell Nora and Elan where we've put them and they'll go and collect them. That's the easy part.'

'But where could we possibly put the plates so they'll be safe for nearly two thousand years?'

'In water. We find the nearest well or spring and drop them in. They'll be very safe with the Nymphs to guard them.'

Jack couldn't imagine anyone trying to steal anything from a water nymph, especially if they were all like Jennet.

'How long do we have in the past before the window in time closes?'

'Now that's the good news. It doesn't close from the other side. It doesn't matter how long we're there. We can fly back at any time.'

'Well that's a relief,' laughed Jack.

Camelin bowed his head and looked thoughtful.

'I was training to be a Druid you know. I was Gwillam's acolyte but then everything changed. Gwillam was killed and I became a raven. I'd only been with him a few years. It took twenty-one years to train to be a Druid. Reading and writing didn't come until near the end, and that's why I never learnt. Anyway, I can see how useful reading could be now.'

'Oh it is,' agreed Jack. 'I can find you some great books to borrow.'

Camelin pulled his face.

'I was thinking more about the menu from the Chinese takeaway, unless you've got any good food books.'

Jack laughed.

'I'll see if I can borrow a cookery book. You'll love the pictures.'

'Before I forget, Nora gave me a message. She said you've got to remember to bring the golden acorn with you on Friday. She can't perform the ritual without it.'

'I wish she'd take it back. I'm frightened I might lose it.'

'I think it's what you're supposed to do, you know, as *The One*. You've got to keep it safe, look after it to prove you're worthy.'

'Is there anything else you haven't told me?'

Camelin pretended to think hard then shook his head. Just then Grandad called upstairs. Jack's supper was ready.

'It must be my supper time too, my stomach's really empty.'

Camelin's stomach always seemed to be empty. Jack wondered if he'd feel hungry all the time once he'd been transformed into a raven.

'See you tomorrow,' he called as Camelin took off.

Jack watched Camelin as he showed off his brilliant skills again; a backwards loop the loop followed by an amazing twisting dive. Jack sighed; it would be great to fly. He just wished he didn't feel so afraid.

It was nearly bedtime before Jack got back to his room. He took out his wand, opened his Book of Shadows and was about to write to Elan when he heard a loud crash. It came from the greenhouse. Jack held his wand up at the window so he could see better, then hid it quickly when he saw Grandad making his way down the garden path. There was another crash, this time from the kitchen. It wasn't Grandad; he was still outside. With his wand unlit, he cautiously made his way to the top of the stairs. Someone or something was definitely in the house. Jack carefully took one step at a time. If it was Peabody, he wanted to sneak up on him. The back door was wide open. Jack could still see Grandad's torch shining inside the greenhouse. Another crash from the kitchen was followed by a strange chittering sound. Jack stopped. Whatever it was in there wasn't alone. He was about to take his wand and burst into the kitchen when Motley came running through the back door. He stood on his back legs and started frantically telling Jack something.

'Hold on, let me put my wand in the other hand.'

Motley started again.

'They've got Orin. I told her not to come… she wouldn't listen and now they've got her. They'll make her into a hat.'

Motley paused for breath. He was very upset and frightened.

'Who are they and who's Orin?'

'Spriggans… in the kitchen… they want to make Orin into a hat. Oh, my beautiful Orin… my baby sister… she should never have followed us tonight.'

'What are Spriggans and why would they want to make your sister into a hat?'

'No time to explain… you've got to save her.'

'What do you want me to do?'

'Get her back… make them give her back. Do whatever it takes… just don't let them go back down the hole with her.'

'Hole!'

'Big hole… in the kitchen… where they've tunnelled through. Best tunnellers in the world Spriggans are; go and have a look.'

Motley ran behind Jack's legs. Jack carefully pushed the kitchen door open a crack to see what was going on. There in the middle of the kitchen floor was a hole. Jack saw three small creatures roped together like mountaineers. They had a very wide mouths and Jack could see their sharp needle-like teeth as they grinned at each other. Soil was ground into their clothes. The middle one was holding a beautiful white rat, upside down, by its tail. The last one was half inside and half out of the hole. At the front was the leader of the gang. On his head was a fur hat with a lighted candle stuck into a holder. It flickered as the Spriggan shouted in a high-pitched voice. They were making far too much noise to notice Jack.

'Puts the rat in the bag,' ordered the leader in a high squeaky voice.

'She's mine,' snarled the second Spriggan. 'I nabbed her.'

'She's got to go to Him. He won't allow anyone else to wears white.'

Jack could see Motley's tiny body shaking as he tried to explain.

'Who are they talking about?' Jack whispered.

'Their Chief. He'll want Orin for himself.

131

Spriggans hunt rats. They make the males pull carts in the mines… eat the females… rat kebab is a delicacy… make their soft pelts into hats. See the leader… that candle holder's a twisted rat's tail… his hat used to be Rolph… one of our Night Guard.'

Jack looked at the beautiful white rat. He couldn't let her end up like Rolph. He had to do something.

'Don't worry Motley, I'll get her back.'

Jack burst into the kitchen. The Spriggans froze. The light from his wand blinded them. He held it high in the air and let the sparks fly out of the tip. He could see the Spriggans hopping around as hot embers landed on their brown leathery skin. Orin twisted up and bit the hand that held her.

'Owwww!' the Spriggan squealed, but he didn't let go.

Jack aimed his wand carefully above Orin and concentrated the tip into a glowing ball.

'Hold still Orin,' he shouted, and watched as her body went limp. He could see the fear in her jet black eyes. He let the ball of light fly towards the Spriggan's arm. This time he dropped his prize.

'Run Orin… over here,' shouted Motley.

'Take her up to my room and stay there,' ordered Jack. 'I'll deal with this lot.'

Motley and Orin disappeared. Jack turned to face the three intruders. The middle one was hopping wildly around the kitchen holding his arm and wailing. He was dragging the other two behind him. If Jack was to do anything he had to do it now while they were confused and tangled by the rope. He'd managed to toss the Bogie out of the bush by waving his wand. It might work again if he tried it on the Spriggans. He pointed it at the Spriggans' feet and willed them back into the hole. To his amazement the three little creatures shot across the kitchen floor and disappeared into the tunnel.

'Close!' Jack commanded the gaping hole in the floor. It sealed itself instantly. No one would ever know the floor had been damaged. Jack put his wand in his pocket and turned on the light as Grandad came in through the door. The kitchen was a bit of a mess.

'That fox got into the greenhouse,' grumbled Grandad as soon as he saw Jack. 'Dug a great hole right under the plant pots. It's taken me ages to fill it in but I can't have it damaging any more of my vegetables.'

Grandad looked at the mess and smelt the air.

'It's been in here too. That's my fault for leaving the back door open.'

'I'll help you clear it up.'

'No it's alright. You get yourself back off to bed and I'll sort this lot out.'

When Jack got back to his room Motley and Orin were sitting on the table. Orin looked shaken. Jack held his wand so he could talk to Motley.

'They've gone.'

'They'll be back but not tonight… hope you don't mind Jack… called the guards in… not safe to go back out yet.'

Jack looked towards the window. He could see several tails hanging below the curtain.

'That's OK, you can all come out.'

As the rats jumped one by one from the window ledge onto the table Motley introduced them.

'Morris… Fergus… Raggs… Berry… Lester… Podge… Midge.'

'Pleased to meet you,' said Jack and nodded back to each of them as they nodded to him.

'All right if we keep watch from the window tonight?' Motley asked.

'Of course you can, but if Grandad comes in make sure you pull your tails up.'

'Have to wake you early... you'll need to let us out,' replied Motley. 'We'll give Nora a full report in the morning.'

Jack could see that Orin was still shaking.

'Orin can sleep on my pillow,' he told Motley. 'She's too upset to keep watch.'

'Orin isn't in the watch... only ever eight of us... usually make a circle so we've got every angle covered.'

Motley and the rest of the Night Guards took up their positions around the circular table, each with their backs facing inwards and their faces out.

'Like a compass!' exclaimed Jack.

'Bright boy,' replied Motley. 'I find North, the rest know where to stand... last thing we do is link tails.'

Jack watched as they all intertwined their tails in the centre.

'Precaution... no one can snatch us without the others knowing... easier to give them a jog too if they fall asleep,' added Motley giving a quick pull on his tail. Seven other tails moved and seven backs straightened up.

'Night watch... dismiss.'

Jack watched as the rats saluted Motley then scampered back onto the window ledge. Motley gave

Orin one more stern look.

'Hope that's a lesson to you!'

'I'm sorry. I won't do it again,' she whispered.

'Don't allow females on the watch... too dangerous... their pelts are softer... make better hats.'

Orin eventually stopped shaking and settled down on Jack's pillow. As Jack's eyes adjusted to the darkness he could see eight small silhouettes on the window ledge. He didn't understand what Orin whispered in his ear but her soft velvety tongue licked his cheek several times before she curled up into a ball.

Jack lay awake for ages. Somehow he had to get rid of the fear in his heart or the ritual wouldn't work. Eventually he came to a decision. Tomorrow afternoon, instead of going through the gap in the hedge and coming straight home from Ewell House, he'd go further along. He'd try and open the Yews. He needed to find his way back into Glasruhen Forest. If anyone would understand and be able to help, Arrana would. He had to see her again before Nora performed the ritual.

PREPARATIONS

'Motley told us how brave you were last night,' Elan said excitedly when Jack walked into the kitchen.

'I was only helping out.'

'You saved Orin. I don't call that just helping out,' replied Nora. 'Motley saw what you did in the kitchen and he was very impressed and grateful. Poor Orin wouldn't have survived if it hadn't been for you.'

Jack's cheeks were burning. He felt proud but also embarrassed.

'Should I have sent you a message? It was very late.'

'You didn't leave anything for us to do,' laughed Nora. 'Besides the trees keep me informed and the Night Guard report here every morning.'

137

Elan laughed. 'Nora gives them breakfast but don't tell Camelin. He'd only get jealous.'

'I won't,' promised Jack. He could imagine exactly what Camelin would say if he knew. 'Motley said he thought the Spriggans would be back. What do you think they were after?'

'Oh anything and everything,' replied Nora. 'We haven't had a Spriggan problem for a long time. They'll think twice about coming back to your house after last night. They don't like magic.'

'But they do like to sneak around looking for anything valuable,' explained Elan. 'They prefer precious stones, silver or gold, but they're just as likely to steal your dustbin.'

'Of course they don't see it as stealing, just taking back what they think belongs to them. Like Gnomes they have underground kingdoms. Whatever comes from the earth they consider is theirs,' continued Nora, 'but it looks like they were hunting rats last night and they won't be very pleased to have lost such a valuable one.'

Jack was relieved they hadn't been after Nora's golden acorn.

'The Spriggans were arguing over Orin. One of them said she was for *Him*, and Motley said she'd be for their chief. Do you know who he is?'

'That would be Chief Knuckle. He's the oldest but probably not the wisest Spriggan. They say he has a cloak made from the fur of pure white rabbits. I imagine he'd have loved a white hat to match. Rat pelts have a built-in candle-holder, which is very useful for a Spriggan.'

'Motley explained that to me last night. They were roped together. Is that so they don't get lost in the tunnels?'

'Oh, goodness no!' exclaimed Nora. 'That's for safety; a Spriggan left on it's own turns into a giant and that could be dangerous for anyone close by. A gigantic Spriggan could crush anything in its way without even knowing what he'd done. They're not the brightest of creatures.'

'Nasty little creatures if you're talking about Bogies,' said Camelin as he shuffled into the kitchen.

'We were discussing Spriggans,' Nora informed him.

'Ergh! They're even worse. You'd recognise one immediately, covered in dirt, great wide mouth, always grinning and at what I've no idea. You can usually smell them first. I swear they never have a bath.'

'Jack saw three last night in his kitchen,' continued Nora.

'He was brilliant,' interrupted Elan. 'Saved Motley's little sister and sent the Spriggans back to where they'd come from.'

'Why didn't anyone tell me? Why do I always miss all the good stuff?'

'Probably because you spend too much time in that basket of yours in the loft,' laughed Nora.

'You should have sent me a signal,' Camelin said to Jack. 'Can you do an owl?'

Camelin threw back his head and hooted loudly.

'That's the call of the *raven owl*; at night it means there's a problem. We'll practice it sometime. Any more trouble and I can come and sort it out for you.'

'Thanks,' Jack replied, 'I wasn't alone last night. The Night Guard were with me.'

'Fat lot of good they'd be if there were Spriggans around. Bet their little legs were shaking like jellies.'

Camelin started to laugh and wobble his spindly legs until he saw Nora's face.

'Any more of that and you can go back to your loft,' she said sternly.

Jack thought he'd better change the subject.

'I came to ask you what time I should arrive tomorrow night. It didn't say on the invitation. Grandad says I should ask if I need to wear my best clothes.'

'It doesn't matter what you wear,' replied Nora.

Camelin began to snigger and everyone looked at him.

'He won't need any clothes at the Raven's Bowl.'

'You're not being very helpful,' Nora said and gave Camelin another stern look. She turned to Jack. 'It's more important that you're ready for the ritual.'

'Don't forget to bring the golden acorn with you,' added Elan.

'Is it your birthday tomorrow?' Jack asked.

'No,' she laughed. 'We just needed a good excuse to invite you to stay.'

'Can we go now?' asked Camelin.

'Go where?' enquired Nora.

'Upstairs. There's something I need to do with Jack before tomorrow.'

Nora and Elan looked puzzled but Camelin wasn't saying any more. Jack shrugged his shoulders. He had no idea what Camelin wanted either.

'That's fine,' said Nora. 'We'll see you later.'

Once they were in the loft Camelin shuffled to the far corner and brought the bottom of the old pizza box over to Jack. He'd neatly pecked it away from the lid. There were bits of tomato smeared on it and what could once have been a mushroom. Camelin flipped it over and looked at Jack.

'I want you to make me a sign. It's got to say *keep out*. I don't want Nora or Elan coming up. I've been practicing my letters and I don't want them to find out.'

Camelin went back for the lid and showed Jack what he'd done. There were three wobbly pictures of a jelly, a pie and a long stick.

'What is it?'

'It's you... *j* for jelly, *a* for apple pie and *k* for kebab.'

'But you've drawn a stick!'

'I copied it from this one,' replied Camelin as he rummaged around and triumphantly produced a grubby bamboo skewer. 'I only keep this bit. I eat the rest.'

Jack wanted to laugh but Camelin was being very serious.

'You need a cake in there too, like this.'

Jack drew the cake in between the apple and the kebab stick and wrote the letters of his name underneath.

'Will you make my sign?'

'Not a problem, but we'll need two holes at the top and some string to put through the holes so I can hang it up.'

Camelin swiftly stood on the lid and used the end of his beak to make two holes, one quite a lot bigger than the other. He skipped off into the corner again to look for some string, whilst Jack took the pencil Camelin had left him and wrote in large capital letters…

KEEP OUT

'That's great. You can put it up on your way out and I'll see you tomorrow. I've got things to do.'

'Things?'

'I've got to look my best for the party. Got some serious preening to do and all my claws to clean. No time to chat today.'

'See you tomorrow then,' said Jack as he hung the sign in the middle of the ladder where it couldn't be missed.

Nora and Elan seemed surprised when he came back to the kitchen alone.

'Camelin's got things to do,' explained Jack. 'Grooming I think.'

'He's so vain,' said Elan. 'He's always looking at himself in the mirror.'

'He told me how he'd got his scar yesterday.'

'That's good,' said Nora and nodded. 'That means he trusts you.'

'Do you mind if I go now? I've sort of got some things I need to do before tomorrow too.'

'Not at all. We'll see you here about 6 o'clock.'

'I've got to come to the front door, Grandad said.'

'I'm sure Camelin will keep a lookout for you. We'll see you tomorrow. I think we've all got things we need to do,' smiled Nora.

Jack made his way down to the bottom of the garden. He looked to see if anyone was watching. Instead of going through the gap in the hedge he went and stood in front of the yews. He took his wand out of his bag and held it firmly. Once the rough bark had become smooth he stood very still and concentrated. He willed the yews to open. Nothing happened. He held the wand higher and took a deep breath.

'Open,' he commanded.

The yews remained closed. Maybe he ought to raise both hands as Nora had done. He was about to try when some of the branches parted. A small nut-brown face shook its head.

'You can't come through without permission.'

'I wanted to see Arrana. I mean, Arrana the Wise, Protector and Most Sacred of All.'

'You still need permission and you're going to have to wait until I get an answer. It's already been sent. Please wait.'

The head disappeared and Jack realised he was still standing with his wand in mid-air. He busied himself and put his backpack on but kept the wand out in case the yews opened. It wasn't long before he saw the message returning. It came rustling through the trees and stopped at the great yews in front of him. The head reappeared.

'Follow me.'

As Jack stepped forward the trees creaked and groaned. They only parted slightly, just enough for Jack to step onto the path. Once he was through they closed behind him. He looked around to find out whose face he'd seen. Behind the first tree was a tall willowy woman. Her long golden hair almost touched the bottom of her flowing robe. She had a circlet of flowers on her head and a belt of ivy twisted around her waist. She smiled at Jack and beckoned him forward. Her feet hardly touched the ground as she flitted from tree to tree. When they reached the end of the yew tunnel she stepped inside the trunk of a large beech tree and disappeared. The trees ahead rustled and another Dryad stepped out. She was similar to the first except her hair was silver and she wore a pale grey gown.

'This way,' she beckoned.

She led Jack into Glasruhen and left him where the oak trees began. The faces of the Dryads he'd seen on his first visit peered at him from behind the trunks of the gnarled trees. They darted in and out of the oaks and flitted on and off the path. Jack followed them deeper and deeper into Glasruhen. His thoughts went back to Newton Gill. It must have been exactly like this before their Hamadryad faded into nothingness and became a hollow tree. He understood why the Gnarles were so lonely and missed the Dryads.

They led him to the clearing; it wasn't long before he stood in front of Arrana again. He bowed low and held the golden acorn flat on his palm towards the Hamadryad. He didn't speak aloud. He spoke with his heart as he had before.

'Arrana the Wise, Protector and Most Sacred of All, I need your help.'

Jack watched as the trunk of the massive oak shivered and quaked. He heard the Dryads whispering. As the trunk became a blur, everyone, including Jack, held their breath until Arrana towered above them. She smiled and nodded.

'You've done well since I saw you last. You've shown compassion and great courage. You've used the twig I gave you well.'

'I don't want to fail you.'

'You won't.'

'But I'm afraid. I don't think I'm going to be able to fly.'

'You'll feel differently when you've been transformed. Camelin felt exactly the same at first. He had to learn to fly without anyone to teach him. He spent the first few months on Nora's shoulder. He was so frightened he wouldn't even try.'

'But Camelin doesn't mind heights.'

'And neither will you. Once you're a raven you'll have the instincts of a bird. You won't feel like a boy.'

Arrana's words made Jack feel a lot better. If the ritual worked he'd overcome his fear. If Camelin had, he could too.

'The ritual will work if you want to be a raven with all your heart.'

'I do. I want to save you.'

Jack remembered the Gnori, the hollowness and emptiness of the dead tree. Tears ran down his face.

'I don't want you to become a hollow tree or the forest to die. I don't want Nora to die either. I want this to work with all my heart.'

'And so it will Jack Brenin.'

The forest erupted with song. Jack turned to see the Dryads. He could hear their beautiful voices, only this time he understood their song. They were singing about him! When he turned around to thank Arrana she was gone. The Dryads parted for Jack to reach the pathway and return home.

They kept him company until he reached the gap in the hedge. He quickly darted past so no one would see, but Elan called to him from the other side of the hedge. Jack froze. How could he have been so stupid? Nora would have known straight away he'd been through the yews. He knew how Camelin felt now.

'I'm sorry,' he said as he entered the garden.

'There's nothing to be sorry about. I've been waiting here to give you something to take home with you. After you'd gone Motley came to speak to Nora and we didn't think you'd mind.'

Next to Elan was a large cage and inside was Orin.

'Nora's already spoken to your Grandad and he says it's all right. You can keep Orin in your room. He was really pleased you wanted a pet.'

'But Orin's not a pet!'

'We know that but Grandad doesn't have to.'

Orin looked pleadingly at Jack.

'I want to help but Motley won't let me be in

the guard. He said I'd be safe with you and I can keep you company and watch from your window at night if you'll have me.'

'Of course I will, and I promise to look after you.'

'Good, that's settled,' said Elan as she passed the cage to Jack. 'See you tomorrow night.'

After supper when Jack was back in his room, he sat with Orin; they talked late into the night. Jack was grateful for the company. He wouldn't have slept too well anyway. Even after speaking to Arrana he was still worried about the ritual.

THE RAVEN'S BOWL

Jack spent the following morning helping Grandad in the greenhouse.

'I can still smell that fox,' he complained as they cleared away the broken plant pots.

Jack looked at the freshly turned soil where the Spriggan's tunnel had been and hoped they wouldn't be back.

After lunch Grandad showed Jack how to tie the small flowers and broad leaves he'd cut into a posy.

'I'm sure Elan will like these,' said Grandad as he admired the delicate pink and white Lily of the Valley flowers.

'Mmmm,' mumbled Jack.

'She will Jack, trust me.'

The rest of the day went really slowly. Jack found it hard to fill the hours before he could go back to Ewell House. He spent the afternoon sorting Orin's cage out until she was happy with it. He was relieved when it was eventually time to set off. Jack checked one last time to make sure he'd got everything. The golden acorn was safely zipped into the jacket he'd packed for the morning. Orin climbed into the side pocket of his backpack. He wasn't too happy about carrying the flowers but there was no other way of getting them to Elan without squashing them.

He'd just turned the last corner before Ewell House when a boy on a bicycle sped past. There was a sudden screech of brakes. The boy stopped then slowly turned the bike around. Jack's heart sank when he recognised the goalie from the playing field.

'Hey pixie boy, got flowers for your girlfriend?'

Jack ignored the boy and carried on walking; he was nearly at the gate. The boy cycled back. As he passed Jack he lunged at his arm and knocked the flowers out of his hand.

'OK pixie boy, you and me, we've got unfinished business.'

Before Jack could do anything the boy was off his

bike. He shoved Jack out of the way then kicked the posy into the air. Pink and white flowers showered onto the pavement. The goalie grinned.

'Ooops! Hope they weren't expensive.'

Jack could feel his heart beating wildly. He wished the boy would go away.

'Thought I told you I didn't want to see you again pixie boy; so what you doin' here?'

'My name's Jack.'

'Ooooh, bit posh aren't we?'

The boy circled around Jack and he mimicked, *my name's Jack*, before pushing him into the hedge.

Jack gasped as a high-pitched squeal came from the backpack. The boy stepped back in surprise. When Jack didn't move he raised his fist. A loud *caw* made them both look up. Jack saw Camelin swoop towards them. The boy's eyes widened. His hands shot up to shield his head but he wasn't quick enough. There was a splat as Camelin bombed him from above. Jack burst out laughing; the boy's hair and face were plastered in ploop. Camelin landed on the gatepost and fixed the boy with his beady eye.

'What's going on here lads?' a deep voice asked from behind.

Jack turned and recognised Don from the

cricket club.

'It's Jack, isn't it?' Don asked as he helped him out of the hedge.

Before Jack could reply the boy grabbed his bike.

'We're not finished yet pixie boy,' he yelled as he pedalled away.

'Was he bothering you?' asked Don.

'He's got it in for me.'

'He ought to pick on someone his own size. I'm just off to see Sam now. I can walk you back if you like.'

'Thanks but I'm going in here,' replied Jack and pointed to Ewell House.

'Well, if you're sure.'

Jack nodded.

As soon as Don went round the corner he carefully took off his backpack.

'Are you OK Orin?'

He put his hand into the pocket and stroked her soft fur.

'No harm done?' asked Camelin.

'No I think she's OK.'

Jack grinned at Camelin, 'That was a great shot.'

'Don't tell Nora. I'm not supposed to do that.'

'You were only helping out. He'd have hit me if you hadn't shown up.'

Camelin shuffled his feet then looked down at the scattered flowers.

'Were they for Elan?'

'Yes, but not to worry.'

Jack gathered the flowers and leaves up as best he could. Once they were inside Nora's garden he took out his wand. He laid the flowers on a stone bench and concentrated hard. He did everything he could to remember what Grandad had done earlier.

'Wow!' croaked Camelin as the posy remade itself. 'You really are a natural.'

'It's not as good as Grandad's.'

'It's beautiful,' said Elan as she tapped Jack on the shoulder. 'Are you alright? We saw that boy push you.'

'I've met him before. He really doesn't like me.'

'He's just a bully. Try not to let him worry you. It's a good job that man came along when he did.'

Jack nodded, then winked at Camelin.

'Let's go inside,' continued Elan. 'Nora's made quite a feast.'

Camelin didn't need telling twice. He took off and swerved around the side of the house so he could be first into the kitchen.

'I hope you don't mind only I've brought Orin. I couldn't leave her on her own, not after I'd promised to look after her.'

'We were expecting her. There's an extra place been laid next to Motley.'

Jack was amazed when he got into the kitchen. The table was piled high. There were homemade rolls, pies, sausages and different cheeses, with jellies and cakes in the centre. Jack could see that Camelin's eyes were as wide as saucers. At the far end of the table nine small plates were arranged on a raised tray. The Night Guard were sitting around it on upturned beakers. Orin scampered up to join them. A large bowl was next to Jack's place and Camelin was hopping from leg to leg in his eagerness to get started.

'This party is really for you Jack,' said Nora when everyone was seated. 'Your last night as an ordinary boy. After tomorrow morning you'll be *extra*ordinary.'

'Like me,' interrupted Camelin. 'A raven boy.'

Everyone laughed and clapped.

'Can we start now?' Camelin asked then added, 'please.'

'We should warn you Jack, his table manners aren't very good,' whispered Elan.

'It's OK, I've seen him eat before,' Jack whispered back.

The party lasted for the rest of the evening. Camelin ate as much as he could before Nora frowned and said he'd had enough. After they'd finished Jack held his wand so he could understand what the rats were saying. Motley and the Night Guard entertained everyone with their singing. Motley introduced Morris who began a rousing song. After the first verse the rest of the Night Guard joined in. Even though Jack was still holding his wand he didn't know what the rats were singing about.

'I can't understand them,' Jack whispered to Camelin.

'Neither can I. They're singing in Welsh,' laughed Camelin.

'It's about saucepans bubbling on the fire,' Orin whispered, 'and Johnny has a scrap with the cat. Motley likes that bit.'

A large, grey, bedraggled rat stood in the middle of the table. He bowed to everyone and introduced himself as Raggs. He told everyone about his adventures as a ship's rat before he'd joined the Night Guard. Orin sang a solo in a high, squeaky voice.

'She's not allowed to sing with the guard choir,' explained Motley.

'Would you like to do something for us?' Nora asked Jack.

'I could sing too,' he replied.

'Oh yes,' the rats said together.

Jack sang one of his favourite songs he used to sing in the choir. When he'd finished everyone clapped. To end the evening Camelin did his shuffle dance. He even let Fergus and Berry, the two youngest rats, join in.

'I think it's time for bed now,' Nora announced. 'Some of us have an early start in the morning.'

Orin climbed onto Jack's shoulder and waved goodbye to the Night Guard.

'Try and get a few hours sleep if you can before we set off for the Raven's Bowl,' Nora said before Jack and Elan climbed the stairs.

'You'll need to be up and off at least an hour before first light,' Elan told him when they reached the door of the spare bedroom. 'Goodnight Jack. I'm sure everything will be fine.'

'Aren't you coming with us?'

'I'm not needed. I'll have breakfast ready for when you get back.'

Jack unpacked the few things he'd brought. He would have loved to join Camelin in the loft but hadn't been invited. He found it hard to sleep. He kept going over the words of the ritual. He was worried he might forget them. There was also the other part he'd been trying to put out of his mind, the bit where he'd have to take off all his clothes. Nora had shown him a large hooded cloak he could use. She'd assured him, even if there were other people on the top of Glasruhen Hill waiting for the sunrise, they wouldn't notice Jack on the rock if he wore it.

Orin had already snuggled down on Jack's pillow. He was glad he wasn't alone; it was going to be a long night. He must have finally dropped off to sleep because the next thing he felt was something hard prodding him awake. It was an effort to wake up but he managed to open his eyes before an extremely hard beak poked him again.

'It's time,' Camelin croaked. 'This is going to be fun!'

It probably would be for Camelin. He didn't have to walk all the way to the summit of Glasruhen Hill. Jack hadn't told Nora or Elan he wasn't very good at getting up in the mornings. This morning was worse. His stomach churned. Camelin must have heard it.

'We can't eat until Nora's done the transformation so the sooner we get on with it the better.'

'I'm fine,' Jack assured him. 'I'm not hungry, just a bit nervous.'

The morning air was fresh and there wasn't a cloud in the sky. As they made their way down to the end of the garden Jack could feel the dew from the grass seeping through his trainers. He'd left his wand in the bedroom but the golden acorn was in his jacket pocket. Nora stood before the Yews and raised her arms. As they parted Camelin flew off towards the hill.

'See you at the top,' he croaked.

The climb through the woods wasn't as strenuous as Jack had imagined. Nora started to explain what would happen, or what she thought was going to happen.

'I've never had to perform a transformation involving anyone changing back again before.'

'I feel a bit shaky. Are you sure this isn't going to hurt?'

'Not exactly. Everyone's different and it's a long time since I've transformed anyone. If you'd been born a shape shifter you'd be able to transform from one form to another without even thinking about it.'

Born a shape shifter... Jack remembered reading the same words in his Book of Shadows. He realised he hadn't fully understood what they'd meant.

Nora continued explaining.

'Some people have the ability to change into something else without having to perform complicated rituals.'

Jack wasn't looking forward to his body being scrunched down to the size of a raven but he'd promised to help. He knew he'd have to go through with the ritual. Although he was nervous, his excitement was greater than his fear and now he longed to be able to fly like Camelin.

'I expect for the first few times it's going to take

some getting used to,' continued Nora. 'But by the end of the weekend you should be fine.'

Jack hoped so.

It wasn't long before they left the gentle incline that led from the bottom of Nora's garden to the slopes of the hill. Here the path grew steeper and every so often Jack had to stop to catch his breath. As they neared the summit Camelin reappeared and reported that the whole area was clear. Not one person had ventured out to watch the sun rise.

'Everyone used to come up here. There'd be feasting and singing but that was such a long time ago now,' said Nora sadly.

'It's too far for most people to be bothered walking up to the top,' croaked Camelin. 'But when you can fly we can come up here all the time.'

Jack thought he'd rather fly to the summit than walk any day. He was out of breath and feeling very hot.

'We're here,' Nora announced as she pointed to an outcrop of rock. 'We'd better get ready. It can't be long now until the sun rises.'

Jack gave the golden acorn to Nora. She gave the wing feather to Camelin and her cloak to Jack. He followed Camelin to a hollow at the base of the rocks. Nora had been right. He wasn't going to be visible from the main path but he was glad he'd got the cloak. He quickly undressed and put his clothes safely in the crevice. It was difficult to climb up the rock in bare feet. There was a strong breeze at the top and Jack shivered as the cloak flapped around his ankles. The air was cool and fresh. He tried not to look down. He felt dizzy and sick.

'Kneel down on the rock,' Nora called. 'We haven't got much time.'

As Jack bent over the rock seemed to rise up and the sky spun around. There was nothing between him and the ground, hundreds of feet below.

'Be careful,' warned Nora. 'When the transformation is complete keep very still, otherwise it could be dangerous.'

Jack had no intention of moving at all now he was on top of the rock.

'You must lie flat and look into The Raven's Bowl,' Nora shouted. 'When the first ray of light from the sunrise hits the bowl make sure you're holding Camelin's wing feather. Touch the water with your forehead and repeat the words of the ritual.'

Camelin for once had been silent and Jack realised why when he turned around. He still had the feather Nora had given him in his beak.

'Take the feather Jack. Camelin will place his wing on your back as soon as he sees the light. That will be my signal to begin the ritual.'

Nora had the book she'd brought from the library open in one hand and in her other the golden acorn lay on her open palm.

'Are you feeling OK?' she asked Jack.

'Yes,' Jack and Camelin replied together.

The sky became lighter. Jack lay still and concentrated on his reflection in the Raven's Bowl. As the first ray of light lit the edge of the water he felt Camelin's wing touch his shoulder and heard Nora softly speaking words he didn't understand. From the corner of his eye he saw the golden acorn send out rays of light. Panic filled his whole body; he knew he should be saying his words. The intense light from the golden acorn distracted him. His hand was sweating. It was hard to hold the feather. The words just wouldn't come. He tried to concentrate. He could feel his heart pounding in his chest. The pressure from Camelin's wing increased. Jack lowered his head and touched the water with his forehead. The sunrise flooded into the bowl and blinded him. At last he spoke...

A feather from a raven's wing,

His voice was shaky as he completed the next line.

This is the token I do bring.

He felt the pressure increase from Camelin's wing, which hadn't left his shoulder...

As sunrise lights the darkened sky,
Transform me so that I can fly.

A crushing pain shot though Jack's body. He tried to curl up but he couldn't. The hood of the cloak had flopped down over his head. His hands wouldn't respond as he tried to push it back. As he writhed around Camelin took the hood in his beak and pulled it aside. Jack caught sight of a reflection in the water. He thought it was Camelin's, then realised it was his own. The ritual had worked. He'd been transformed into a raven!

'Caw!' he exclaimed. 'Nora, look!'

'Is everything alright?'

'Yes,' they both replied.

'Touch your foreheads together and you should be able to change back again.'

Jack hadn't anticipated changing back so soon. He hadn't got used to the sensation of transforming into a raven and now he was going to have to do it again in reverse. The cloak felt heavy as it engulfed him. Camelin leaned forward and they put their foreheads together. A bright light, as dazzling as the sunrise had been, flashed outwards from the point where their brows touched. Again Jack was blinded. He must remember to close his eyes the next time he transformed.

The crushing pain returned for a few seconds but he knew instinctively, without looking at his reflection, that he was a boy again. His whole body ached. It was painful climbing down the rocks to the crevice where his clothes were hidden. He found it difficult to dress, his hands were shaking so much.

'I'm glad we don't have to come up here every time I need to change into a raven,' he told Camelin.

'Now the ritual is complete. All you have to do is put your foreheads together and the transformation will take place. You can do it anywhere you want in future,' explained Nora.

Jack felt very tired and walked a little way behind Nora as they made their way back to Ewell House. Camelin had offered to fly ahead and report back to Elan. Jack secretly wondered if he'd been eager to get back first so he could find out what was for breakfast.

By the time Nora and Jack entered the kitchen Elan had scrambled eggs, toast and a pot of tea ready.

'That's just what I need,' said Nora gratefully. 'Help yourself.'

'Don't mind if I do!' croaked Camelin as he tucked into more than his fair share of breakfast.

Jack slumped into the chair and slept.

When he woke he ached all over. Nora was busy in the kitchen.

'How long have I been asleep?'

'Since we got back from The Raven's Bowl. About a couple of hours. How do you feel?'

'Like I've been squashed.'

'It'll wear off. I don't think you'll feel like this every time you transform, I'm sure it will get easier.'

Camelin swooped into the kitchen and landed gracefully on Nora's shoulder.

'OK,' he croaked. 'When you've eaten we might as well make a start on your flying lesson.'

'So soon?' groaned Jack.

'No time like the present. I'll see you upstairs when you're done.'

Jack hadn't realised he'd be transforming again so soon. So much had happened since he'd arrived at Grandad's. He knew he'd never be the same again. Now he was a raven boy, just like Camelin, but would he feel differently about flying and have the instincts of a bird as Arrana had said? He was about to find out.

FLYING LESSONS

Jack couldn't eat much breakfast and when he'd finished he went up to the attic. He stopped at the bottom of the ladder. His *KEEP OUT* sign was still there. He shouted to Camelin.

'Can I come up?'

'Are you alone?'

'Yes.'

'Then it's OK. Come up.'

Jack wondered why Camelin was being so secretive but as soon as he put his head through the trap-door he understood. The contents of Camelin's emergency ration basket were strewn over the floor. He'd begun sorting them into piles.

'Just counting,' he explained. 'I'm good at counting.'

Jack watched as Camelin lovingly replaced his stash piece by piece into the basket.

'Did you bring me anything for your flying lesson?'

Jack had some chocolate bars packed in his bag. He'd remembered to put a couple in his pocket when he returned the golden acorn to his bedroom.

'Hope you like these!'

Camelin took the bars and tossed them into the basket. He looked very pleased.

'That's twenty-nine,' he announced, 'and milk chocolate is one of my favourites.'

Jack suspected anything to do with chocolate would be a favourite for Camelin. He checked to make sure there was nothing sticky around the trap-door before pulling himself into the loft.

'Mind where you put your feet and try not to move things around or I'll never find anything.'

Jack waited until Camelin made a space then quickly undressed.

'Are you ready?'

Jack nodded and bent his head towards Camelin. They touched foreheads. The blinding flash hurt Jack's eyes again even though they were tightly shut. When he opened them he'd transformed into a raven.

'Wow!' This is fantastic. What do I do?' he croaked as he flapped his wings up and down in the small loft space.

'Slow down! Slow down! Stop! You've got to learn to walk first before you can fly.'

Jack didn't realise Camelin was being serious but when he stopped flapping and took a couple of steps he found walking wasn't as easy as he'd thought it would be. It wasn't what he was used to. His feet wanted to hop, skip and shuffle. Walking became more like dancing.

'Not bad,' encouraged Camelin, 'but you look a mess. What's wrong with your feathers?'

Jack inspected his wings and tried to look at his back.

'No, on your head. Some of them are sticking up.'

Camelin tried to flatten the feathers but just when he thought he'd got them all straight one would spring out again.

'I give up,' he croaked, and raised both wings in the air.

'I can never get my hair to stay flat either.'

'I thought that's because you hadn't combed it. I don't seem to be able to do much about your feathers; you'll have

170

to do. Come on. We're wasting time. Let's get outside; we'll have more room to practice in the garden.'

Jack made his way to the window and looked down. His spindly legs started to wobble.

'It's a long way down to the garden.'

'Not that way. Follow me. Elan's got a surprise!'

Jack followed Camelin as best he could down the ladder. They made their way to an open window on the other side of the room. There was a large basket hanging outside with a very thick rope attached to it.

'Come on, climb in,' said Camelin excitedly.

Jack shuffled up a plank that had been leant against the window ledge.

'Going down!' shouted Camelin when they were both inside.

Elan was below operating a pulley. She lowered the basket steadily onto the grass below.

'I didn't expect both of you to be inside. You should have flown down Camelin.'

'I had to make sure Jack was all right,' he told Elan before winking at Jack.

'You're just a very lazy raven,' she replied trying to look cross.

Camelin hopped out. Jack managed to hop onto the rim then down onto the grass.

'OK. Let's start with the basics,' Camelin said and demonstrated to Jack what he wanted him to do by hopping around on one foot first, then the other, then both together. 'Now you.'

Elan laughed and gave Jack a clap when he managed to follow Camelin around the garden.

'See you later,' she shouted before disappearing into the house.

Jack listened carefully to Camelin and followed his instructions. The basic groundwork seemed to go well and in no time at all he was hopping, skipping and scurrying around the lawn.

'What do you want to do now?' asked Camelin.

Jack didn't want to think about flying just yet. He was happy keeping his feet on the ground for as long as possible.

'We could play football.'

'Don't know how to play football.'

'I'll teach you, but we'll need a ball.'

'Let's go and ask Nora. She might have something we could use.'

Nora rummaged in one of the kitchen drawers and eventually found an old table tennis ball.

'Will this do?'

'Great,' Camelin replied.

'What on earth are you going to do with it?'

'Football,' Jack and Camelin said together before hopping back into the garden.

'OK,' said Jack. 'Let's get started.'

He explained the rules and between them they made two goals at either end of the lawn with some empty plant pots. An interested pigeon settled onto the repaired bird table to watch them. It was harder than Jack imagined trying to kick a ball with claws. He managed to get the ball through the goalposts twice. Camelin had yet to score. When it was Camelin's turn to start with the ball Jack hopped towards him to tackle. Camelin bent over, picked the ball up in his beak and skipped off towards the goalmouth.

'Handball,' yelled Jack. 'You can't do that! It's against the rules.'

'Haven't got any hands,' Camelin tried to shout back with the ball in his beak.

'Beak ball then,' said Jack indignantly. 'That's not allowed either.'

Camelin grudgingly brought the ball back to the centre.

'You didn't say anything about *beak ball* when we started,' he grumbled.

The play continued for a while until Elan came out

and shouted to them to see if they wanted a drink.

Jack had begun to walk towards the patio when Camelin yelled. He turned around; the ball was between the plant pots.

'You cheated!'

'Didn't,' replied Camelin.

'It doesn't count if you picked it up.'

When Camelin didn't answer Jack went over to the pigeon.

'Did you see what he did?'

The pigeon didn't answer and Camelin burst out laughing,

'You won't get an answer out of him. He won't understand you.'

'I thought I'd be able to speak to all the birds once I was a raven.'

'Only *intelligent* birds, like ravens. Pigeons don't talk.'

It was then that Jack saw the dent in the side of the ball.

'You did use your beak. You've squashed it!'

'Ooooh look!' exclaimed Camelin, quickly changing the subject. 'Elan's got some cake.'

He left Jack and flew over to the picnic table where Elan had put the tray.

'Come on Jack, it's chocolate cake,' he shouted excitedly.

Jack left the ball and hopped over to the bench but couldn't get up. Elan leant the broom against the table and Jack managed to do a sideways shuffle to the top.

'I'm starving,' he said when he saw the cake.

'See. I keep telling everyone. It's hungry work being a raven.'

'Jack didn't have much breakfast unlike some I could mention,' said Elan looking directly at Camelin.

They were both allowed two pieces of cake, which they ate greedily.

'What are we going to do now? We haven't got a ball to play with any more.' Jack said when he'd finished.

Camelin was working his way around the table making sure they hadn't left any crumbs.

'Don't be so mean,' said Elan. 'Leave some for the sparrows.'

'But they're my crumbs!' exclaimed Camelin in horror. 'I'm not allowed on the bird table so why should they be allowed on the picnic table?'

'I thought it was only starlings you didn't like,' said Jack.

'Starlings and sparrows,' confirmed Camelin. 'They'd steal the crumbs out of your beak if you let them.'

'Take no notice of him Jack,' continued Elan. 'He's got a problem about most of the birds that come in the garden.'

'What's wrong with sparrows?' asked Jack.

Elan sighed, picked up the tray and left Jack to hear all about sparrows from Camelin.

'They're stupid,' he began. 'They get all nervous because they think a wolf might jump out and eat them up.'

'Wolf!'

'Yes,' confirmed Camelin. 'Centuries ago Dagbert, king of the sparrows, was eaten by a wolf and the story's been passed down from sparrow to sparrow for generations.'

'But there aren't any wolves left in Britain.'

'You try telling a sparrow that!' replied Camelin. 'I told you they were stupid.'

Jack would liked to have heard more about Dagbert and the wolf but Camelin decided it was time to continue with Jack's lesson. He shuffled over to the broom and kicked it away from the table.

'Ready to try a small glide now?'

Jack had been having great fun playing football but this was different. He'd no idea what to do. Any instinct he should have, as a bird, hadn't appeared yet.

'Watch me,' said Camelin as he spread his wings and glided gracefully onto the ground. 'Now you.'

Jack's claws gripped the table. His spindly legs shook. He spread his wings, took a deep breath and stepped off the edge. He wobbled rather than glided to the grass and had to skip a couple of steps so he didn't topple over as he landed.

'That wasn't too bad was it?' he asked.

'You're going to have to do a lot better than that,' grumbled Camelin.

'Well I can't get back up on top to have another go. Someone kicked the broom away.'

Camelin looked around the garden.

'I know. Follow me.'

They went down to the rockery by the hedge where Camelin had his secret cave. There were large rocks dotted around the raised bank but the far side had a vertical drop into the flowerbed.

'This is perfect,' croaked Camelin.

Jack had to agree. The top of the rockery wasn't as high as the picnic table.

Jack felt a bit more confident practising gliding from here. It would be easy to climb up the rocks and the landing would be soft if he crashed.

Stepping off wasn't easy, but once Jack plucked up

the courage to leave the highest rock he managed to glide down with his wings outspread. His landing wasn't very graceful but it was only his second try. After half an hour he'd improved considerably. Camelin showed Jack how to use his wings for assisted hopping. They practised on the lower branches of the fir trees by the picnic table. Soon Jack was able to hop from the grass to the branch, onto the table then glide back onto the grass.

'This is great. Can we go higher?' he asked.

'No problem,' replied Camelin.

Jack was on the second branch when Nora and Elan came out to check on his progress.

'What are you doing?' cried Nora. 'Stay there, I'll come and get you.'

It was too late. Nora's cry startled Jack. He lost his footing and his concentration. He croaked loudly as he toppled off the branch.

'Jack!' Nora shouted.

Instead of plummeting to the ground, he spread his wings instinctively, then raised and lowered them powerfully. He rose rapidly into the air.

'Look, I'm flying!' he croaked excitedly.

He fell even faster than he'd gone up.

Camelin covered his eyes with his wings. Nora and Elan stood with their mouths open then dashed towards Jack as he crashed into the flowerbed.

'You have to keep flapping your wings if you want to fly,' croaked Camelin.

Jack groaned.

'Come on, If you don't get up we're in trouble,' Camelin whispered when he saw Nora and Elan rushing over to where Jack lay.

Nora fussed over him then frowned at Camelin.

'I thought we agreed you'd just to do the basic training today. Groundwork we said. There wasn't any mention of trees.'

'It's my fault. I asked to go higher,' admitted Jack. 'I'm OK, nothing's broken.'

'Well, I think you've probably done enough for today.'

Nora went into the herborium and came out with her cloak. She draped it over Jack so only his head poked out.

'If you transform down here you won't have a problem getting upstairs.'

Jack and Camelin touched foreheads. The flash of light frightened several sparrows from the bird table. Jack was sure he heard Camelin laugh.

'We'll have a picnic lunch by the lake, so when you're ready come and join us,' said Nora.

'We'll tell you more about the cauldron,' added Elan.

'Can I tell him about the Treasures of Annwn,' Camelin asked excitedly.

'I don't see why not,' agreed Nora, 'but just keep to the facts.

By the time Jack was changed he felt hot and sticky. Even with the window open the heat in the loft from the midday sun was almost unbearable. It wasn't much better on the patio. When he got down to the lake everyone was underneath one of the great willows. Nora had spread a rug out and Elan was helping her to unpack a large basket. It was cooler by the water and the long slender leaves of the willow swayed gently to and fro providing them with a constant breeze.

'I've brought these to show you Jack,' said Nora as she took something from the bottom of the picnic basket.

Jack watched as Nora laid a package, wrapped in cloth, carefully on the rug. It was tied with a cord but instead of undoing the knot she took out her wand and tapped the package three times. The cord fell apart and the cloth peeled itself back to reveal three metal objects. They were the same shape and size, one piled on top of the other. They didn't shine or sparkle and didn't look expensive but the green metal they were made from made them look old. He'd seen something like them before, but not this shape. These were like the shin pads he wore for football, only with holes down each side.

'When you go through the window in time you'll be looking for three plates like these,' explained Nora.

'The cauldron plates!'

'Yes. Each has a different tree embossed in the bronze.'

Elan pointed to each of the plates in turn.

'These are the beech, pine and holly, which I look after.'

'I've got the hazel, apple and elm and Arrana keeps the rowan, ash and birch safe,' explained Nora.

'The missing plates are the ones I collected from the hawthorn, oak and willow wells,' sighed Camelin. 'Those are the ones we'll be looking for.

Jack looked puzzled.

'But I thought there were thirteen altogether?'

'The last one isn't this shape,' explained Elan. 'It's the base plate…'

'…and it's round and it's on the wall by the front door!' interrupted Jack when he suddenly remembered where he'd seen a tree on a green metal plate before.

"That's the one,' Elan replied.

'The name of the house and the surname I adopted should tell you where it used to hang,' added Nora.

'Ewell,' said Jack. 'The *yew* well!'

Camelin flapped his wings and hopped around to show Jack how pleased he was that he'd been able to work out the answer without being told.

'The embossed trees represent a special time of the year. Each plate hung on its own tree, which stood by a sacred well. Whenever there was a festival on Glasruhen Hill the keepers of the wells would bring their plates. I'd lace them together and we'd use the cauldron and the golden acorn in our rituals,' explained Nora.

'The well in this garden is the Yew Well. Gwillam looked after the Oak Well in the Sacred Grove and the one on the edge of Glasruhen Forest, where you saw Jennet, is the Hawthorn Well,' croaked Camelin.

'When it's all laced together it looks like this,' Elan said as she took out one of Nora's books from the picnic basket. She opened it and showed Jack a drawing of the cauldron. Nora tapped the page with her wand three times. The drawing came to life, rose from the page and began rotating. Jack was fascinated. As the cauldron slowly turned he looked closely at the plates. He couldn't see any of the holes now the plates were joined. The cauldron was larger than Jack had imagined.

'Where did the holes go?'

'If we didn't use a little bit of magic it would leak,' laughed Nora. She gave one of the plates a gentle tap with her wand and the holes sealed; another tap and the holes reappeared.

'The cauldron is one of the four treasures of Annwn,' began Elan.

'You said I could tell Jack,' interrupted Camelin and looked pleadingly at Nora.

'Go ahead,' she smiled, 'and when you've finished we can eat.'

'There were four great treasures,' Camelin began rapidly. 'The first was the Sword of Power, a great magical battle sword, which made its owner invincible as long as it was used for good.'

Camelin picked up a twig and lunged at Jack.

'And the second?'

'That was the Spear of Justice. It didn't harm anyone who told the truth. The third was the Stone of Destiny, which could reveal your future.'

'And the fourth was the cauldron?' said Jack.

'Yes, but I'm telling this,' Camelin grumbled, then quickly carried on when he saw Nora's frown, before she could say anything. 'The cauldron was the only way of transporting objects between the two worlds. It was known as the Cauldron of Life. You could open the Western Portal with it and bring back the leaves from the Crochan tree to make the elixir, or Hamadryad acorns to plant. Did I miss anything out?'

Nora shook her head and smiled at Camelin before turning to Jack.

'Each one of the treasures has the power, when used with a Druid's golden acorn, to open a portal into Annwn. The others are no longer on Earth and their gateways have been sealed. The only entry left is through the Western Portal on Glasruhen Hill but it's impossible to open without the cauldron.'

The recovery of the cauldron plates suddenly became very real to Jack. While the others chatted over lunch, he ate in silence. A lot was depending on him.

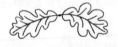

After lunch Nora got the boat out and they rowed over to Gerda's island. Instead of flying, Camelin sat on the prow like a figurehead. They showed Jack around the island and Gerda waddled happily over to greet them. On the way back Jack and Elan got out and paddled in the shallows and splashed each other.

'I think you'd better go and get some dry clothes on,' laughed Nora when she saw Jack's soaked jeans.

They repacked the basket. Jack carried the rug back to the kitchen then went upstairs to change. Before he opened the bedroom door he knew something was wrong. A familiar smell hit his nostrils. As he peeped round the door he gasped. The duvet was half off the bed, the bedside cabinet had been turned over and his Book of Shadows lay open on the floor. Soil had been trailed everywhere. Jack looked in horror at the wrecked room.

'Elan!' he cried.

'What's wrong?'

'Somebody's been in my room.'

Elan looked at the mess.

'I didn't do this!'

'I know.'

Jack began frantically searching through the mess.

'The golden acorn, it's gone!'

INTO THE TUNNEL

Jack continued to search his room while Elan went to find Nora and Camelin. The golden acorn was nowhere to be found.

Nora stood in the doorway and sniffed the air.

'I left it on the table,' Jack told her. 'I know I did.'

'Spriggans!' she gasped.

He fought back the tears.

'When was the last time you saw it?'

'After breakfast. You gave it back to me after the ritual. I put it on the table, with my Book of Shadows and wand, when I came upstairs. I don't understand how they knew where to find it?'

'Spriggans can smell gold easily and once they've

got the scent they don't give up. Maybe they weren't just hunting rats when they tunnelled into your greenhouse and kitchen the other night,' said Nora thoughtfully.

'Look at this!' croaked Camelin who had his head out of the window. 'Down there in the grass.'

Everyone crowded around. Jack could see a hole, exactly like the one he'd seen in the kitchen.

'Well that explains how they got in. They've obviously tunnelled under the hedge and climbed up the trellis. Look, all the ivy's been pulled down,' said Elan.

Nora began pacing up and down.

'It must have happened while we were on the island. The trees wouldn't be able to get a message to us there. For them to do this in broad daylight isn't good. They usually do this sort of thing at night, and never here, not with all the protection we've got. I'm not happy about this.'

Jack sat on the edge of the bed and bit his knuckle.

'I'm sorry. I'm so sorry. You gave me the acorn to look after and now it's gone.'

'Don't worry Jack,' said Nora kindly. 'This isn't your fault. I thought the acorn would be safe here. I was wrong. I never expected anyone or anything to come under the hedge.'

'But you need the acorn for the ritual. Can you get it back?'

'We're going to need some extra help,' said Elan.

'We are,' agreed Nora. 'Elan, you go and find Motley, and Camelin can fly over to see Timmery later. We'll have a meeting tonight to decide what to do.'

Jack was too upset to ask Camelin who Timmery was.

'Leave this to us,' said Nora as she gently squeezed Jack's shoulder. 'There's nothing else we can do at the moment.'

Jack felt awful, and then an even more terrible thought struck him.

'Where's Orin? She was asleep on my pillow the last time I saw her.'

'Orin,' they shouted.

Nora, Jack and Camelin rushed around the house searching for her.

'She's gone,' sobbed Jack. 'They've taken her too; it's all my fault.'

Nora put her arm around Jack's shoulder.

'We'll get her back if we can,' she told him. 'Get yourself out of those wet clothes. We'll meet in the kitchen in ten minutes and start making plans. This can't wait until tonight.'

Jack changed as quickly as he could. How was he going to tell Motley his sister was gone? Tears streamed down his cheeks. This was no time to cry. He dried his eyes. He had to be strong and help the others find Orin. He took the stairs two at a time and dashed into the kitchen. Motley was standing on the table talking to Nora. He didn't need his wand to understand that Motley was upset.

'What's happening?' he whispered to Camelin.

'Nora's going down the tunnel after the Spriggans to try to rescue Orin and get the golden acorn back, Motley wants to go too but Nora said no. It's too dangerous. He's agreed to gather the Night Guard and circle the hole. They'll keep watch until Nora comes back.'

'I want to go too,' said Jack in a loud wobbly voice.

'You're too big for the hole,' said Nora.

'I can squeeze down there if you can.'

'Mmmm,' said Nora thoughtfully. 'There's something I haven't told you. To go down the tunnel, I'm going to have to shape shift.'

Jack remembered the words from his Book of Shadows.

The Seanchai, Keeper of Secrets and Ancient Rituals, Guardian of the Sacred Grove, Healer, Shape Shifter and Wise Woman; that's you isn't it?'

189

'It is. You've been using your Book well, but it's too dangerous for me to let you go down the tunnel.'

'I'm going to be flying back into the past. You don't mind me doing that.'

Jack was close to tears again.

'I've got to do something to help. Camelin and I can transform, I can use my beak and claws to defend myself if I have to.'

Camelin frowned at Jack.

'I think we should stay here,' he croaked.

'And I say we should go.'

Jack straightened his back, folded his arms and clenched his teeth.

'I agree with Jack,' said Elan as she came in from the garden.

'Are you sure?' asked Nora.

'Sure,' Jack and Elan said together.

'We'd better work out a plan quickly. We don't know how long Orin's been gone,' said Nora.

'I think we should follow their trail through the tunnel and find out where it leads first,' said Elan. 'Agreed?'

'Agreed,' everyone replied.

'We might have to make some quick decisions because we don't know what we're up against,' added Nora before turning to Jack and Camelin. 'And if there's any sign of trouble I want you to promise me you'll get back to the house as quickly as you can.'

'Promise,' said Jack and Camelin together.

'Good, that's settled. Now once we have Orin and the acorn back I'll close the tunnel so well they'll never get back into the garden again,' added Nora. 'Are we all ready.'

Everyone nodded. As Jack touched foreheads with Camelin the kitchen lit up. His clothes fell in a heap on the floor. He struggled out then waddled over to Camelin. He watched Nora raise both arms. She turned slowly and with each rotation her body got smaller and smaller until she'd shape shifted into a large ferret with beautiful silver fur. She darted over to join Jack and Camelin. To Jack's surprise Elan also raised her arms and turned slowly. She too started to shrink.

'I didn't know Elan could shape shift!' Jack whispered to Camelin.

'She can do exactly what Nora can,' explained Camelin. 'Watch.'

Jack's eyes grew wider as Elan got smaller and smaller until a chestnut-coloured ferret appeared. She shook her fur and looked around the kitchen. Her green eyes flashed as she darted over to join the rest at the door.

'Close your beak,' Camelin said to Jack. 'Nora says it's rude to stare.'

Jack was too shocked to say anything.

'Come on,' said Nora. 'But not a sound once we're inside the tunnel.'

To Jack's surprise, the tunnel was well made. The Spriggans had compacted the earth on the walls and floor making it smooth to the touch. Nora led, Jack followed, Camelin came next and Elan last. Jack found it hard to keep up with Nora. She scurried along and he kept stumbling. He hadn't really got used to his new feet yet.

Once they'd left the entrance the tunnel got darker and darker. No one spoke. They'd been travelling for about ten minutes when Nora suddenly stopped. Jack almost bumped into her. There was a rustling of feathers when Camelin crashed into Jack.

'Shhh,' Nora whispered. 'I can see a light ahead; we need to slow down.'

By the time Jack could see the flickering light he could also hear angry high-pitched voices. They'd stopped at the end of the tunnel where it led into a circular cave. Beyond it, the tunnel carried on. Three Spriggans were crouched around a small fire. A pot of water hung from a tripod over the flames. Each Spriggan wore an old felt hat with an unlit candle perched on the brim. The nearest Spriggan had his foot on a drawstring bag. Jack thought he saw something move inside.

'I says we skins her now and cooks her,' the nearest Spriggan squeaked.

'Are you mad, Grub,' the middle one replied. 'Chief would skins us alive if he finds out.'

'Whiff's right,' the third Spriggan wheezed. 'How'd you explains where the middles went? You knows he always get to eat the best meat. When's the last time you had a nice tender female rat. We only gets the tough ones.'

'Go on Grub, tell Pinch and me hows you'd explains it to him,' said Whiff.

'I just don't sees why he has all the best meat?' Grub grumbled.

'Because he's the Chief, that's why,' explained Pinch.

'OK, I'd tells him she was dead when we found her and she wasn't fit to eat so we skinned her and throws the meat away.'

There was silence. The other two Spriggans were nodding at Grub. Jack knew they were going to have to do something soon or Orin was in danger of being eaten.

'Yeh, why shoulds his lordship get all the bestist meat. It's us what goes a hunting for him,' agreed Whiff.

Grub and Whiff looked at Pinch. Before he replied Nora turned and nodded.

'Now,' she whispered.

Nora and Elan darted forward. The Spriggans jumped up.

'Ferrets!' cried Grub as he jumped behind Pinch.

Nora grabbed the drawstring bag in her strong teeth and Elan went over to the fire. As Nora turned and fled back up the tunnel Jack and Camelin touched foreheads. There was a blinding flash. Before it disappeared they touched foreheads again. Once more the cave filled with light. The Spriggans' high-pitched squeals echoed around the cave. Elan pulled one of the tripod's legs with her paw and the water tipped onto the fire. The flames hissed and died as the cave went pitch black.

'Over here,' Elan shouted to Camelin and Jack.

They raced over towards where Elan stood at the mouth of the tunnel. They ran as fast as they could away from the cave. They'd only got halfway when they heard shrill voices shouting and screeching not far behind. The Spriggans were after them! Every so often Jack saw a light flicker in the tunnel. The Spriggans were closing the distance between them.

'Run faster,' Elan shouted.

It wasn't easy but Jack and Camelin managed to reach the garden before the Spriggans caught up with them. The sunlight blinded them for a moment. They stood panting, waiting for Elan. Motley and the Night Guard had broken the circle around the mouth of the tunnel.

'Where's Nora,' Camelin gasped.

'She's gone in the house,' Motley said in a very shaky voice. 'Are there Spriggans down there?'

'Run!' shouted Elan as she bolted out of the hole. 'There'll be Spriggans up here soon. Don't let them catch you.'

As the rats scattered Nora came out of the kitchen. She'd already transformed and held her wand high in the air. Jack expected her to seal the entrance but instead she waited. First one head appeared, and then all three Spriggans tumbled out of the tunnel.

'Stop!' cried Nora.

The Spriggans stopped. Light burst out of Nora's wand.

'You have something which belongs to me.'

'You got something what belongs to us and we

wants it back,' screeched Pinch.

No one spoke. Nora waited patiently for the Spriggans to hand over the golden acorn. The Spriggans shielded their eyes from the light coming out of Nora's wand. They shuffled expectantly, waiting for Nora to return the drawstring bag. All of a sudden a smell of burning reached Jack's nostrils. The others smelt it too and were looking from Spriggan to Spriggan to see if their candles had set fire to their hats.

'No!' shouted Nora when she saw what was burning.

The rope that secured Grub to Whiff was on fire.

It was too late. As the rope burnt through Whiff and Pinch shot back down the tunnel. Grub began to grow and grow, and grow. Soon he'd passed the kitchen window. He didn't stop until he'd reached the bottom of the roof.

'Giant!' warned Elan.

Grub started blundering around the garden. He crushed the picnic table and flattened the benches. Nora pointed her wand at the bottom of the trellis and twirled it around in an upward spiral. The fallen ivy picked itself up and started to wind its strong tendrils around Grub's feet, legs and finally his body and arms. In seconds he looked like an old tree trunk with only a small part of his face visible. When Nora was completely satisfied that Grub was immobile she lowered her wand.

'That should make sure he doesn't trample on anyone. Now, is everyone alright?'

Whiff and Pinch were nowhere to be seen. Motley and the Night Guard peeped out from behind the shed, then came to join everyone else by the kitchen door.

'And I don't want to hear another word from you,' Nora cautioned Grub.

The gigantic Spriggan frowned down at everyone.

'Did you get her back?' whispered Motley.

'We did,' replied Nora.

Everyone cheered.

'She's in the kitchen but she's a bit shaken. You can see her in a minute.'

'What about the golden acorn?' Jack asked.

'I'd hoped it was going to be in the bag, but it wasn't.'

Everyone looked worried.

'How did the fire start?' asked Elan.

'With this,' croaked Camelin as he waddled towards Nora. In his beak was a small lantern dangling from the top of a long silver stick.

There was something strange about the lantern.

Instead of a light Jack thought he could see a tiny green shape inside.

'What have you got there?' Nora enquired.

'Please don't hurt me,' said a very frightened voice from inside the lantern cage.

'My goodness me!' exclaimed Nora. 'It's a dragon.'

'Dragon!' exclaimed Jack.

Everyone crowded around to see the small creature.

'No one's going to hurt you,' Nora assured him. 'Let's get you out of there and you can tell us what you're doing in the company of Spriggans.'

Elan took the lantern from Camelin and looked for a catch to open. It was completely sealed.

'There's no escape from the cage,' the dragon explained sadly. 'It's made from a special magnetic metal. The Spriggans welded it together so you'll not find an opening. I've tried melting it with my flames. It's no use. I'm going to be trapped in here forever.'

'Shield your eyes,' Nora warned the tiny dragon.

Once its wings were wrapped tightly around its face and body. Nora waved her wand and aimed it straight at the top. It shattered into tiny pieces. The lantern sprang open and a small green dragon with beautiful shiny scales and tiny purple wings tumbled out.

'Oh thank you,' he cried as he bowed to Nora, 'Charkle at your service.'

'I haven't seen a dragon for years,' Nora exclaimed.

'I've never seen a dragon at all!' gasped Jack, staring with his beak open.

'They captured me when I was a baby,' explained Charkle. 'They wanted me for my flames, you know, in case their candles went out in the tunnels. They'd pull my tail and use my flames to relight them. They pulled my tail all the way through the tunnel just now when they were chasing you. I'm sorry about the giant but it was my only chance to escape. They're not allowed to take me outside but they were so intent on getting their rat back, Grub must have forgotten he'd got me in his belt.'

'I hate Spriggans,' croaked Camelin.

All the rats nodded in agreement.

'Well you're free to go home now,' said Nora kindly.

'Free,' repeated Charkle. There was a hiss of steam as tears ran down his cheeks, 'to go home.'

'Where is home?' enquired Jack.

'My family has a roost in one of the caverns in Westwood,' replied Charkle.

'Why don't you stay with us for a few days and we'll take you home,' said Nora. 'Jack's going to need somewhere to have a practice flight soon and Westwood's a perfect place to go.'

'That's very kind,' said Charkle as he wiped away the last of his tears.

'Well that's settled,' said Nora, smiling kindly at the dragon.

'But what's going to happen about the golden acorn,' Jack asked.

'Excuse me,' said Charkle politely, 'did you say a golden acorn?'

Everyone looked expectantly at the little dragon.

'A little man with a very long nose told Chief Knuckle where he could find a golden acorn. He said a boy had picked one up not long ago. Whiff, Pinch and Grub were sent to collect it.'

'A Bogie!' exclaimed Elan. 'We should have known.'

'The little man showed Chief Knuckle something called a torch. The Chief was very impressed with a light he could turn on and off without using a flame. He agreed to trade the torch for the golden acorn.'

'But I still don't understand how the Bogie knew about it,' said Jack.

'Bogies make it their business to know everything. Information is their main trade and I wouldn't be surprised if this particular Bogie is Peabody. I intend to find out what's been going on,' said Nora thoughtfully.

Jack was worried. He'd not liked the look of Peabody when he'd seen him in Newton Gill Forest and he'd been frightened when the Bogie had appeared at his window.

'The little man was in the chamber just before you arrived,' Charkle explained. 'He took the golden acorn and went on ahead to give the torch to Chief Knuckle.'

Jack frowned.

'But how will we get it back if the Spriggans don't have it any more?'

'We don't have to worry about that. Very soon I shall make it clear to Chief Knuckle that he's got a problem. He'll realise he's made a big mistake. It won't be long before he'll be falling over himself to get my golden acorn back,' Nora replied.

Jack looked puzzled.

'But I don't understand.'

'Spriggans believe all gold belongs to them but they can lay no claim to any gold which comes from Annwn. To make matters worse his men have stolen from a Druid. I don't think Chief Knuckle's going to be very happy about that when he finds out. I shall send him a message and arrange to meet him. If he doesn't return my golden acorn by the end of the month I shall shrink him to the size of a matchstick. He won't be Chief then. Only the biggest Spriggan is allowed to be Chief.'

'If only we knew where to find them.' said Elan, 'There are miles of tunnels down there.'

'I could show you,' said Charkle. 'I know all the tunnels. I ought to; I've been jogged up and down them in that lantern for years.'

'I won't have you going down the tunnels again,' said Nora firmly. 'We'll send Timmery. When he arrives later you can tell him how to find Chief Knuckle. Timmery has an excellent sense of direction, and he's very brave.'

Camelin was waggling his head from side to side behind Nora's back as she spoke and mouthed the words *he's very brave*. Jack was looking forward to meeting Timmery, but there was someone else he wanted to see first.

'Can we go and see Orin now?' he asked.

They left the giant Spriggan in the garden and went back into the kitchen where everyone gathered around Orin. Her fur was ruffled and some of her whiskers were bent. She looked tired. They were all glad she was back safe.

'I'm sorry,' Jack said. 'Will you forgive me?'

'There's nothing to forgive,' replied Orin. 'Those Spriggans were after the golden acorn. If I'd kept still I don't think they'd have seen me but I panicked and shot under the duvet. All that mess in your room happened when they tried to catch me.'

'We ought to make sure they don't come back up the hole,' said Elan.

'I agree,' replied Nora and took her wand out into the garden.

Jack watched from the kitchen window as Nora grew a prickly bush on top of the hole. He suddenly felt all scrunched.

'Can we transform?' he asked Camelin as he wriggled into his pile of clothes.

'Close your eyes everyone,' Camelin said before he touched Jack's forehead.

'When will Timmery be here?' Jack whispered to Camelin.

'After dark. He sleeps during the day and spends all night being brave.'

'Now Camelin,' chided Nora as she came back into the kitchen. 'I don't want to hear you telling Jack anything bad about Timmery.'

'Is Timmery a badger?' asked Jack.

Camelin exploded in laughter.

'That's a good one!' he spluttered, 'Timmery's about the size of a matchbox. He's a Pipistrelle; you know, a bat.'

'A bat!'

'A bat,' repeated Camelin. 'He gets a bit much sometimes. He's very enthusiastic. You wouldn't like him.'

'That's enough Camelin,' warned Nora. 'Now I suggest we all have a rest and meet at dusk when Timmery arrives. Don't forget you've got to go and tell him about the meeting will you Camelin?'

Camelin pulled a face. Jack wondered if he was jealous of the little bat. As he climbed the stairs with Orin on his shoulder he felt very tired. He lay on his bed with Orin curled up on his pillow. It had been an eventful day and it wasn't over yet. When Timmery arrived there'd be the meeting. He thought about all the strange happenings since he'd looked into the Raven's Bowl that morning. Camelin was right; it was hard work being a raven. Jack yawned; it wasn't long before he fell asleep.

MEETINGS

A tapping on the window woke Jack. He sat bolt upright and Orin scampered onto his shoulder and began to tremble.

'Don't worry. I think it might be Camelin,' he reassured her, when he saw a familiar black shape perched on the window ledge.

'Time for the meeting,' Camelin informed him. 'Nora says to bring your wand so you'll be able to understand everything.'

'Aren't you coming?'

'I've got to go and tell Timmery it's time. Won't be long.'

Jack picked up his wand and made his way to the

kitchen. Motley and the rest of the Night Guard were already sitting on their upturned beakers. Jack sat on the empty chair between Nora and Elan. Orin ran down Jack's shirt onto the table and joined Motley. Charkle was perched on Elan's shoulder and Gerda sat by the patio doors.

'Timmery won't be long,' Nora announced, 'and then we'll get started.

Jack heard the flapping of wings as Camelin swooped in through the kitchen door. He was beaten to Nora's shoulder by a tiny bat that darted in through the window. Camelin circled round and landed gracefully on Nora's other shoulder.

'I think you can perch on the stool,' Nora told him.

Camelin frowned at the little bat as he jumped onto the table and waddled over to the high stool next to Elan.

'For those of you who don't know,' Nora began, 'this is Timmery.'

Charkle fluttered briefly in front of Nora's shoulder and introduced himself.

'I'm Charkle of the Dragonette family from the Westwood Roost.'

'Lovely to meet you,' fussed Timmery.

'And this is Jack,' said Nora, as Jack stood and

smiled at Timmery.

'Oh Jack Brenin! I've heard so much about you. I'm so pleased to meet you too. If I can do anything to be of service just let me know.'

Camelin gave a great sigh and looked bored.

'Pleased to meet you,' replied Jack.

'Oh I'm honoured, honoured I am…' began Timmery, but Nora interrupted him by calling the meeting to order.

'We have an important matter to discuss. Some of us have had a long, tiring day. The sooner we sort this out the better. I need to arrange a meeting with Chief Knuckle. The golden acorn must be found and returned or we won't be able to perform the ritual to open the window in time. Most of you know this already. I think Elan's told you about our problems Charkle?'

'Oh yes,' he replied. 'What do you want me to do?'

'You can explain to Timmery how to find Chief Knuckle so he can deliver my message. I've made a tiny hole at the bottom of the prickly bush to allow Timmery to enter the tunnel.'

Charkle began to explain to Timmery the way through the tunnels to Chief Knuckle's chamber. As he spoke Nora drew his directions on a piece of paper.

'Go into the tunnel and carry on until you come to the first cave, then take the opposite tunnel and keep going until you're in a big cavern. There'll be lots of tunnels leading off in different directions. Sniff each entrance to find the one you're looking for. Chief Knuckle's is the smelliest of the lot. He's the one you'll want to talk to. None of the rest can do *anything* without his permission. The Chief's chamber is massive. There'll be candles lighting up the whole place. Even though they live underground, Spriggans don't like the dark. At the far end you'll see a great golden chair which looks more like a throne. That's where you'll find Chief Knuckle.'

'Have you got all that?' Nora asked Timmery.

Timmery nodded then floated down to the table and scrabbled along the route Nora had drawn on the paper.

'Got it,' he chirruped. 'This is going to be a great adventure, a story to tell all my relatives. What should I call it? *Timmery in the Spriggans' Lair* or what about *Timmery and the Spriggan Chief?*'

Everyone laughed except Camelin. Nora tapped the table with her wand for quiet and gave out more instructions for the evening.

'Now, I suggest the Night Guard stick together Motley. There'll be safety in numbers. If you all patrol around the garden tonight it would help. My main concern is to make sure the Spriggans don't come up somewhere else in the garden before I've spoken to Chief Knuckle.'

Motley nodded but looked very apprehensive.

'Don't worry,' said Nora kindly. 'If they come back up the tunnel they'll have a problem getting past the prickly bush I've put over the hole. You'll have plenty of time to raise the alarm. If you see any sign of a Spriggan scatter in as many directions as you can. Being roped together will slow them down.

Motley put on a brave face but Jack could see he wasn't happy.

'Timmery, when you've delivered my message, come back as quickly as you can and let me know you're safe. Then you can join the night watch and report anything unusual.'

'They can report to me,' said Camelin with an air of importance. 'I can raise the alarm if there's a problem.'

The kitchen was suddenly filled with a loud hooting as Camelin demonstrated the call of the raven-owl.

'Well if you're sure,' said Nora.

'I'm sure,' replied Camelin, looking pleased with himself.

'Now that only leaves Gerda,' said Nora, 'I'd like

you to sleep in the kitchen tonight. You know what to do if anyone or anything breaks in.'

Gerda nodded and waddled round to a basket of straw Nora had placed by the dresser. She shook her tail several times before settling down with her head tucked under her wing.

Nora took a tiny envelope addressed to Chief Knuckle and placed it in front of Timmery.

'Ready to go?' she asked him.

The little bat nodded, picked the envelope up in his teeth and flitted out of the kitchen.

'While Timmery's gone I'll make some supper. We'll eat when he comes back and then prepare to go back down the tunnels. I'd like you to stay here Camelin. If there's a problem, call Timmery and send him back down the tunnel to find us.'

'Why do I always miss the good stuff?' Camelin complained bitterly.

'This isn't a game,' chided Nora.

'What do you want me to do?' Jack asked.

'You can come with us. I've got a special job for you to do. You'll be able to stay in the tunnel while I meet Chief Knuckle and you won't be seen.'

'I might as well be in my loft while you're gone,' announced Camelin. 'I can co-ordinate everything from up there and keep a look out at the same time.'

Jack suspected Camelin was secretly pleased he didn't have to go. He hadn't been keen to go down the tunnel earlier. 'Co-ordinate' probably meant he'd be having a sleep until everyone returned.

Timmery reappeared just as Nora finished laying out the supper. He darted through the kitchen window and attached himself to the front of Nora's cloak.

'Chief Knuckle wasn't pleased but he's agreed to meet you.'

'Excellent! Shall we eat? By the time we've finished it will be time to go.'

After supper Jack made his way up to the attic where he'd arranged to meet Camelin for his transformation. He could hear Camelin in the loft above but instead of coming down his head appeared at the top of the ladder.

'Come up here first. I've got a surprise for you.'

Jack climbed up and poked his head into the loft.

'Look, it's for you!'

Jack looked over to where Camelin was pointing. A beanbag lay next to Camelin's raven basket.

'Oh, cool!'

'Do you like it?'

'It's great. Does that mean I can sleep up here with you tonight?'

'It was Nora's idea, but it would have been mine if I'd thought of it first. She thinks it would be safer for you and Orin to sleep up here. I can protect you both from trouble. I'm the only one who can do the call of the raven-owl.'

Elan shouted to Jack from the garden. She was waiting to lower him down in the basket. Jack and Camelin touched foreheads and once the transformation was complete Jack waddled back down the ladder, onto the window ledge and into the basket. Once he was on the grass Nora joined them.

'Ready?'

'Ready,' they both replied.

Nora pointed her wand at the prickly bush and a hole, big enough for them all to get through, appeared. Both she and Elan turned around slowly and spiralled down. As they shrank their bodies changed into the silver and chestnut ferrets Jack had seen earlier.

'I want you to carry this for me Jack. I'm going

to need it when we get to the cave,' Nora said as she pushed her wand towards him with her paw.

Jack picked up the wand in his beak and waddled after them both into the tunnel. They didn't stop until they reached the entrance to the cave where they'd rescued Orin.

'You two stay here. I'm going to wait in the chamber for Chief Knuckle,' Nora whispered.

She stepped into the darkness of the empty cave and shape shifted back into her usual form, then took the wand from Jack's beak. He was surprised how small Nora looked as she sat hunched on the floor. Jack and Elan crouched in the mouth of the cave so they wouldn't be seen. They didn't have long to wait before a strange looking creature stepped out of the far tunnel. He was taller than the other Spriggans Jack had seen. His eyes were so closely set together they almost touched and one was slightly higher than the other. His wide mouth was crooked and full of needle like teeth. His large nose was almost as wide as his mouth.

'That's another reason why he's the Chief,' Elan whispered to Jack as she nodded at his nose. 'He's got the best sniffer.'

Some of the other Spriggans had long noses, some had small, but Chief Knuckle's was wider and rounder than any of the rest.

'Spriggans need a good sense of smell. The wider their nostrils, the more important they are,' continued Elan.

Chief Knuckle swaggered toward Nora. His guard hurried behind him carrying an assortment of curved picks, sharp prodders and long crowbars. The Chief's pure white cloak of rabbit fur swept the floor. On his head was a grey rat pelt, the tail having been stiffened into a candleholder. The candle was unlit but wax had dripped down the rat's pelt hat onto his hair and beard. In his hand he carried the torch.

'Shuts up the lots of you!' the Chief piped, in a very high squeaky voice, to the rest of the Spriggans who'd clambered behind him into the chamber.

'Chief Knuckle,' began Nora, but before she could say any more he interrupted her.

'I don't welcomes visitors, especially not ones what makes me walk a long ways out of me chamber.' He stopped speaking and sniffed the air slowly in the direction of the tunnel mouth where Jack and Elan were hiding. 'I don't likes what I smells.'

'We both have a problem. I've come to suggest a solution....'

'Problem! Problem!' Chief Knuckle screeched as he glowered at Nora. 'The only problems I've got are unwelcome visitors demanding to sees me. Binds her up,' he hissed though his sharp teeth.

Jack watched as a group of three Spriggans brought a long coil of rope as close as they dared.

'Don't be ridiculous,' said Nora quietly, 'I wish to speak to you about a golden acorn?'

'Well I didn't come to speaks. I came to ties you up and feeds you to me rats, not that there's much meat on an old hag like you.'

'Enough!' said Nora as she stood.

A gasp rang around the cave as she towered above the Chief. Her head nearly touched the roof. The Spriggans with weapons pointed them at her.

'Enough I say,' Nora announced firmly as she produced her wand. 'I could turn you all into gherkins if I wished, but you've stolen something which belongs to me and I want it back. Not only that, I've got something which belongs to you. I've got no room in my garden for a giant Spriggan. You can come and take him back once I've got my golden acorn back.'

All the Spriggans had scurried away from Nora. They were all trying to hide behind the Chief. Their small legs were trembling so badly the chamber was filled with a knocking sound. Only Chief Knuckle stood his ground.

'Spriggans never steals. They only takes what belongs to them,' he informed Nora with as much courage as he could muster.

'And yet you stole my golden acorn. I'm Eleanor, Seanchai and Guardian of the Sacred Grove. I presume you've heard of me.'

Every Spriggan in the room fell flat on its face, except Chief Knuckle.

'All the gold from the earth belongs to us,' he pronounced defiantly.

'But this gold wasn't from the earth. It came from Annwn. It's Druid's gold and belongs to me.'

This final revelation brought Chief Knuckle to his knees.

'Forgives us, oh Seanchai, we didn't knows. The Bogie said it was his.'

'What exactly did the Bogie tell you?'

'He said he'd lost it on the path and a boy picked it up and wouldn't give it back. He told us the boy was staying with an old woman at the big house. He gaves me this in exchange for his gold.'

Chief Knuckle held up the torch with a very wobbly hand so Nora could see his prize.

'The Bogie lied. The golden acorn belongs to me and if I don't have it back by the end of the month I'll shrink you down to the size of a matchstick.'

Chief Knuckle gasped and turned pale.

'I promises you it will be brought back to you, oh great Seanchai.'

'When you bring it back you can come and shrink your friend down to his normal size and take him away. I never expect to see you in my garden again and you'll never hunt rats on my land anymore. Do you understand?'

The Chief nodded and bowed as he backed away from Nora. As she turned to go she held up her wand and sent sparks flying around the cave from its tip. All the Spriggans crouched down and shielded their bodies. There was a terrible shrieking as they all tried to talk at once. In the confusion Nora turned around slowly and transformed back into a ferret. Jack picked up her wand in his beak.

'Time to go,' she whispered. 'I think we made an impression don't you?'

Once they were back in the garden Nora sealed the hole in the bush again. By the time they reached the kitchen Jack couldn't stop yawning.

'I think it's time we all went to bed. You can tell Camelin all about it if he's awake and tomorrow we can continue with your flying lessons.'

Jack climbed into the basket and Elan raised him up to the attic window. He waved his wing to her once he was inside. He hopped up the stairs into the loft and waddled over to Camelin.

'Nothing to report here. It's all been quiet,' said Camelin after he'd transformed Jack back.

'I've got lots to tell you.'

'Don't want to talk tonight,' Camelin announced abruptly. 'I need some sleep.'

'Tell you in the morning then,' said Jack.

He wasn't offended. As he lay on the beanbag Orin came and snuggled in the crook of his arm. He watched the stars though the round window. Moonlight streamed in and bathed Camelin's raven basket in a pale, ghostly light. It was peaceful in the loft and his thoughts drifted from Chief Knuckle and the Spriggans to Peabody, Orin and Camelin. Jack listened to the loud squeaking from Motley and the Night Guard as they patrolled the garden. Camelin's rasping snore changed into soft rhythmic breathing. Jack was dozing off when a flapping of wings jolted him awake. Timmery had flown into the loft. Jack reached for his wand so he could understand why Timmery had woken them. He managed to catch the end of his report.

'… moved from the wall; they're under the tree now…'

'Spriggans?' asked Jack getting ready to leap off the beanbag.

'No, cows,' grumbled Camelin. 'He's woken me up to tell me the cows in the opposite field have moved from the wall and are under the tree.'

'… and I've seen a car on the main road,' continued Timmery.

'Nora told you. It's *unusual* things you need to report, not cows and cars.'

'But the cows don't usually go over to the tree until dawn,' explained Timmery.

'It's not important. Now go away and leave me in peace,' Camelin croaked loudly.

'Only doing my duty,' twittered Timmery as he flittered out of the window.

By morning Jack and Camelin were both shattered. They hadn't seen Motley at all but Timmery had disturbed them another three times.

'He's taking his duty far too seriously,' grumbled Camelin, 'and no matter what I've said, he's intent on reporting every single movement he's seen.'

Jack nodded in agreement but he was too busy yawning to reply. Camelin began yawning too.

'I'm going to have to speak to Nora. We can't have another night like that.'

By the time Nora came into the kitchen Jack and Camelin had been up and waiting for nearly half an hour. Camelin was dozing on the window sill and Jack was grooming Orin.

'Sleep well?' she asked cheerfully.

'No,' Camelin croaked grumpily through a stifled yawn. 'None of us did. I need to talk to you about Timmery. He doesn't understand that it's only suspicious things he needs to report. He woke us up about cars and cows and at three o'clock this morning he reported there were twenty-three starlings roosting in the dovecote. I hardly think they pose a threat but I'll go and evict them later; they really shouldn't be there.'

'He'll be here soon. I'll explain it to him again,' replied Nora. 'But you can leave the starlings where they are. They aren't doing anyone any harm. If the doves are happy to share their roost then I'm not going to interfere, and neither are you.'

Camelin didn't express his opinion about starlings. It was obvious to Jack that Nora had quite a soft spot for them.

'She never tells them off about their manners,' Camelin whispered to Jack. 'They're a lot worse than mine. In fact they're disgustingly messy eaters.'

'That's enough Camelin,' Nora chided.

'But you will speak to Timmery, won't you?' he pleaded.

'I will. Have you had breakfast yet?'

Jack had seen Camelin help himself to a light snack from the bird table on his way from the loft to the kitchen. Camelin didn't mention this to Nora.

'I'm starving!' he croaked.

'I doubt that very much,' laughed Nora. 'Don't worry, we'll be eating soon.'

It wasn't long before Elan, Charkle and Gerda joined them.

'Peabody must have been watching Jack all week,' said Elan, 'but I'm surprised no one saw him and sent word to us.'

'There was someone in the bell tower under my roost last week,' said Timmery as he flitted through the window.

Everyone looked at the tiny bat.

'And you didn't report that!' croaked Camelin very loudly. 'For the last few hours you've come to tell me about cows, cars and starlings, but you didn't mention you'd seen someone watching the house!'

'He was there in the daytime and you only said to report anything I saw at night. He didn't disturb my sleep. He was very quiet up there.'

'Well I'm glad you didn't lose any sleep,' Camelin grumbled. 'Some of us hardly slept at all last night.'

'Time for me to get back to the bell tower. Hope you all have a lovely day and I'll see you all again at dusk.'

'Out!' croaked Camelin as loudly as he could.

'Just being sociable,' replied Timmery as he darted around the kitchen.

'Well ravens aren't sociable at this time of the morning, so unless it's really important don't come back.'

'Some ravens aren't sociable at any time of the day,' laughed Elan.

Camelin frowned, hunched his shoulders and closed his eyes. He dozed on the window sill until breakfast was ready.

'Are you ready to try flying today?' Nora asked Jack.

'Oh! I er… suppose so,' Jack replied.

'You'll be fine, a natural if ever I saw one,' Camelin

said sarcastically.

'Don't worry,' Elan said as she smiled encouragingly at Jack. 'You *will* be fine. Camelin might be grumpy but he's an excellent teacher.'

Although Jack was still apprehensive he was also excited. It would be great to try some real flying. He longed to be able to soar, swoop and dive. Camelin made it look such fun. He was about to find out if it was.

FLIGHT

'Why didn't Chief Knuckle say anything about Charkle?' Jack asked Nora as they cleared away the breakfast dishes.

'He won't know for sure that he's here. He'll be safe as long as he doesn't go down any tunnels.'

'That's exactly how I got caught in the first place,' said Charkle as he hovered in front of Jack. 'I was exploring a cave with my two brothers, Norris and Snook. We'd been a few times before and not had a problem until we found a dark hole and those nasty little creatures grabbed us.'

'Did they capture Norris and Snook too?' asked Jack.

'Oh no! They were older than me and already breathing fire. I was just a baby and I couldn't defend myself. Norris set two of the Spriggans' felt hats alight and Snook scratched the other one with his talons but they couldn't rescue me. I got taken down to their workshop and sealed in that lantern. They used me to light their candles once I started breathing fire.'

'It must have been awful,' said Jack. 'I don't know much about dragons; I thought they were all big.'

Charkle laughed.

'Dragons are easy to understand. Dragonairs are red, Dragonors blue and Dragonettes green. You don't want to go messing with red ones. They're big, fierce and usually bad-tempered. Both the males and females breathe fire. The blue ones are about your size. They're usually quite friendly and they don't breathe fire at all, but they've got the sharpest teeth so it's always as well to keep out of their reach just in case they haven't had breakfast.'

'Are all green dragons small?' Jack asked.

'Oh yes… we're Dragonettes… small, friendly and very good-natured. Only the males breathe fire.'

Charkle stopped beating his wings and sank down to the table.

'It's been so long since I've seen my family. I've missed them so much.'

'I can take you over to Westwood today if you'd rather not wait until next weekend,' offered Nora.

'No, thank you. If you don't mind I'd rather stay here with all of you for a few days. It's so long since I've had any company. I'm really enjoying being here.'

Nora smiled at Charkle before turning to Jack.

'Do you understand now why I didn't want you to go down the tunnel? Spriggans enjoy roasting birds, as well as rats, when they can catch them. That's why Camelin doesn't like going underground.'

'Can you blame me?' grumbled Camelin. 'At least I'm not scared of heights.'

'Who on earth's scared of heights?' asked Elan.

Jack frowned at Camelin who shuffled from foot to foot and hunched his head into his neck as far as it would go.'

'Sorry Jack,' he whispered.

'Well why didn't you say?' Nora said. 'Fancy keeping that to yourself!'

Jack didn't say anything; he was too embarrassed. He'd thought his secret would have been safe with Camelin and he'd hoped he'd feel differently once he was a raven.

'Straight down to the herborium with you. I've got just the thing. You'll never have a problem with heights again.'

Once they were in Nora's room she rummaged around the shelves looking for the right bottle. Jack felt very grateful.

'When you've drunk this you can transform in here. Save you going back upstairs. Camelin will have you flying in no time.'

Jack drank the bitter-tasting liquid. It felt hot in his throat and made his mouth taste awful.

'Sorry Jack,' Camelin said again. 'It sort of slipped out. I didn't mean to tell.'

'It's not a problem and if this helps I could be flying soon.'

Camelin shuffled around until Nora left them alone.

'Did you bring me anything, you know, for the flying lesson?'

'I did but I'm only giving you half. I need something to get rid of this awful taste.'

Jack undid the small cake he'd brought from his room for Camelin. He broke it in two. In one gulp Camelin's half was gone.

'OK, let's go.' He croaked and touched Jack's forehead. 'We'll start with a bit of gliding, only a bit higher this time.'

They skipped over to the beech tree at the far end

of the garden and hopped from branch to branch until Jack was higher than he'd been before. It would be a long glide to the grass but he felt confident.

'Here goes!' Jack croaked as he opened his wings and stepped off the branch.

For the first time in his life he didn't feel sick when he looked down. The ground wasn't swirling below him. Instead of gliding as he'd agreed instinct took over. His wings seemed to know just what to do. He brought them down powerfully and then up again and again and again. Suddenly he was gaining height.

'I'm flying!' he croaked excitedly. 'This time I'm really flying.'

Jack saw Camelin's beak open as he rose past him.

'Close your beak,' Jack croaked. 'I thought you said it was rude to stare.'

Jack gained more and more height. He felt no fear. flying was the best feeling in the whole world.

'Look at me!' he cried.

'Come down now before you get me into trouble,' Camelin called after him.

'This is brilliant! Whatever Nora gave me, it's working.'

'Set down on the grass,' shouted Camelin.

It was too late. Jack had already started an

approach towards the branch where Camelin sat. The touchdown didn't quite go as planned. Jack overshot and went careering into the next tree.

'We need to work on your landing skills!' laughed Camelin.

'Oh wow!' exclaimed Jack. 'I need to do that again.'

For the rest of the morning Jack practiced his new skill. Camelin helped him to refine his technique and taught him how to estimate where his feet needed to go when he came in to land.

'I think I need a rest,' gasped Jack. 'I didn't realise how tiring flying would be.'

'Let's go and get some food,' suggested Camelin. 'Follow me!'

Jack presumed they'd be making their way towards the house but instead he followed Camelin as the raven flew over the hedge, across the main road and around the back of the shops next to the Church. They landed on a flat roof behind a fish and chip shop.

'Leave this to me,' Camelin whispered.

He swooped down, landed on the window ledge and tapped on the window. He puffed out his chest and walked proudly up and down once the two women in the back, who were preparing chips, noticed him.

'Oh look!' exclaimed the younger woman. 'That crow's back!'

'Ah look, he's brought his girlfriend too!' replied the other woman pointing towards Jack.

The two women put their head on one side and smiled at Jack. He wasn't sure he liked being mistaken for a female crow.

'Here he goes,' the older woman said and nudged the younger one in the ribs.

Camelin shuffled along the window ledge performing a kind of jerky dance. He nodded his head and hunched his wings up and down. After a bit of bobbing he lifted one leg then the other. Eventually he flew back and joined Jack on the roof.

'Any minute now,' he said excitedly. 'But be careful, the chips are usually red hot!'

They didn't have to wait long before the back door opened. The younger women brought out a polystyrene tray piled high with chips and slid it onto the roof.

'There you go,' she said kindly. 'Brought your lady friend out for lunch have you?'

Camelin strutted around and gave the woman a display of his gratitude by doing a few one legged twirls then promptly tucked in to his reward. Jack was ravenous. He managed to grab a few chips before Camelin could eat them all.

'Do they always feed you?' he asked when the tray was empty.

'Oh yes, and they always call me a crow. Now you know the kind of indignities I have to put up with.'

'Well at least they don't think you're a female!' laughed Jack. 'But it was worth it. Those chips were great.'

'Not a word when we get back,' warned Camelin. 'If they think we've eaten we won't be allowed any lunch and it's a roast today with apple pie for afters.'

'Not a word,' Jack promised.

'Come on, time to go. We've got someone to see.'

Camelin took off and Jack followed. He circled around the top of the church tower before landing on a parapet which ran around the bottom of the belfry. Once he'd landed and looked around Jack gasped; the view was amazing. He could see the whole area. Glasruhen Hill loomed high above them. He could see the Forest where he'd met Arrana and Newton Gill further along. Below was Ewell House. It wasn't hard for Jack to understand why Peabody had climbed the bell tower to spy on him.

'Won't they be worried about us. We've been gone a long time now?'

'That's why I've brought us up here, so we've got an excuse when we get back. We're visiting!'

Jack looked around but couldn't see anyone.

Camelin threw his head back. 'Timmery,' he shouted as loudly as he could.

There was a movement from the ceiling of the belfry. A sleepy face peered down at them from the far corner. As soon as Timmery realised who'd called he got really excited and flittered down.

'Hello, hello, this is an unexpected pleasure. So good of you to drop in.'

'Just being sociable,' Camelin said sarcastically. 'And I've got a message for you from Nora.'

Camelin seemed disappointed that the tiny bat wasn't annoyed. He didn't seem to mind being woken up in daylight and looked genuinely pleased to have visitors.

'Does this mean you can fly now Jack Brenin?' he fussed. 'You'll be as good a flyer as Camelin in no time, just you wait and see.'

Camelin coughed loudly and frowned at Timmery.

'Jack's going home this afternoon and Nora says you're to keep a watch over his house tonight. Orin's going to be with him too… but most importantly, I don't need you to report anything to me at all unless there's a really big problem… understand?'

Timmery nodded vigorously until Camelin was satisfied that he'd understood.

'Well, we mustn't disturb your sleep. It's about time we got back.'

'Oh dear,' piped Timmery. 'Aren't you going to stay a bit longer?'

'Nope,' replied Camelin. 'Just a flying visit.'

'Oh do come again,' Timmery fussed. 'I love visitors, any time, night or day.'

'Well I only have visitors during the day,' Camelin grumbled, 'so there's no need for you to come calling on me in the middle of the night.'

He took off before Timmery could say anything else.

'Goodbye,' said Jack politely. 'Must fly!'

As Jack flew over the hedge of Ewell House he saw Nora on the patio with her arms folded looking crossly at Camelin. He could hear her telling him off. He landed on the grass and hopped over to them.

'You were supposed to have stayed in the grounds. What would you have done if you'd had a problem?'

'I only took Jack to see Timmery and to give him your message. I wouldn't have taken him if he wasn't flying so well,' Camelin said with as much innocence as he could muster. 'And it's such a great view from the top of the belfry, I thought it would help Jack have a better understanding of where everything is.'

'I don't suppose any harm's been done, but next time you must tell me when you intend to go out. We were very worried. It's only Jack's first time out and I can't believe you woke Timmery up in the middle of the day. You were supposed to give him my message after supper.'

Camelin winked at Jack as he hung his head down as far as it would go.

'Timmery was very pleased to see us,' added Jack. 'He didn't seem to mind being woken up.'

'I'm very sorry,' said Camelin. 'I won't do it again.'

He gave Nora his pathetic, forlorn look and she forgave him.

'Your Grandad's calling round for you after dinner on his way home from the Cricket Club. I invited him to eat with us but he said he was having a pub lunch with some friends from the Gardening Club.

Jack and Camelin waddled over to the herborium. Jack lay on the floor once he'd transformed back. His arms and legs ached very badly, worse than they'd done before.

'Take this with you,' Nora said as she put a brown jar on the table. 'Rub that on your arms and legs tonight before you go to bed. It's for aching muscles.'

'Thanks. It was worth the pain. Being able to fly is the best thing in the whole world.'

The rest of the day went quickly. It was a hot afternoon and the animals settled down to sleep. Elan, Nora and Jack got their wands out after lunch and went into the garden. Nora wanted to make Grub look more like a tree and turned his clothes into bark. Elan made his hair into branches and Jack added the leaves.

'That's better,' Nora said as she stood back to make sure Grub's face couldn't be seen. 'The sooner we hear from Chief Knuckle the better. It took nearly twenty minutes to feed him this morning.'

'When do you think he'll get the acorn back?' asked Jack.

'It depends where Peabody is,' replied Nora. 'With any luck he'll still be hiding out in the Gnori at Newton Gill. If he is we'll have it back in no time.'

'Are you ready for tomorrow?' Elan asked Jack as they watched Nora repair the picnic table.

'Tomorrow?'

'School! It's your first day, isn't it?'

'It is,' sighed Jack, 'I don't want to go. I wish you were coming with me.'

'I don't think I'd fit in. I can learn what I need to know from Nora's library.'

'I'm worried about those boys I saw on the field last week.'

'I'll come and meet you if you want. Nora's already asked your Grandad if you can come round and do your homework here every night after school. She just didn't tell him what kind of homework you'd be doing!'

Jack and Elan laughed.

'The day won't go quick enough. Now I can fly I just can't wait to do it again.'

'Do you want me to meet you?'

Jack didn't know what to say. It would be good to walk home with someone but that someone was a girl and if the boys saw him they'd probably torment him about it. Then he thought of a solution.

'If you don't mind I'm going to see if Grandad will meet me, just for the first few days. You could come along with him if you wanted.'

'That's a great idea,' Elan agreed.

The thought of school was a bit more bearable now Jack knew he'd be back at Ewell House every night.

'I might have other homework to do as well and I'm going to have to do it before I go home.'

'It's not a problem. Nora and I can help you if you get stuck and we'll make sure Camelin doesn't disturb you until you've finished.'

'Thanks,' replied Jack. He couldn't believe he'd only been at Grandad's for just over a week. So much had happened in that time.

Before Grandad arrived Jack went up to see Camelin and collect Orin.

'I'll see you tomorrow night then.'

'Naw,' Camelin laughed. 'Why wait that long? I'll be round later tonight. When I see your bedroom light go on I'll tap on your window.'

'Brilliant!' We'll be able to carry on with your lessons. Grandad won't hear us because he has the television on loud and the lounge is at the other side of the house.'

'Can't have you flying better than I can read, can we?'

Camelin chuckled so loudly he woke Orin.

There was a loud knock on the front door. 'Time to go,' said Jack wistfully.

'See you later, and don't forget I'll be hungry. It's hard work reading.'

It was Jack's turn to laugh. Orin jumped onto Jack's hand and made herself at home in his pocket. Jack collected his backpack from the spare room and went down to meet Grandad. He found everyone in the kitchen.

'Just been getting my things,' he explained.

'Nora says you've all had a good weekend.'

'The best,' replied Jack. 'Thanks for an amazing time.'

'You can come over next weekend and stay again if you like,' Nora said. 'I know Elan will be glad of the company and I'm sure you've got things already planned Sam.'

Grandad nodded.

'It's a busy time, what with the gardening and cricket, but I don't want him to be a nuisance or be in the way.'

'If Jack wants to come he'll be more than welcome,' said Nora and gave Jack a wink that Grandad didn't see.

'Bye,' called Elan from the gate as she waved to them. 'See you tomorrow night.'

Jack smiled as they walked back along the lane. He was happy. It had been a long time since he'd felt like this. He hadn't wanted to come and live with Grandad but, now he was here, he couldn't think of anywhere on earth he'd rather be. His life had been changed forever. He was a raven boy like Camelin now and could fly. He looked towards Glasruhen Forest and wondered if Arrana was alright. He knew she'd be kept informed about his flying lessons. She'd also know it wasn't his fault the golden acorn was missing. He'd have to ask Nora if he could fly over with Camelin into Glasruhen Forest at the weekend to see her. Flying really was going to have lots of benefits. He hoped his muscles would get used to it soon; he still ached. Camelin had told him they had a lot of things to practice before they'd be ready to go through the window in time but Jack didn't care. He couldn't wait to fly again.

BAD NEWS

Jack's first day at school went quicker and better than he'd expected. He'd worried about what his new classmates would be like and if he'd fit in, but it hadn't been as bad as he'd thought. None of the boys he'd met on the playing field were in his class and all the teachers had been friendly. At the end of the afternoon Grandad and Elan were waiting for him by the back gate which led into the lane.

'Good day?' Grandad asked.

'It was OK. I've put my name down for the choir auditions. They're doing a concert at the end of term.'

'Good for you,' said Grandad and patted Jack on the back. 'Got a lot of homework tonight?'

'I've got things I have to do,' Jack replied. He didn't want to lie to Grandad but he couldn't tell him about the flying lessons.

'Nora said Jack can use her library for his homework,' said Elan.

'That's really kind. I've only got a few books and most of them are about gardening,' Grandad replied.

'See you later then,' Jack said as they reached Grandad's gate.

'Dinner's at six. Don't be late.'

'I won't,' Jack promised.

'Were you OK today?' Elan asked when they were alone.

'It was fine apart from my aching muscles and not being able to concentrate too well.'

Jack looked around.

'Where's Camelin?'

'Keeping watch,' laughed Elan, 'just in case you had any trouble. He said he wanted to be ready for those boys if they showed up and started anything.'

Camelin must have heard his name. He appeared above them and spiralled into a nosedive. He pulled out at the last moment with a backwards flip.

'Wow!' exclaimed Jack.

'Don't encourage him!' laughed Elan. 'He'll get

bigheaded.'

Camelin swooped round and landed carefully on Jack's shoulder.

'Ready for your lesson?' he croaked, then whispered in Jack's ear, 'See you later for mine.'

Jack only had two things he needed to find out for homework and Elan knew exactly where to look in Nora's library. It wasn't long before he was able to transform. He worked on landing and taking off and managed to fly in and out of Camelin's loft. The time went too quickly and Jack had to hurry down to the gap in the hedge and run all the way back to Grandad's.

Later when Jack was in his room, Camelin tapped on the window. He had a piece of paper in his beak. Jack thought it was a letter from Nora until he saw the drawings. There was a circle filled with smaller circles, a raspberry, an ice cream and a lot of long lines which Jack recognised as noodles.

'Can you put the letters on?' Camelin asked. 'It's for Orin.'

Jack looked again at the pictures and realised the first had to be an oatcake. He wrote *O R I N* in big capital letters and pegged it onto her cage.

'Not bad,' he said. 'I'm sure she'll love it.'

'Of course she won't know the letters but she'll be able to read my pictures,' croaked Camelin, obviously pleased with himself.

By Thursday night Jack had settled into his new routine. The school wasn't the same as he'd been used to but he liked his teacher and no one had bothered him. Elan came to meet him at the gate and they'd talk about the things he'd done during the day. As soon as he arrived at Ewell House he went to the library and did his homework, then concentrated on flying. After dark Camelin would arrive for his lesson and once he'd gone Jack played with Orin until she snuggled down on his bed. It was then he'd get out his Book of Shadows and ask as many questions as he could. He learnt more about Hamadryads, the High Druid and the sacred groves. He found out about the four main festivals which used to take place on top of Glasruhen Hill. He'd tried discussing what he'd read with Camelin but the raven wasn't interested, so instead he told Orin.

On the Thursday night he made a discovery which worried him. It was something he needed to speak to Elan about and it couldn't wait until tomorrow. He opened his book at the first page and wrote her name at the top. He glanced at the clock; it was getting late. He hoped she hadn't gone to bed. He hesitated. It was hard to begin to write what he wanted to say.

The book says that to open the window in time everything must be equal. It says that those performing the ritual must have the same powers. Is this right?

Jack watched the words fade into the page. He paced up and down the room. This was going to be a big problem. Nora had said she was the last Druid on Earth. Without someone with the same powers they'd never be able to perform the ritual. What would they do? Where could they find another Druid to help them? He tapped his wand in his hand impatiently.

'Look!' Orin squeaked. 'You've got some writing.'

Jack quickly read Elan's answer.

Yes, that's right.

He felt even more anxious,

Who will help her?

The reply wasn't what Jack expected.

I will.

We'll talk about it tomorrow.

Jack was going to have to wait. He tried asking the book more questions about the ritual but wasn't able to get any more answers. Eventually the book snapped shut and refused to open again. There was nothing else he could do but go to bed and wait until after school to find out more from Elan. He didn't sleep well.

'What's wrong?' asked Elan as they walked towards Ewell House.

'I don't understand how you're going to help Nora. You've got to have exactly the same powers; how can that be?'

'Some things aren't as they appear.'

'That doesn't answer the question.'

Elan sighed deeply.

'There are still some things we haven't told you.'

'Like what?'

'Well, you know I can shape shift…'

'Into a ferret.'

'…not just into a ferret. I'm like Nora.'

Jack's mouth fell open. He stopped walking and stared at Elan.

'You mean you're not a girl?'

'No.'

'What are you? I thought you were my friend. I thought Nora was your aunt.'

'I am your friend but Nora isn't my aunt.'

'Are you a Druid?'

'No, I'm a nymph.'

'Not like Jennet?'

'No, I'm one of the Fair Folk of Annwn.'

'Did you shape shift into a girl on purpose to trick me?'

'Oh Jack, no, I wouldn't do such a thing. When the cauldron plates went missing I got trapped here with Nora. There was a group of us waiting to make the last journey into Annwn but, as you know, we couldn't go. While we waited for someone to help us Nora chose to be old and I chose to be young.'

Jack shook his head in disbelief. This meant Elan had to be the same age as Nora.

'So what do you look like?'

'When you find the cauldron plates and we reopen the Western Portal into Annwn you'll be able to see me as I really am, but not until then.'

Jack didn't know what to say. He hadn't even considered that Elan was anything other than she appeared. He thought she'd learned how to do things with her wand from Nora, just as he had.

'Will I ever see you again if we succeed?'

'I have to return to Annwn to renew my strength. Like Nora and Arrana I won't survive forever on Earth, but it doesn't mean I won't see you again.'

Jack swallowed hard. His eyes watered as he fought back the tears. Saying goodbye to Nora, Elan and Camelin wasn't something he'd be able to do easily. They'd probably soon forget about him once they went through the portal. No matter what Elan said he might never see them again. He swallowed hard and straightened his back. He'd promised to help and he would. He'd been having fun and had forgotten it was a matter of life and death for Nora and Arrana and now, it seemed, for Elan too. They were his friends and he wouldn't let them down.

'Are you all right?' Elan asked as she put her hand on Jack's arm.

'I am now,' he replied and managed to smile. 'It was just a bit of a shock.'

'That's why we didn't tell you everything at once. We didn't want you to be frightened and run away.'

'I probably would have done. I'm good at running.'

'Bet you're not as fast as me,' she laughed. 'Beat you to the sundial!'

They ran and laughed all the way into Nora's garden. As they sped past the bird table a flock of starlings took off.

'Told you I could beat you!'

Jack was too out of breath to answer. As he gulped for air he noticed Camelin waddling on the roof shouting something to the startled birds as they flew past. He was too far away to hear but he had a good idea what his friend had been saying.

'Next time you can have my backpack on and then we'll see who wins,' Jack said when he finally got his breath back. 'I think you had a bit of an advantage.'

'Big day tomorrow,' Nora said as she joined them. 'A longer flight for you Jack and a visit to Westwood to reunite Charkle with his family.'

Jack didn't want to have to say goodbye to Charkle; he really liked the little dragon.

'Will he come back and visit?'

'I certainly hope so,' replied Nora. 'He'll probably bring Norris and Snook with him too. It's a good job they're only small or we wouldn't all fit in the kitchen.'

'Did someone say kitchen? Is it tea time?' Camelin asked as he swooped down onto Nora's shoulder.

'You know very well it's not, but now we're together I've got some good news. I'm meeting Peabody tonight at dusk.'

'Where?' Camelin asked.

'Here. He's going to use the tunnel. We'll leave your flying lesson until later, if you don't mind Jack, and have an early tea. We need to be ready for our visitor. Once he's returned my golden acorn we'll put it somewhere very safe until its needed for the ritual.'

As the sun sank behind Glasruhen Hill they left the kitchen and went over to the hole in the garden. Nora raised her wand and removed the prickly bush. They didn't have to wait long before they heard footsteps inside the tunnel. They grew louder as they came closer to the entrance. In the half-light Jack saw the end of a very long nose appear before the rest of Peabody stepped out onto the grass.

'Oh great Seanchai,' Peabody began as he took off his cap and bowed low before Nora. 'I've come to speak with you.'

'Speak!' exclaimed Nora. 'I thought you'd come to return my golden acorn.'

'It's the golden acorn I wish to speak of, most wise and kind Guardian of the Sacred Grove,' continued Peabody as he bowed again.

'Where's my golden acorn? You know it's Druid's gold don't you?'

'I do now but I no longer have it.'

'Explain yourself before I turn you into a Brownie.'

Peabody straightened and replaced his hat.

'I came to explain. You see my brother Pycroft has the acorn and I can't find him anywhere. He made me lie to the Spriggans. He's the one who gave me the torch for Chief Knuckle. He's the one you should be talking to. It wasn't my fault.'

When Nora didn't answer Peabody began shuffling his feet and took a step towards the tunnel. Gerda settled herself down in front of the hole and eyed Peabody suspiciously. He stepped away from her.

'Can I go now?' he asked quietly.

'Not until I've made a small adjustment to your nose,' replied Nora.

'No, no, not my nose,' wailed Peabody.

Nora raised her wand and aimed it straight at Peabody's face. There was a green flash and a cry of surprise. For a few moments the light blinded them all. As their eyes grew accustomed to the twilight again Jack saw Peabody's glasses lying on the grass. He bent down and picked them up.

'My nose, my nose!' sobbed Peabody.

Everyone looked to see what was wrong. A small button nose, which wasn't long enough for Peabody to sit his glasses on, replaced the long, pointed one he'd been so proud of.

'Now we both have a problem,' said Nora sternly. 'I'll restore your nose once you return my golden acorn. I suggest you find your brother quickly. You have ten days. Go, and don't return without it.'

Peabody snatched his glasses from Jack's hand and put them in his pocket. He stumbled towards the hole. Gerda moved to the side and he dived in. They heard his retreating footsteps. No one spoke.

'That wasn't what I'd expected,' Nora said eventually.

'Will he get the acorn back?' asked Jack.

'I've just made finding it the most important thing in his life. I just hope he can get it back from Pycroft in time.'

'There are only fourteen days to the Solstice,' explained Elan.

'Until the ritual?' Jack asked.

'Until the ritual,' confirmed Nora.

They went to bed subdued. Jack didn't go up to the loft. He was tired and needed a good night's sleep. He was woken early by a loud rasping noise coming from the garden. He squinted as he opened the window to find out where the noise was coming from. He finally located the sound. It was coming from the new tree by the shed. Grub was snoring.

'Does he do that every night?' Jack asked Camelin at breakfast.

'All night and most of the day. He sleeps more than I do.'

'He doesn't snore when he's eating,' added Charkle.

'That's something else he does more than me too. You should see the amount of food he gets through in a day.'

Nora had insisted that they eat an enormous breakfast.

'It's a long flight to Westwood. If you get tired and want to stop we'll be right behind you in the car,' Nora told them. 'Now, off you go and transform whilst Elan and I pack the boot. We'll take your clothes along just in case you get tired and want a lift back.'

Jack was used to transforming now. Each time it got easier and the more he flew the less he ached. He thought he'd probably suffer for a few days after a long-distance flight. This was going to be his first big test as a raven.

When they flew down to the car Charkle was sitting on Elan's shoulder.

'Are we all ready?' Nora asked.

Everyone nodded.

Jack and Camelin set off across the fields. For a while Jack could see Nora's Morris Traveller snaking its way along the roads but soon it was lost from sight. Their plan was to fly in a straight line towards the river, then follow it's course. It appeared suddenly over the brow of a small hill they'd soared over, and then meandered gently over the landscape. They flew past farms and what looked like an endless patchwork quilt of greens, yellows and browns. They saw a ruined Abbey, remains of an old Roman fort and several large hills. Jack was beginning to tire.

'Do you know anything about Westwood?' he called to Camelin.

'It's a bit like Glasruhen Hill only smaller. There used to be a portal there but it got sealed up when the Romans came. It's not far now. See the trees over there? Come on, race you.'

It wasn't much of a race. Jack was out of breath when he finally landed next to Camelin who looked pleased with himself for having arrived first.

'Nora can't get the car up here so we'll have to meet them down there in the car park,' Camelin explained.

They flew down and landed on the branch of a large oak tree.

'This was once a Hamadryad like Arrana,' Camelin explained. 'Nora used to visit her before, but now it's just a hollow tree.'

The hollowness of the tree made Jack feel sad. He thought about Arrana's plight.

From their position they could see the Morris Traveller winding its way along the country roads. It stopped next to a densely wooded area. Nora and Elan, with Charkle on her shoulder, got out and disappeared into the trees.

'That's where the Westwood Roost is,' explained Camelin, 'but there's not much point flying over there. They'll be back in the car before we arrive.'

It was a beautiful morning. The bright sunshine made Jack's eyes smart. He closed his eyes and almost fell asleep.

'Here they come,' croaked Camelin as he nudged Jack in the wing. 'We'll go and say goodbye to Charkle on our way home, give him a bit of time to see all his family again.'

It wasn't long before Nora drove into the deserted car park. Jack heard a strange noise as they got out of the car. It was Charkle. He was on Elan's shoulder, engulfed in steam, sobbing his heart out.

'What's wrong?' croaked Jack and Camelin together.

Charkle couldn't speak.

'They've gone,' explained Nora. 'His whole family has disappeared without a trace.'

THE WESTWOOD ROOST

Jack and Camelin fussed around Charkle.

'What happened?' they both asked.

'Gone!' was all Charkle could say and began sobbing again.

'We found the roost without any problem but as soon as we entered the cave we knew Charkle's family wouldn't be there,' explained Nora.

'The smell inside made your nose curl,' interrupted Elan.

'What kind of a smell?' Camelin asked.

'Hag smell,' replied Elan.

'Ergh!' Camelin croaked as he turned his head to one side and coughed several times.

'Hags!' exclaimed Jack. 'You mean like witches?'

'Not quite,' continued Nora. 'Hags don't like sunlight and tend to live in dark places. They're not very big, about your size.'

'As a boy?'

'No, as a raven. You'd know one if you met one and you couldn't mistake their voices.'

Camelin thrust his head forward and made a strange high-pitched sound, then continued describing Hags in the same voice as he circled round Jack.

'They're really ugly, got great beak like noses, long claw like hands and feet, a mass of purple-black hair, which reaches the floor and they're grossly messy.'

Charkle choked back another sob.

'Are there Hags still in the cave?' asked Jack.

'Hag,' replied Elan. 'They live alone, don't get on with anyone. We think this one might be Finnola Fytche. *FF* is scrawled on the entrance to the cave.'

'She might be able to tell us what happened to the Westwood Roost and where they went,' said Nora kindly as she smiled at Charkle before turning towards Jack. 'You ought to eat something after your long flight.'

'Great. I'm famished,' said Camelin.

'I wasn't talking to you. I didn't think you'd need

any encouragement to eat. Let's go further up the hill before we unpack the food. Elan can go over to the roost and try to find the Hag. I'll go and talk to the Dryads in the forest. Someone has to know something about Charkle's family.'

'Can I come with you?' Charkle asked Elan.

Nora scooped Charkle up in her hand and brought him close to her face.

'You can come along with everyone later. Stay with Jack and Camelin for now.'

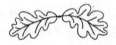

Once the picnic was laid out Nora turned again to Jack.

'Make sure you eat something.'

Camelin had already got too much in his beak to speak. Jack wondered how Elan was going to get back to the Westwood Roost. It would be a long walk. It was only when she raised both arms and began turning slowly that he realised she was going to shape shift. With each rotation her body got smaller and began to reform. He'd expected to see the chestnut ferret but instead a beautiful eagle owl appeared. She shook herself. Jack was amazed at how big she was, at least three times bigger than Camelin. Her feathers were different shades of brown and she had two ear tufts which were almost flat against her head. Her eyes, instead of being deep amber, were dark green.

'See you later,' she hooted as she spread her wings and gracefully flew off towards the roost.

Jack watched in admiration as Elan rose effortlessly higher and higher. There hadn't been a sound from her wings as she'd flown away.

'Come on you two,' said Camelin through a beakful of sandwich. 'Get stuck in.'

'I'm not hungry,' Charkle replied as he sniffed back another tear.

'Well, do you think you could warm this up for me? You know send a bit of a flame over. Only I love toasted cheese sandwiches.'

'Camelin,' said Jack sharply, 'Can't you see Charkle's upset,'

'You're beginning to sound just like Nora,' grumbled Camelin as he looked longingly at the sandwich. 'Everyone knows cheese tastes better when it's toasted.'

Charkle moved away from the rug where the picnic was spread and flew up onto the lower branch of the nearest tree. Jack followed him.

'I'm sorry about your family. I know what it's like to feel alone, I'm never going to see my mum again. She died not long ago, and my dad's living hundreds of miles away. I haven't got any brothers or sisters either. I've only got Grandad and I still feel sad inside.'

Charkle's eyes filled with tears again.

'All the time the Spriggans had me in that cage I kept hoping one day I might escape and come back to my family. Do you think I'm ever going to see them again?'

'I don't know but try not to worry. Nora will do her best to find them. You'll never be alone any more now you've got us.'

Jack smiled at Charkle and the little dragon managed to smile weakly back.

'We ought to do what Nora said. Try to eat something. It might be a long day.'

They joined Camelin who was still grumbling to himself. Jack didn't really feel hungry but if he wanted to fly back he'd have to eat. Charkle sat hunched up, looking forlorn until Nora returned.

'Did you find out where they went?' he asked eagerly.

Everyone looked at Nora; even Camelin stopped eating.

'Not quite, but if Elan's been able to flush a Hag

out of the roost we might find out a bit more. The Dryads in Westwood live in silver birch trees. They haven't got good memories at the best of times. As soon as they lose their leaves in autumn they curl up and sleep until the new buds appear in the spring. They think Charkle's family left after a Hag moved into the cave but it was so long ago now they can't remember any more.'

Charkle let out a puff of steam and two huge tears.

'Come on you two, help me to get this lot cleared away and we'll go and find Elan.'

Camelin looked wistfully at all the food that hadn't been eaten and sighed. Once everything was back in the basket they made their way to the car.

'Do you want to come with me Jack or do you want to fly over to the roost with Camelin?'

'I'll fly. I feel OK now I've had a rest.'

'You'll have to come with me Charkle. It wouldn't do for anyone to see you flying around.'

Charkle didn't protest; he still looked very sad.

As Jack and Camelin circled around the roost they could see Elan on the ground with her wings outstretched in front of the entrance. The tips of her wings almost touched each side of the rock. Her feathers were all puffed out and her head jutted forward as she fixed her gaze on something inside the cave. It was strangely quiet as they landed. The trees were still and not a bird could be heard. Camelin kept his distance and landed on a branch in a nearby tree. Jack alighted on the ground nearer the cave. It wasn't long before they heard the engine of the Morris Traveller.

Once Nora stood before the entrance Elan lowered her wings and straightened up.

'Come out,' Nora commanded.

'No!' came a high-pitched reply.

'Then we're coming in.'

Nora walked straight into the cave. Everyone followed. The smell was revolting. It made Jack gag and he could see it had the same effect on Camelin. Nora held up her wand and sent an arc of light, shaped like an umbrella, above their heads.

'Aaaaaaaahhhhhhh!' screeched the Hag. 'Too bright, too bright, put it out, it's hurting my eyes.'

'The light stays until you give us the information we need,' replied Nora sternly.

Jack looked around the cave. There was rubbish strewn everywhere on the floor, reminding him a bit of Camelin's loft. The screeching had come from the back of the cave but even with Nora's light Jack was unable to see who had made such a dreadful noise. From the darkest recess the voice spoke again.

'We don't give information. You need a Bogie for that.'

Jack saw Nora frown.

'And which Bogie would you recommend?'

There was silence for a while, then the Hag started screeching again.

'Go away! Coming in here uninvited, frightening the life out of me with that great ugly bird, making my eyes hurt. Go away and don't come back.'

Nora didn't answer. Instead she pointed her wand in the direction of the voice and gave it a quick flick. A small bundle of purple hair, claws and black ragged clothes tumbled out into the open. Nora raised her hand, held her palm out flat towards the rolling jumble of arms and legs and made it come to an abrupt halt.

'Aaaaaaaaaaahhhhhhhhhh!' the Hag wailed as she shielded her eyes.

'Finnola Fytche I presume,' began Nora.

'Who wants to know,' snapped the Hag.

'The Seanchai. I command you to answer my questions unless you want to become lunch for my owl?'

Elan raised her wings and hopped a couple of steps towards the cowering Hag.

'All right, all right, call the bird off. I'll tell you what you want to know.'

Elan stopped but didn't lower her wings.

'You are?' asked Nora.

'Finnola Fytche, but why bother asking if you already know?'

'Which Bogie were you referring to and where might I find him?'

Finnola shook herself and carefully rearranged the ragged cloak. She ran her claw like hands through her mass of purple hair before she spoke again.

'That would be Pycroft. He visits here; we trade.'

Jack wondered what kind of things the Hag and Bogie might trade. There were a lot of bones lying around the cave floor and what looked like a sheepskin near the entrance.

Nora tapped her wand, waiting for Finnola to continue.

'Don't know where you'd find him. Unpredictable

he is. Here one day, gone the next. Never know when he'll reappear. Have you done now with your questions?'

'Just a few more... when did you last see a family of Dragonettes?'

Charkle peeped out from behind Nora's neck and stared at Finnola.

'Few hundred years ago I'd say. Don't have much to do with Dragonettes, not much meat on them. You need at least three to make a decent meal.'

Charkle shot back behind Nora who frowned again at Finnola.

'They didn't stay long after I arrived. Left in the winter when the great earthquake brought the back of the cave down. Not seen any Dragonettes since, not till now anyway.'

Jack wished he could go outside into the fresh air. The smell was making him feel sick and he didn't like to think what he might be standing in.

'I'm putting a watch on you,' Nora said quietly to Finnola. 'I intend to know everything you do from now on, so if you see Pycroft before I do tell him he's got something which belongs to me and he needs to return it as quickly as his little legs will carry him. Understood?'

'Don't do messages,' Finnola grumbled.

'And I don't take kindly to rudeness so if you want the light to disappear you'll do as I ask.'

Finnola grumbled under her breath in her squeaky, high-pitched whine.

'If I hear anything I don't like, I'll come back and *permanently* light this cave. Is that clear?'

Finnola nodded.

Nora turned and walked towards the entrance. With every step she took the light inside grew fainter and fainter until only darkness remained. It was a relief to be outside and Jack gulped in the clean, fresh air.

When they were back in Westwood Elan shape shifted back. No one spoke until they got to the car.

'Do you think Pycroft is around here somewhere?' asked Elan.

'He could be anywhere,' sighed Nora, 'but at least we learnt a bit more about Charkle's family.'

'You don't think she ate them all do you?' whispered Charkle who was close to tears again.

'No,' replied Nora. 'I doubt she'd have caught any of your family. I expect they moved out because of the smell. I'm sorry Charkle but I don't think it's going to be easy to find them. You're welcome to live with us, but I'm going to have to transform you into something a little less conspicuous or you won't be able to fly around very easily. Now what's it to be?'

'Can I be a bat like Timmery?'

'Not another bat like Timmery,' groaned Camelin.

'I think that will be perfect,' said Nora, ignoring Camelin's remark. We'll sort that out as soon as we get home. Now are you two flying back or do you want a lift?'

'Flying,' Jack and Camelin said together.

The flight back seemed to take ages. Jack was exhausted when they reached Ewell House. Nora was nowhere to be seen and he realised Elan still had his clothes in the car.

'I'm going to have to stay like this till they get back, but I'm so tired I'm finding it hard to stay awake.'

'I keep telling them its tiring being a raven but they never listen to me. Food and sleep, those are the two main things a raven needs and lots of them.'

All Jack could do was nod in agreement.

'I've got a surprise for you,' Camelin said excitedly. 'Follow me, but when you get to the window you've got to close your eyes!'

Jack could hardly lift his wings as he flew after Camelin up to the loft. When he was safely on the window ledge he did as Camelin had asked.

'Surprise!' croaked Camelin.

Jack smiled when he opened his eyes. There on the floor of the loft was a second cat basket.

'It's for you. A raven basket just like mine. I know it's the right size because I tried it last night.'

Camelin looked expectantly at Jack.

'Do you like it?'

'It's great,' said Jack as he hopped into the basket.

It was a perfect fit and soon they were both on their backs, with their feet in the air, snoring loudly.

By the time Jack and Camelin woke the heat in the loft was oppressive.

'Emergency rations,' announced Camelin as he rummaged around in his basket before throwing a chocolate bar to Jack.

Jack had never tried to unwrap anything with his beak and claws. It wasn't easy, especially since the heat in the loft had melted the chocolate. Camelin was on his second by the time Jack got into the wrapper.

'Come on, let's go outside. It'll be cooler flying,' Camelin said once Jack had finished.

'I'd like to go and see Arrana but I think we ought to ask Nora first.'

'OK, race you to the kitchen.'

'It's not time to eat,' Nora said as Jack and Camelin swooped past her and landed on the back of the chairs.

'We haven't come for food,' replied Camelin.

Nora looked genuinely shocked.

'Do you think it would be alright if we flew over to Glasruhen Forest to see Arrana?' asked Jack. 'We won't be long.'

'I think she'd enjoy a visit and by the time you get back I'll have transformed Charkle. No one will ever know he's a dragon unless he sneezes.'

Jack and Camelin left Nora in the kitchen. It was

a relief to be out of the sunshine. Jack enjoyed flying in the shade of the trees; he liked the rush of air under his wings.

'Watch this,' croaked Camelin as he turned over and flew on his back. 'Now you.'

'I don't think I'm ready for upside down flying yet.'

'Just have a go. You never know when you might need it.'

Jack tried to flip over but ended up rolling in a complete circle. He tried again, this time managing several wing beats before his head bumped into a branch. He went careering down.

'Pull up!' yelled Camelin.

Jack flapped his wings wildly as he fell. His wing almost touched the ground before he managed to pull down hard and rose steadily into the air.

'The main thing to remember is not to lose track of where you are,' advised Camelin as he flew alongside Jack. 'Try again.'

'Maybe tomorrow.'

'Don't worry,' Camelin said cheerfully. 'We can't all be good at everything.'

Jack didn't rise to the challenge. He thought he'd leave the more spectacular flying to Camelin and concentrate on the skills he needed.

Jack watched the trees sending their message to Arrana. They flew faster trying to reach the centre of Glasruhen before the last Dryad could announce their arrival but the trees were too quick. By the time they reached the centre of the forest a group of Dryads had gathered around the ancient oak.

'Something's wrong,' Jack called to Camelin. 'They look worried.'

As soon as they landed the Dryads circled around them. They all began speaking at once until the tallest raised her arms and everything went quiet.

'What's wrong?' asked Jack.

'We couldn't deliver the message. Arrana won't wake up. She's been like this before but never this sleepy,' the Dryad explained.

Jack hopped back a little way and in his loudest voice addressed the Hamadryad.

'Arrana the Wise, Protector and Most Sacred of All Dryads.'

Everyone held their breath. Arrana didn't stir.

'Try singing,' the Dryad suggested, 'and we'll all join in. That might wake her.'

Jack thought carefully. He didn't know which song would be best, and then he remembered *The Tree in the Wood*. He opened his beak to sing but instead of his lovely voice a terrible croaking sound came out.

'Oooh, I know this one,' said Camelin enthusiastically as he joined in with Jack.

Together they made a terrible racket. All the Dryads put their hands over their ears. Jack and Camelin threw their heads back and croaked the chorus as loudly as they could…

'*…and the green grass grew all around, all around, and the green grass grew all around.*'

Their song rang through the forest. The noise was awful but it seemed to be having an effect on Arrana. The Hamadryad quivered slightly. Jack and Camelin croaked even louder until the whole trunk began to vibrate and eventually became a blur. As Arrana transformed leaves began to fall from her branches. When eventually she stood where the gnarled trunk had been, everyone gasped. Arrana's copper coloured hair was flecked with silver, her face was pale and Jack could see through her smooth, nut-brown skin. He didn't know what to say.

'It's started,' she whispered. 'I'm beginning to fade.'

THE SEARCH

The message had already reached Nora by the time Jack and Camelin returned but she still wanted to hear what they both had to say about Arrana.

'This is very worrying,' she said as she paced up and down. 'And you say you could see right through her?'

Jack and Camelin both nodded.

'She was sort of transparent,' explained Jack. 'Is there anything we can do?'

'Not until we open the window in time and send you two back to find those missing cauldron plates. We don't have much time and we're still no nearer to getting the golden acorn back.'

The atmosphere was subdued. No one spoke. All were lost in their own thoughts.

'Elan's out now, looking in all the obvious places where Pycroft might be. I don't understand why the trees haven't seen anything of either Bogie.'

'Could Pycroft be in Newton Gill with Peabody?' Jack asked.

I doubt it. If Peabody knew where he was he'd have got him here somehow. He'll want his own nose back as soon as possible. I imagine he's looking everywhere for his brother too.'

Jack thought about Camelin's secret cave at the bottom of the garden and the Hag in Westwood Roost. Pycroft had to be in a place with no trees or Nora would know his whereabouts.

'Somewhere underground then, like a cave,' suggested Jack.

'I've got Timmery and Charkle checking them,' Nora replied. 'But so far he's left no trace'.

'I think we need to have a look at the map and start a systematic search. We have so little time and such a lot of ground to cover.'

Nora went over to the dresser and brought out her map.

'Now let's think, areas where there aren't any trees.'

Nora tapped the map in several places.

'The top of the hills to the north of Glasruhen are sparse and bleak. Then there are the old quarries, disused mines, caves and more Spriggan tunnels than I care to think about.'

A worried silence filled the room. Again no one spoke until a fluttering of wings announced the arrival of Charkle and Timmery.

'Any news?' asked Nora.

The two tiny bats fluttered around Nora's head. Jack tried to see which one was Charkle. They looked almost identical except one had a purple sheen to his wings and was slightly bigger. Timmery flew over the map. He fluttered around the drawing of a group of hills.

'We've looked in all the caves around the bottom of the Ridgeway and Elan's looked in all the crags and caves on top. There's no trace of anyone living there. She said to tell you she won't be back until later. She's going to carry on for a while.'

'What can we do to help?' Jack asked. 'It seems a waste of time for us to sit around doing nothing.'

'You're right,' said Nora. 'There's a lot we've got to do before the solstice and at least you two can be putting in some practice.'

'I meant looking for Pycroft and the golden acorn.'

'I know you did, but there's something Camelin has to teach you before the ritual. If you don't get it right, you won't be able to break through the thin veil that separates the window in time from the here and now. You might as well make a start.'

Jack looked at Camelin who puffed his chest feathers out importantly and eagerly began to explain.

'You know how everything has to be equal?'

Jack nodded.

'Well, we'll have to go to the top of Glasruhen Hill to where the old hill fort used to be. It was built around the summit. Then we've got to start off flying towards each other from either end of the old gateways at exactly the same speed. When we pass each other in the middle, at exactly the same time, we'll break through the window into the past.'

'It's the only way the window in time can be opened,' continued Nora.

'But I thought you were going to perform a ritual to do that!' exclaimed Jack.

'The ritual is to make sure we send you back to the right time and place. It's bad enough you've got to return to such troubled times. You don't want to be there any longer than you need be.'

Jack realised it wasn't going to be easy flying at the same speed as Camelin. He was a far stronger flyer, with years of experience.

'You're going to have to be very careful, both of you, when you go back into the past, especially you Jack,' continued Nora. 'Once you've transformed into a boy you're going to have to keep out of sight and avoid being caught.'

'But... I thought I'd be staying as a raven.'

'You will until you locate the plates. Once you find them you'll need to get them into the nearest well or spring and you won't be able to do that as a raven. The plates will be too big and heavy to lift in your beak. Camelin can't transform into a boy anymore so you'll have to move the cauldron plates on your own.'

Jack hoped they'd be able to find the missing plates quickly. He'd been reading about the Roman occupation of Britain and if he was caught with a Druid's cauldron plates he'd be in real danger. He might never make it home again.

For the rest of the day Jack and Camelin practiced flying towards each other. As Jack predicted, it wasn't easy. When Elan returned she took a pole with a large hoop attached to the top down to the bottom meadow. She paced out the length they'd each need to fly and pushed the pole into the soft ground exactly in the middle.

'If you use this it will make it easier for you to practice,' she told them. 'It needs to be perfect. You'll only get the one chance when we perform the ritual. And, don't forget, with the sun going down the light will be fading.'

Even after hours of practice it wasn't any easier. Jack felt frustrated and cross because he couldn't get it right. Camelin tried to compensate for Jack's lack of speed, but even that didn't help.

'We've got the next two weeks to practice,' Camelin said cheerfully. 'We'll get it right eventually.'

The next few days passed quickly. Jack made his way to Ewell House on his own each night after school. Elan was busy searching the countryside with Charkle and Timmery for signs of the Bogie. He continued to do his homework in Nora's library as quickly as he could, then he transformed and practised with Camelin until it was time to go home.

It became a nightly routine for them to take off from opposite ends of the meadow and try to pass each other as they flew through the hoop. Jack had to learn how to tip his body at the last minute. He had to keep his wings tucked close into his body so he didn't crash into Camelin as they passed each other.

Each night before bed Camelin tapped on Jack's window and came for his reading lesson. Before they began Jack would ask if there was any news. He always got the same answer; there wasn't any.

'They've looked everywhere, twice,' Camelin told him on the Friday night.

It was the first weekend since Jack had arrived that he hadn't been over to Ewell House. Everyone was busy searching. He spent Saturday afternoon reading to Orin about the Romans. He needed to know as much as he could so he'd be prepared for his journey into the past, as long as the acorn could be found in time.

With only three days to go Jack finally perfected flying past Camelin at precisely the right time and speed.

'Again!' he cried as he hopped around the meadow feeling elated.

By the fifth time Jack knew they'd got it right.

'Well at least we're ready,' he said thankfully to Camelin.

'You're a great flyer,' Camelin replied, 'a natural.'

'I couldn't have done it without such a brilliant teacher.'

Jack watched Camelin puff out his chest feathers; he knew he was pleased.

'Come on, race you back to the house. I've got something for you in my bag.'

They flew at speed back up to Camelin's loft, weaving and swerving around the bushes and trees and landing at exactly the same time on the window ledge. It took them both a few minutes to get their breath back.

'Well at least we know we can get away in a hurry if we ever need to,' laughed Camelin. 'Now, what've you got for me?'

Once Jack had transformed and dressed he took a large bag out of his backpack and put it into the middle of his own raven basket, the only clear space he could see in the entire loft.

'It's a thank you, for you, for teaching me to fly.'

Camelin's eyes grew wide; he began rocking from

foot to foot in his excitement. He sniffed the air and then sniffed around the bag.

'Are they doughnuts?'

'Have a look.'

In no time Camelin had the top off the bag. Inside was an assortment of mini-doughnuts.

'I wish I had an Oracular Frog. They're the perfect pet you know.'

'Oracular Frog!'

'Yes, they know everything. It could take one look in the bag and tell me exactly how many doughnuts were in there.'

'I can do that,' laughed Jack and peeped into the bag. 'Thirty.'

'Wow! Thirty! How did you do that?'

'Easy, that's how many I asked for at the baker.'

Camelin poked his beak into the bag, brought out one of the small doughnuts in his beak, flipped it and gulped it down.

'Mmmm! Raspberry, my favourite. I didn't know they made *raven doughnuts*. Do they do anything else for ravens at the baker?'

Jack laughed and watched Camelin flip and swallow another mini doughnut. There wasn't anywhere for Jack to sit. Camelin had covered the beanbag with rubbish.

'You really ought to have a dustbin up here you know.'

'What for?' Camelin asked as he sucked the raspberry jam out of his third doughnut.

'Because it's getting to look like a rubbish tip.'

Camelin began speaking with his mouth full but Jack wasn't listening.

'Tip!' he exclaimed as he quickly made his way to the ladder. 'That's it, the rubbish tip!'

He dashed down the stairs as fast as he could and arrived out of breath in the kitchen. 'Tip!' he managed to say to Nora, 'Rubbish tip.'

'What about the rubbish tip?' Nora asked.

'Could Pycroft be hiding there? Has anyone checked? It would be an ideal place to hide and there aren't any trees or anything growing there. He'd find lots of things he could use to trade, things a Hag might want. There were all kinds of rubbish and broken things in her cave.'

'That's a brilliant idea Jack, a job for Motley and the Night Guard. If anyone can find anything in a pile of rubbish the rats will.'

Camelin flew in through the patio doors.

'What's wrong?'

'I think Jack might have worked out where to

find Pycroft.'

'At the rubbish tip,' Jack explained.

'I wonder what made you think of that!' replied Camelin.

Jack winked at Camelin but didn't tell Nora about the terrible mess in the loft.

'Can you go and find Motley for me?' Nora asked Camelin.

He shuffled his feet for a few seconds before reluctantly flying off.

'I was beginning to give up hope,' said Nora. 'I really think there's a good chance he might be there. If he is we'll need a plan to make sure he can't escape. I'm sure he knows we want the acorn back and the last thing he'll want to do is return it, especially after he's gone to all that trouble to acquire it.'

'But it doesn't belong to him. He can't keep it,' Jack said crossly.

'I'm afraid that as long as Pycroft has the acorn he'll believe it's his. Bogies are like that. They don't have a better nature you can appeal to. I'll send Camelin over to you later to let you know if he's there or not and what we intend to do.'

'Can't I go with you?'

'I wouldn't know how to begin to explain to your

Grandad that we're visiting a rubbish tip after dark. Would you?'

Jack had to agree with Nora. He'd have to wait for her to send him news later.

It was a long wait. For hours Jack watched from his bedroom window for any sign of Camelin. It was useless to write to Elan in his Book of Shadows. He knew she'd be out with the others. Orin kept Jack company until she yawned and scampered onto his pillow, where she fell fast asleep. It was nearly midnight when Jack finally saw Camelin's silhouette swoop over the trees. He opened the window wide and Camelin flew straight in and landed on the back of Jack's chair. He was really excited and began noisily telling Jack the news.

'We've got the tip surrounded. You were right, he's in there. Motley found him. He won't escape.'

'Jack,' shouted Grandad from his bedroom, 'is that the radio? It's a bit late. Turn if off, there's a good lad.'

'Sorry Grandad,' Jack shouted back then whispered to Camelin. 'You're going to have to keep your voice down and start again slowly from the beginning.'

'Nora sent Motley and the Night Guard over to the tip. They came back and said they'd found a burrow, a big one made out of rubbish, and someone was living in it. Elan's keeping watch and as soon as he returns she'll help Motley and the Night Guard bring him over to Ewell House.'

'Won't he put up a fight?'

'Naw. Bogie's don't like anything with teeth and claws. Besides, Charkle's going to be there. If the Bogie gives them any trouble Charkle can persuade him to be good by directing his flame in the right place. I doubt any Bogie would want a singed bottom.'

Jack laughed then remembered that Grandad was sleeping in the next room.

'You're going to have to go now.'

'What about my lesson?'

'We'll have a double one in your loft tomorrow night. I hope I'm there when Pycroft returns the acorn.'

Camelin was very excited when Jack arrived at Ewell House after school the next day.

'They've got him,' he cawed loudly before Nora could tell Jack the news. 'Motley said they'd captured Pycroft and they'll bring him to the house as soon as it's dark.'

'We must be ready,' said Nora. 'We can't afford any mistakes. We must have the acorn back. The solstice is tomorrow night.'

Camelin puffed his feathers out, strutted along the table and interrupted Nora again before she could continue.

'Timmery's gone to let Chief Knuckle know the good news. As soon as we've got the acorn back the Spriggans can come and shrink Grub back down to size.'

'I shan't be sorry to see him go,' sighed Nora. 'He's such a size to feed. I'd better go and re-open the tunnel. Have you two got something to do before it goes dark?'

'Yes,' Jack and Camelin replied together.

They went up to the loft. At the end of Camelin's double reading lesson Jack congratulated him.

'You're nearly there. A bit more practice and you'll be able to read anything.' Camelin looked pleased.

Once Jack had transformed they went outside to practise flying through the hoop for the last time.

After supper Jack and Camelin kept watch from the chimney pot.

'Are you feeling OK about the ritual tomorrow night?' Camelin asked.

Jack nodded. He was a bit nervous and anxious but at the same time curious and excited. He was just wondering how to explain his feelings when they saw something move by the gap in the hedge.

'It's them!' Camelin cawed excitedly.

Jack watched the procession as it made its way towards the house. Motley marched proudly at the front with his head in the air. The rest of the Night Guard surrounded the Bogie. It looked like Peabody, with the same mean pinched look, only this Bogie still had a long, sharp, pointed nose. He wore a green jacket and red hat which had a beautiful white feather tucked under the hatband. His brown trousers looked more like shorts and his green and red striped stockings came over his knees. His feet were the longest Jack had ever seen, longer than Peabody's, and his flat, narrow shoes ended in points. A chestnut ferret brought up the rear and a small bat, with a purple sheen to its wings, flitted around the Bogie's head. Jack and Camelin swooped down and circled the group. As they passed the tunnel opening Timmery joined them.

'Halt,' Motley commanded when they reached the patio door.

Nora stepped out.

'The Bogie,' Motley announced as he and the Night Guard bowed low.

'I believe you've got something to return,' Nora said loudly.

The Bogie looked annoyed. His eyes were cold and Jack felt a shiver run down his spine as Pycroft glowered at Nora. Eventually he reluctantly fished into his waistcoat pocket and brought out the golden acorn. But instead of giving it to Nora he wrapped his fingers around it.

'I'd like to know what you wanted it for?' Nora asked.

The Bogie planted his feet firmly apart in a defiant gesture.

'I haven't got time for this,' continued Nora and quickly withdrew her wand. 'If I don't get an answer in the next couple of seconds I'm going to shrink your nose so it matches your brother's.'

Unlike Peabody he didn't protest or squeal or bob up and down. Instead he continued to scowl angrily at Nora.

'I wanted it for my collection.'

'You had no right of ownership to my golden acorn.'

'Why not? I saw one of those birds bounce it off a boy's head a while back and presumed nobody wanted it.'

Camelin coughed and looked embarrassed when Nora gave him a cross look but she soon turned back to Pycroft as he continued to explain.

'If I'd been quicker I'd have grabbed it then and there but the boy picked it up.'

'So you got the Spriggans to steal it for you?' continued Nora.

'Not at first. I followed the boy and then told my brother about him. He had him cornered in Newton Gill Forest but somehow the boy got away so I got him to search the boy's room, but he couldn't find the acorn. Then he followed the boy here. I had a look at this place from the bell tower and realised that getting in without being seen would be a problem. That's when I got my brother to go and see the Spriggans. I knew they'd be able to get in and out again.'

Jack realised he hadn't imagined someone watching him that morning on the back lane. It must have been Pycroft behind the trees. Jack shuddered again.

'So you involved Peabody in your scheme.'

'Yes, yes.' Pycroft replied gruffly. 'I'm very busy. Peabody runs a lot of errands for me. I knew Chief Knuckle would send a band of Spriggans here once he'd seen the torch I had to trade. Peabody got them to dig under the hedge. They were happy to go and get it. Saved both of us a lot of effort. They don't mind digging and they had no problem finding the acorn. Spriggans can sniff out gold quite easily'

Nora folded her arms. Pycroft still looked cross and defiant.

'And is that all you've got to say?' asked Nora.

'Nothing else to tell,' Pycroft replied rudely, 'so I'll be keeping the gold then.'

'I don't think so,' Nora said sternly.

'Don't see why not. Finders keepers. If the acorn was important or belonged to anyone why was it being thrown away?'

'That is none of your business. Besides, you didn't find the acorn, you got others to steal it for you. Give it to me.'

Everyone held their breath expectantly and looked

at Nora as she held out her hand.

'Hasn't anyone told you my acorn is Druid's gold?'

Pycroft shrugged his shoulders.

'You should have taken better care of it. That bird didn't want it and what use could a boy possibly have with Druid's gold?'

Jack could see Nora was getting angry. She raised her wand and pointed it at Pycroft's hand. His fingers sprang open. As he fought to close them again his palm began to shake. The golden acorn rolled off his trembling palm onto the ground. He was rooted to the spot and try as he might he couldn't bend over to retrieve it. Motley picked it up in his paws and scampered over to Nora's feet and offered it up to her.

'Thank you,' she said kindly, then turned her attention back to Pycroft.

'An apology would be nice.'

Pycroft closed his lips tightly and scowled. Nora lowered her wand and Pycroft took a step back but Nora had seen him. She raised her wand again and froze him in mid-stride.

'You had your chance to put things right and you chose to be rude. Now it's my turn to choose what to do with you.'

Pycroft's whole body was frozen, his face twisted in

a scornful look. With a quick flick of her wand a flash of light exploded in front of Pycroft's face. His eyes crossed as he tried to see what she'd done. Nora had replaced his long sharp nose with a pig's wide snout.

'This will be permanent unless you find some manners and change your ways. For every good deed you do your nose will begin to change shape but each time you're bad or rude it will shrink again. Now go back to where you belong and don't come bothering me again.'

Pycroft moaned. As soon as Nora released him his hand shot up to examine his new nose.

'You'll pay for this,' he screamed and scurried towards the hole as fast as his little legs could carry him.

Jack thought he could still hear Pycroft complaining but not for long. A great cheer erupted from everyone in the garden as Nora held up the golden acorn. They'd got it back at last.

WHEN ALL IS EQUAL ALL THE SAME

18

THAT WHICH WAS LOST IS FOUND AGAIN

INTO THE PAST

When they were sure that Pycroft had gone everyone spoke at once and continued chatting until Elan shook her chestnut fur and shapeshifted back.

'That's better,' she said as she stretched her arms and legs. It's almost midnight. Shall we go over to the hole and wait for the Spriggans?'

They didn't have to wait long for no sooner had they rounded the corner than the first head poked out of the hole, followed by another and another until twelve Spriggans almost filled the kitchen garden.

'The Bogie returned your property?' Chief Knuckle asked as he bowed low.

'I have it back,' confirmed Nora. 'Would you like

to shrink Grub down to size?'

The Spriggans shuffled over to Grub who was sleeping soundly. They made a circle around him and started joining hands. Once the last pair were clasped together a series of small explosions began from inside the ivy that surrounded Grub. He woke with a cry and struggled to free himself from the tangle of leaves. He began to shrink rapidly. Whiff threw him the end piece of their rope and he tied it securely around his waist.

'Please accepts my sincere apologies,' the Chief said as he bowed again. 'I hopes this is an end to the matter.'

'It will be when you've left my garden and backfilled the hole,' Nora replied.

'Before we goes, you haven't seen a Dragonette anywhere have you? One of my bands seems to have lost one and they thoughts it might have been in your garden.'

'We've only got ravens, bats and a goose at the moment. I expect your Dragonette went back to its roost. Have you any idea where that might be?

The Chief shook his head, 'Sadly no,' he replied before shouting to three Spriggans who stood near the hole. 'Digging party, makes good.'

It was impressive how quickly they all disappeared through the hole. Earth from inside the tunnel appeared and when Elan pushed the turf back into place it was hard to tell anything had ever disturbed the ground.

'We'd better all get off to bed now,' said Nora. 'You two have an important flight tomorrow.'

'I wonder where Peabody is?' Elan said as they made their way back to the kitchen.

'Here,' a small frightened voice replied from the shadow of the house.

'Step forward where I can see you,' Nora commanded.

Peabody stepped into the light from the kitchen. He had a scarf wrapped around his face to hide the shame of his shrunken nose. His knees began to knock loudly. Everyone stared at him.

'He wouldn't listen to me,' he sobbed. 'Pycroft never listens to me, always thinks he knows best, said he was keeping the acorn for good and no one would ever find out where he was going to hole up. Even I couldn't find him or I would have come and told you, and now it's too late.'

Peabody began to sob even louder when he saw Nora raise her wand slightly.

'I'm sorry. I couldn't find him. I came in through the tunnel but now that's gone I'm trapped. I can't get out of your garden.'

Nora held her wand high and pointed it down at Peabody's nose. His teeth began to chatter and tears soaked into his scarf.

'You'll be glad to know we found your brother and I now have my golden acorn back. I think we've both been misused,' she said kindly. 'You shall have your nose restored.'

A green light flashed from the end of Nora's wand. There was a crackle and Peabody squealed excitedly as his scarf began to stretch. He quickly unwound it.

'My nose, my nose, my distinguished wonderful nose,' he cried as he jumped up and down. 'Oh thank you great Seanchai, thank you. I'm forever in your debt. If there's ever anything I can do, you only need ask.'

'I think I'd like you to leave my garden,' Nora told him as she pointed her wand at Peabody's feet and raised him into the air. When he was level with her face he began thanking her again.

'Oh great Seanchai, oh Mighty One, thank you, thank you.'

They could still hear his voice in the distance after Nora had transported him to the other side of the hedge.

'What will happen if Pycroft finds out Peabody's got his nose back?' Jack asked.

'Unless Pycroft wants a pig's snout for a nose for the rest of his life he's going to have to start treating Peabody better, and everyone else he comes into contact with for that matter,' replied Nora.

There was a grunting sound. Everyone turned to where the noise had come from.

'Camelin!' Nora chided, but Jack could see she was trying not to laugh.

Jack flew back to the loft with Camelin and transformed.

'Are you worried about tomorrow night?' Camelin asked Jack again before he left the loft.

'A bit but I feel a lot better now Nora's got the golden acorn back.'

'Are we still going to watch that cricket match you wanted to see tomorrow afternoon? There'll be lots of sandwiches.'

'We are, but we're not going to steal anything. Besides they'll be watching out for you.'

Jack could hear Camelin grumbling to himself as

he left the loft. When he finally got into bed he couldn't sleep. This time tomorrow he might still be in the past searching for the lost plates. He had to succeed, but what then? Once the cauldron was restored Nora would reopen the portal. Would he be left on his own again? Would he ever see any of his friends once they went back into Annwn? It would be painful to say goodbye. It would be worse if he failed. He'd never had this kind of responsibility before. He was afraid but he'd keep his promise. He'd do his best.

It was late when Jack woke the next morning. The sun was already streaming in through the curtains. He listened but couldn't hear anyone else moving about in the house.

He found everyone, apart from Camelin, sitting in the garden.

'Breakfast?' asked Nora.

'I'm not very hungry. I'll wait for Camelin.'

'Are you OK?' Elan asked.

Jack nodded even though he didn't feel too good.

His stomach was churning.

'Is it all right if Camelin and I fly over to the Cricket Club this afternoon? There's a match I'd like to watch unless you need us for anything else.'

'I don't think there's anything else we can do now. Everything's ready; we just need to wait until sunset.'

Jack had a long wait for Camelin. When he finally appeared he looked as if he'd had a sleepless night too.

Later that afternoon Jack and Camelin flew over to the pavilion. They found a good perch which gave them a grandstand view of the whole pitch. Jack explained the game but Camelin seemed distracted.

'Is there anything you want to talk about before we go into the past?' Jack asked.

'Not really. I'm not looking forward to going back to when it all happened. You know, my bash on the head. I don't think I'm going to be able to watch what the soldiers did to me.'

'I'll watch,' said Jack with more confidence than he felt. 'We'll find out what happened and get those

299

plates back in no time.'

'Thanks,' Camelin replied. 'You know, I didn't think you were going to be any use at first but I'm glad you're *The One*. You just didn't seem to fit the prophecy but I realise now you don't have to be big and tough to be strong and brave.'

Jack smiled. He didn't tell Camelin how rude he'd thought he was when they'd first met.

'Do you know what this prophecy says? I tried asking the Book of Shadows but it didn't give me an answer.'

'It's written around the bottom of Jennet's well but it's so overgrown now I doubt anyone could read it.'

'What does it say?'

Camelin coughed and puffed out his feathers.

'A Brenin boy you need to find
Born at Samhain of Humankind.
The One you seek is brave and strong
And his true heart can do no wrong.
The Golden Acorn he will see
And listen to the Dryad's plea.
Underneath Glasruhen Hill
He'll make a promise he'll fulfil.
When all is equal, all the same,
That which was lost is found again.'

'That's me?'

'Hope so.'

'I understand most of it but what does the bit about all being equal and the same mean?'

'That's the ritual tonight. You know, Nora and Elan, you and me. It's the only way to get through the window in time. Everything has to be the same.'

'So now we've got all that right, the prophecy says we're going to find the lost cauldron plates. It means everything's going to be OK.'

'As long as we get them into water once we've found them, don't get caught and get safely back through the window in time, then everything will be OK.'

Jack realised he hadn't even considered what might happen after they'd found the cauldron plates. Camelin started shuffling from foot to foot.

'Can we go now? Only if I'm not allowed to have a sandwich I'd rather go back and have a little snack out of my basket. Anyway, I've got a surprise for you in the loft.'

Jack had also lost interest in the game; he'd other more important things on his mind. They raced back to Camelin's loft and Jack transformed. He sat down on the beanbag after removing the empty doughnut bag and waited expectantly.

'I've been practicing,' Camelin croaked as he hunted

through a pile of rubbish. He picked out a worn leaflet and put it at his feet in the centre of the loft. He looked as if he was under a spotlight as sunlight streamed in through the window and illuminated his feathers.

Jack could see it was the takeaway menu from the Chinese restaurant. Camelin coughed twice before he began.

'I'm not going to read it all, just my favourites,' he explained. 'Special Chop Suey, Mushroom Omelette, Sweet and Sour Pork Balls, Pancake Roll and…'

'You're making me hungry,' cried Jack.

'But what about my reading?'

'Brilliant, you're a natural.'

Jack gave Camelin a clap and congratulated him again.

'I'm impressed.'

'Do you think Nora will be?'

'Of course she will, but we might have to find something else for you to read from. It might be a bit difficult to explain how you've got a liking for Chinese food!'

'It makes me hungry too.'

'Everything makes you hungry!' laughed Jack.

They heard Nora calling them.

Camelin was already perched on the back of the chair by the time Jack arrived in the kitchen. His eyes were as wide as saucers. On the table Jack could see all Camelin's favourite foods, at least the ones Nora knew about. It was a very special meal. Everyone had been invited. Motley and Orin sat at the end of the table on their upturned beakers surrounded by the rest of the Night Guard. Timmery was on Nora's shoulder and Charkle on Elan's. Even Gerda waddled in and settled down to watch them eat.

'Just for tonight,' Nora told Jack and Camelin, 'you can eat as much as you like. You've both got quite a journey before you.'

When everyone had eaten their fill Elan stepped out onto the patio.

'The light's fading. Time to go.'

Nora took the golden acorn between her finger and thumb and held it up high so they could all see it.

'This is the moment we've all been waiting for, thanks to Jack.'

Everyone cheered and wished them well. Jack stroked Orin and told her he wouldn't be gone long, at least he hoped he wouldn't. On his way up to the loft he took his wand back to his room and put it safely in the spine of his Book of Shadows. He sighed. He felt quite nervous. He had to succeed. This was their only chance.

'Ready?' Camelin asked when he was in the loft.

'Ready,' Jack replied.

They transformed and made their way to the top of Glasruhen Hill to wait for Nora and Elan to join them.

'I want you to promise me you'll come straight back through the window in time if you're in any danger,' Nora said to them both once they were all together again at the summit.

'We'll stay out of trouble,' Jack replied.

'Be careful,' added Elan.

'We will,' Jack and Camelin said together.

Nora patted them both on the head and Elan stroked their sleek, black feathers. They all watched as Nora carefully placed the golden acorn on a bare rock in the exact centre of the hill fort before nodding and taking a deep breath. They took up their positions in the middle of each gateway directly opposite each other, Nora and Camelin at one end, Elan and Jack at the other. They watched and waited as the sun began to sink slowly below the horizon. When the sun had almost disappeared Nora and Elan began the ritual. They recited words Jack didn't understand, words they'd been waiting to say for such a long time, words to send Jack and Camelin back to the right moment in time. Jack listened to Elan; he could hear Nora's voice in the distance. Both began quietly, almost whispering, but growing louder and louder as the sun sank lower. The golden acorn began to glow brighter and brighter. When the sun disappeared golden rays of light spread upwards from the ground. Jack could see a shimmer in the sky overhead as the light from the acorn illuminated the thin veil of the window.

It was time to fly. Jack and Camelin took off from the ground, as they'd practised time and time before. They built up speed and rose into the air until at last they were an equal distance from the ground, high above the mid-point. Jack felt the air rushing past his head as he twisted his body; they flew towards each other at speed. In the split second before they flew past each other they pulled their wings in tightly to their bodies. Jack felt the warmth from the golden light of the acorn. He heard Nora calling to them.

'Take care. Come back safe.'

Then everything went dark. There was a loud crack as they flew into the past.

It was difficult for Jack to reduce his speed. He'd been too busy concentrating on several things at the same time and hadn't given much thought to what would happen once they'd passed through the window. He finally slowed and turned, then made his way back towards the centre of Glasruhen Hill, dropping in height as he searched the sky for Camelin. He knew they'd made it. Nora and Elan were nowhere to be seen and the top of Glasruhen was no longer deserted. Jack could see fires burning in the distance. The smell of wood smoke also came from various buildings, which were scattered around the summit. Instead of the usual bracing fresh air he so enjoyed every time he'd climbed to the top of the hill, the more unpleasant hint of a farmyard hung heavy in the atmosphere. The acrid smell of burning reminded him of Bonfire Night, only it was the wrong time of the year.

He saw a suitable tree for landing and swooped down. Once he was settled on a branch he looked closer at the scene below. Round houses of various heights and sizes were scattered over the hilltop. Lower down at ground level were more of the same. Apart from areas of dense forest the rest of the landscape, as far as he could see in the moonlight, was very similar to the one they'd just come from. The people who lived here were obviously farmers; fences and small fields surrounded each building.

'Are you all right?' Camelin enquired as he landed next to Jack.

'I think so,' he replied hesitantly as he adjusted to the different sights, sounds and smells. 'Is this right? Did we come through at the right time?'

'We did. Can you see the flames in the distance?'

'Yes. Is that one of the sacred groves the Romans burnt?'

Camelin took a deep breath. There was sadness in his voice as he began to explain everything he could remember about the fire.

'Only one of many they burnt to the ground. I collected the second cauldron plate from the grove you can see burning in the distance, then I made my way back to the sacred grove where Gwillam was waiting, just over there.'

Camelin nodded towards a dense area of forest beyond where Jack's house should have been.

'All these oak trees will be gone by tomorrow night,' he sighed. 'When the Roman soldier attacked me and left me for dead they torched Gwillam's grove too. Nora rescued me from the flames. The trees were traumatised by the fire. There was nothing Nora could do to save them.'

'Didn't the people try to stop the Romans from killing Gwillam?'

'I found out later he'd chosen to stay in the Grove and face the Romans alone instead of putting anyone in the village in danger. Word spread fast that the Romans were only after the Druids; they didn't damage any of the farms. Gwillam rejected the idea of hiding. Not all Celts liked fighting and the Cornovii, who'd settled here, were a peaceful tribe, mainly farmers and craftsmen. The Romans left them alone as long as they didn't cause any trouble and paid their taxes. The fortress, not far from here at Viroconium, got most of its supplies from the farmers in this area.'

It was unusual for Camelin to offer so much information; whilst he was in a talkative mood Jack wanted to make the most of it.

'Were you born into the Cornovii tribe?'

'Oh no, my people were here long before the Celts. The original people of this area were tall with dark hair, like Nora. Long before the first invaders arrived Glasruhen Hill was a place of worship. It only became a hill fort a lot later. All the people from around would gather here on special nights and celebrate together. Marriages would take place and acolytes would be assigned to Druids, but that was all a long time ago. I went with Gwillam to see some of the festivals; we'll see them again once we get back into Annwn. We were lucky. In those early days the Cornovii were more interested in the land. They didn't bother our people and they let the Druids continue to tend the sacred wells and groves. They realised how much knowledge the Druids had and allowed them to be their religious leaders. The two peoples sort of became one and the Romans just called everyone in the area Celts.'

Camelin paused but continued looking sad.

'If only I'd been quicker and got back to the grove before the Romans got there. Gwillam would have been saved. Nora could have re-made the cauldron, opened the portal and we could all have gone into Annwn until the troubles were over.'

'What do we do next?'

'We need to be at the edge of the grove by first light, that's where I was attacked, and then we can see what happened. With any luck we'll be back through the window by breakfast time.'

Jack was glad they'd had such a big meal. He hadn't

thought about food until Camelin mentioned it. No matter what Nora might say it really was hungry work being a raven; since the first time he'd transformed he was ready to eat whatever and whenever he could, as well as his regular meals.

'Speaking of food,' continued Camelin as if he'd read Jack's thoughts. 'I could do with a bite to eat now while we're waiting.'

'Where are we going to get food from at this time in the morning? We're not going to find a takeaway here.'

'There'll be food near the entrance to the shrine. The people looked after the Druids and their acolytes by bringing food. They weren't allowed inside so they'd leave it by the entrance. Whatever we find there was really meant for Gwillam and me so we'll not be stealing it, just rescuing it before it gets burnt. The Celts were very superstitious you know; in fact, most Romans were too.'

They flew towards the grove and just as Camelin predicted, there on a low stone platform, by two large oak trees, was a pile of food.

'It's not as exciting as a takeaway but at least it's edible.'

'It's probably a lot healthier,' observed Jack as he saw the collection of fruit, nuts and brown bread.

'Oh, by the way,' added Camelin, 'Roman soldiers were always hungry too. They'd eat anything they could get their hands on and raven was on the menu!'

'They ate ravens!' gulped Jack.

'Oh yes. It wasn't anything personal. They ate crows, jackdaws, peacocks, geese and swans too; anything they could catch. We're both going to have to keep well hidden and out of range of any arrows. I used to have a really hard time at first when I started flying around the area.'

Jack and Camelin ate their fill. They found a tree close to where Camelin thought he'd been attacked and settled down to wait for first light. As Jack rested he realised that Nora had been right. Returning to the past might be dangerous; the last thing he wanted was to end up being roasted by hungry Romans.

REVELATION

This was the first night Jack had ever spent in the open. He'd never slept on a branch before either. Not only was it uncomfortable but each time he nodded off he relaxed his grip and almost slid off his perch. He understood now why Camelin liked his raven basket so much.

Jack was still awake when the dawn chorus began. He wondered how Camelin was able to sleep through all the noise. People in the houses below were stirring too and starting their daily chores. He could see a woman in a woollen cloak visiting one of the fenced off areas. She stooped low and opened the door of a small hut; hens scurried out eager to leave their coop. They quickly made their way to the front of the round house and started scratching around a pile of grain. He watched the woman collect eggs from the hut and carefully place them in a basket. There were pigs in an enclosure next to the house and sheep in the adjoining field. He'd seen pictures like this in history books at school but this was real. It was happening before his eyes!

There was light on the horizon.

'It's morning,' said Jack as he gently nudged Camelin.

'I know. I've been awake for hours.'

Jack didn't think that was true because mingled in with the dawn chorus he distinctly thought he'd heard Camelin snoring. He wasn't about to argue the point; they'd got more important things to think about.

'What next?'

'We wait. It can't be long. The Romans will be breaking camp about now and getting ready to march. They're somewhere in the trees. You'll see them soon.'

'Now we're here do you remember anything else about what happened?'

Camelin took a deep breath and sighed.

'I remember running. I kept off the road and out of sight. I used the tall grasses and reeds for cover but their razor-sharp edges cut into my arms and legs. I couldn't afford to stop and rest. I had to get back to Gwillam as quickly as possible. The two plates I'd already collected were safe inside my tunic. It was starting to get light when I arrived at the edge of the grove. I knew something was wrong; I'd expected Gwillam to be waiting for me. I kept out of sight and moved as quietly as I could from tree to tree until I reached the shrine. Gwillam was slumped across the well.'

Camelin stopped talking. Tears welled up in his eyes; he swallowed hard before continuing.

'I was too late. I knew he was dead. I thought the Romans had taken the plate; the whole shrine had been ransacked. I remember sinking to my knees and biting my lip so I wouldn't cry. I didn't know what to do next. I couldn't move or take my eyes off the well. It was then that the first rays of sunlight hit the water and I caught a glimpse of the plate's reflection. It was still hanging on the sacred tree; they hadn't taken it. I ran and grabbed it, stuffed it into my tunic with the other two, then ran as fast as I could towards Glasruhen Hill. It was too late to save Gwillam but I knew if I could get the plates to Nora it wouldn't be too late to save everyone else. I didn't get very far. As I left the grove I ran straight into one of them.'

Camelin sighed again and hung his head. They sat in silence watching the trees.

There was a flicker of movement.

'Look!' Jack whispered. 'What's that over there?'

Camelin had seen it too, a glint of metal and a flash of red.

'Romans!' he gasped. 'This is it. You're going to have to watch. I don't want to see what they did to me.'

Jack didn't want to watch either but if they were ever going to succeed he'd have to be strong and brave as the prophecy foretold. He had to know what had happened to the cauldron plates.

'Wait here. I'll go and have a closer look.'

'Don't let them see you,' warned Camelin.

Jack glided down from the tree and landed as quietly as he could on a branch near the entrance to the grove. He felt quite shaken at the sight of a tall muscular soldier coming out of the trees. The leather straps hanging from his belt were studded and tipped with metal. They clinked together noisily as they bounced up and down on his red tunic. Another soldier appeared. He was obviously in command. On his head was an impressive helmet with the red plume of a centurion. In his hand he carried a tall stick with a silver top. Each segment of his polished armour glinted in the morning sun as he paced up and down. The first soldier saluted him. Two more came out of the trees and joined them, one leading a horse, the other a heavily-laden mule.

The centurion was about to speak when a boy bolted out from the trees and ran straight into his chest knocking the long stick out of his hand onto the ground. The first soldier Jack had seen quickly bent down and picked it up.

Jack gasped; the missing part of Camelin's life was about to unfold.

He watched in horror as the centurion shouted angrily and struck the boy's face. He gripped him hard around his shoulders and shook him violently. The boy struggled as he tried desperately to escape. More soldiers ran out from the trees and surrounded them.

'Stand still,' one of the soldiers commanded, as he thumped the boy hard in the back.

It must have hurt but the boy didn't cry out, though he stopped struggling. The centurion took one hand off the boy's shoulder and retrieved his long stick from the soldier who was holding it. He must have relaxed his grip on the other shoulder because the boy squirmed and wriggled out of his grasp. Once free he turned and kicked the soldier who'd punched him, as hard as he could, on the shin. He started to run. He dodged between the first two soldiers and sidestepped a third before the centurion bellowed loudly.

'Kill him!'

The scraping of metal filled the air as every soldier drew his sword. One struck the boy on the back of the head. His knees buckled; his limp body dropped onto the damp grass. It was over so quickly. Jack could see blood flowing from the wound. He was frozen to the branch, his whole body rigid from shock and fear. He felt sick and was finding it hard to breathe. If he didn't know better he would have thought Camelin was dead. The centurion prodded the body with his long stick.

'Search him,' he commanded.

Jack held his breath as one of the soldiers rolled the boy over and put his hand inside his tunic. He pulled out the three cauldron plates and examined them.

'Only these,' he said as he offered them to the centurion.

'Nothing of value here,' the centurion replied and tossed them into the grass. 'Is the building alight?'

'All is done centurion,' the soldier announced. 'The trees will be ablaze shortly.'

Jack could hear the crackling of branches as the fire began to spread.

'We march to Viroconium,' the centurion commanded as he mounted his horse.

The soldiers started to shoulder their packs and equipment and form rank. The soldier at the back bent over and picked up one of the cauldron plates. He examined it closely and then retrieved the other two from the grass. Before he shouldered his pack he slipped them into it. This was the information Jack needed. This was the soldier they'd have to follow. He looked carefully at the man's face so he'd recognise him again. He had a scar on his chin but, apart from that, his uniform was identical to those of the other seven foot soldiers in the group. As they marched past Jack could see they each carried different tools. The one with the scar was going to be easy to follow; dangling from the back of his pack were the company's cooking pots.

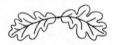

Jack flew back to Camelin. They watched in silence as the soldiers crossed the field and eventually joined the road. The sound of marching feet, rattling packs and clanking belts faded into the distance. The smell of burning drifted on the air towards them. The woman from the farm had smelt it too and ran inside the round building shouting something Jack couldn't hear.

'I couldn't watch,' Camelin said apologetically.

Jack didn't want to talk about what he'd just witnessed. He nodded sympathetically to show Camelin he understood.

'How long will it be before Nora finds you?'

'I don't know. I don't remember. Nora said that when I didn't arrive, and they saw the grove was alight, she came as fast as she could. Luckily I was this side of the fire. If I'd been caught at the other side or in the middle I don't think she'd have found me at all.'

'They're heading for Viroconium,' explained Jack. 'The soldier at the back, with a scar on his chin, has all three plates inside his backpack.'

'Time to go,' said Camelin.

They took off and followed the soldiers. Jack needn't have worried about long-distance flying. They had to stop several times and wait so they didn't get too far ahead. In just under two hours the fortress came into sight.

'I know this place well,' Camelin told Jack. 'Come on, we'll fly on ahead. Follow me. There's a good place to hide near the main gate. We can watch from there and see where the soldier goes.'

319

Once they were positioned in a large tree which overlooked a well-fortified gate Jack had a chance to look around. The fortress was rectangular with a gate in each wall. There were several small towers around the perimeter with larger ones on each of the rounded corners; a walkway ran around the inside of the wall. The most imposing buildings were near the centre and wide roads led into the fort from each of the four gates. Outside the perimeter wall were farm buildings and barns with the river behind. An important looking man stood in the doorway of one of the largest buildings.

'That's Quintus Flavius Maximus,' whispered Camelin. 'He's the Camp Prefect.'

'I thought there'd be soldiers everywhere. Why's it so quiet?'

'The Fourteenth Legion marched out of here a few weeks ago. I was here when they left. Some of us acolytes had been taking it in turns to watch the fort. I was in the barn down there; it was an amazing sight. It was only later we found out they'd been sent to the island of Mona on the Emperor's orders. He'd commanded that all Druids be killed. Hundreds had fled there thinking they'd be safe with a stretch of water separating them from the mainland. They should have gone through the portals but they didn't realise how much danger they were in. Maximus was left in charge when the legion marched. One morning, not long after the legion had left, a centurion rode out with a tent party, set fire to one of the groves and killed the Druid Dryfor. That's how we knew we were in trouble. Nora said it wouldn't be long before they reached Glasruhen and Gwillam started making plans for everyone to go into Annwn. You know the rest.'

'He looks too fat to be a soldier.'

'He is. He used to be one but now he's too old to fight so he organises the running of the fort. He also makes sure that if any of the centurions find anything worth having he gets to keep it. Once I'd recovered I used to fly over here a lot. I've watched him sorting out his plunder. You should see what he's got stashed in his quarters, gold torcs, brooches and a pile of metal objects. He's greedy.'

'What's inside that open square behind him?'

'It's a shrine, dedicated to their goddess of wells and springs.'

'Like Jennet?'

'Not quite. This is a Roman Goddess; they call

her Appias. They think she's a beautiful maiden, a bit like the statues in Nora's garden. When the commander left he gave Maximus instructions to make sure he honoured the goddess. He's supposed to throw gold into the shrine so the water never dries up. He won't because he's too greedy to part with any of his gold. I've even seen him fishing out the offerings other soldiers have thrown in too.'

'Why isn't the centurion we saw this morning with the rest of the legion?'

'I don't know, but he's the one who's been killing the Druids and torching the groves in this area. He brings back any valuables he can find from the local shrines and give them to Maximus; I think he gets a share.'

Jack could see the centurion's armour flash and his red plume bobbing up and down through a clump of trees in the distance.

'They'll be a while yet,' said Camelin. 'Are you hungry?'

'Every time I transform I'm hungry,' confessed Jack.

'Well I might just know where we can get fed. Follow me.'

Camelin led the way round to the far end of the camp. They used the trees and stayed hidden. Eventually he stopped opposite a group of long buildings.

'These are the barracks. I used to fly over when they were cooking. Each barrack has its own bread freshly baked every morning.'

Camelin nodded towards a group of beehive-shaped ovens near the perimeter wall.

'They won't be using many of them today because there aren't many soldiers in camp.'

Jack could smell cooking but it smelt more like bacon than bread. He wasn't sure he wanted to find out what it was, just in case it was barbecued raven.

'Somebody's having a fry up,' Camelin said excitedly.

'Is that bacon I can smell?'

'Yes, course it is. Each barrack has its own frying pan. They won't be short on rations at the moment; looks like pig's on the menu.'

'So they might not be interested in raven if they've got bacon,' said Jack hopefully.

For a few minutes they enjoyed the delicious smells, then Camelin puffed out his chest feathers, which was always a sign he had something important to say.

'Stay here. I'll go and get our breakfast.'

He was off before Jack could answer. It wasn't long before he came back with what looked like a rather large flat bread cake in his beak.

'Mind you don't burn yourself, it's only just come out of the oven.'

It wasn't quite the kind of bread Jack was used to but it tasted good and he was grateful that Camelin's speciality was finding food. It didn't last long but at least they'd eaten. Camelin was keeping a keen eye out in case they were disturbed but Jack was more interested in what he could see through an open doorway.

'Is that a wolf's skin in there?' he asked.

'It is,' confirmed Camelin. 'It belongs to one of the standard bearers. There are three of them; they go at the front of the legion. They each carry poles with different things on top and either wear a bear, lion or wolf skin over their helmet. It's an honoured position.'

'Why haven't they taken this one with them?'

'It's an old one,' replied Camelin. 'I know about this skin. It belonged to that wolf I told you about, you know, the one who ate Dagbert, King of the Sparrows. He stole a chicken and choked on one of the bones; everyone thought it served him right.'

Jack wasn't sure if Camelin was making it up but it seemed a fitting end for a wolf that liked eating sparrows. His thoughts were interrupted by a sudden loud noise.

'What's that?'

'It's a horn. You get used to it. It means the soldiers have arrived,' explained Camelin. 'Come on, back to the gate.

'Look!' exclaimed Jack excitedly as the fort sprang into life.

Soldiers appeared and lined the walkway above the gatehouse.

'Titus Antonius Agrippa,' the centurion shouted up to the guard.

The gate began to open and soldiers saluted as Titus Antonius rode into the fort. He dismounted and dismissed the tent party. Jack and Camelin watched as the centurion strode down the main street. The foot soldiers turned and made their way back to their barracks. Camelin nudged Jack. They flew back to the long huts and watched the soldier with the cooking pots go into the middle one.

'What do we do now?' Jack whispered.

'Wait till there's no one around, then you can slip in, grab the plates, drop them in the well and off we go. This is going to be easier than I thought.'

They settled down but before long the middle door opened again and a soldier came out. He was carrying something.

'It's him,' said Jack, 'the soldier with the scar on his chin and he's got the plates.'

Camelin groaned, 'I think I know where he'll be going.'

They watched the soldier go back to the important looking buildings. He stood outside the middle door and knocked loudly. A voice from within shouted something and the soldier replied, 'Marcus Cornelius Drusus, I have something which might be important.'

The door opened and Drusus entered the office. It was important that Jack and Camelin knew what was being said so they risked being seen and flew onto the roof. Maximus was already speaking.

'...and it was the young boy you killed, not the Druid, who was carrying these plates?'

'Yes Prefect,' Drusus confirmed.

'And you thought you'd get a reward for bringing me two worthless bits of metal?' the Prefect shouted. 'They're only good for smelting. Don't any of these people use gold or silver?'

Camelin and Jack looked at each other. Jack couldn't risk saying anything but he knew Camelin was thinking the same. Why hadn't Drusus taken all three plates to show the Prefect?

'My apologies for bothering you,' Drusus replied. 'I thought they might be of some importance. The boy had them hidden in his tunic; he lost his life trying to escape with them.'

'That will be all Drusus,' the Prefect said gruffly.

Jack heard the clang of metal from inside the office before the door opened and Drusus stepped out. Jack's heart sank; the soldier's hands were empty, the plates were gone.

'Looks like we've got a problem,' sighed Camelin when they were safely back in the tree outside the fort. 'We could have done without the plates being in two different places and especially when one of those places is the Prefect's office. It's going to be twice as difficult and more dangerous trying to retrieve them now.'

THIEF

Jack was worried; he didn't want to stay inside the fort a moment longer than he had to.

'Do we wait until it's dark?' he asked.

'No, they double the guard at night. It's probably best for you to go into the Prefect's office when he goes out to brief the soldiers. He does it every morning. When I used to come over here, spying for Nora, it was always the best time to help myself to any breakfast leftovers. The whole camp assembles in the big space in the middle, the bit they call the forum. Maximus always keeps them standing there for ages. After he's given them their daily orders he comes back to his office until lunchtime.'

Three long blasts from the horn they'd heard earlier echoed around the fortress.

'What's that mean?' asked Jack.

'It means Quintus Flavius Maximus is ready to address the camp. You'll be able to get in there now. Come on, follow me.'

They flew low over the buildings, avoiding groups of soldiers as they hurried towards the forum.

'When you've got these plates you'll have time to find out what Drusus did with the other one. The soldiers don't go back to their barracks until later.'

Jack was feeling nervous. Although the plates didn't belong to Maximus he didn't feel right about searching the Camp Prefect's office. If they caught him they'd think he was a thief.

He'd tried to memorise the plan of the camp while they'd been up in the tree. It was useful being able to fly. Having a bird's eye view of a place made it easier to understand where everything was. He thought he'd be able to make his way back to the well without any trouble once he had the plates.

'Are you ready to transform?' asked Camelin.

'Ready,' replied Jack.

They landed on the ground behind the office buildings. The street was deserted. In the distance

Jack could hear the Prefect's loud voice. They touched foreheads. The blinding light still penetrated Jack's eyes even though he'd had them tightly closed. When he opened them he'd transformed, the only problem was that he was naked.

'Oh!' he moaned. 'I'd forgotten about this part of the transformation.'

Jack carefully made his way to the end of the first building. He was glad it was June and not the middle of winter; even so, it was cool in the shade. He was shaking but that was probably because he was afraid rather than cold. His first priority was to find something to wear. His feet hurt from the gravel on the road but he doubted he'd be able to find any shoes to fit. He could still hear Maximus shouting orders but now he'd transformed he couldn't understand what he was saying.

He hadn't thought what he'd do if the door was locked. Luckily it wasn't. He slipped in through the doorway and looked around for something to put on. The room was lighter than he'd anticipated. All the walls were white; the one without a window was decorated with a battle scene. There was a large table, its legs carved in the shape of lion's feet, with matching chairs. A long reclining seat under the painted wall had a brown woollen blanket draped over the back. He grabbed it and wrapped it around his shoulders. His feet were freezing on the cobbled floor. Jack went and stood on the rug in the middle of the room while he looked around. Near the table was a large basket full to the brim with metal objects. On the top were two large bronze plates. He grabbed them, quickly looked outside to see if it was safe to go, and then made his way back to the place where he'd transformed.

'Camelin,' he whispered, 'I've got them.'

Camelin swooped down.

'Look, I've got them,' Jack said triumphantly.

'Those aren't the ones.'

'They're not!' exclaimed Jack in disbelief as he examined them closely.

They were made of bronze and looked about the right shape and size. One plate was decorated with a man sitting cross-legged holding a snake, and the other had some kind of four-legged animal. To his horror Jack realised his mistake; not only were the pictures wrong, they didn't have any holes in the sides either. Nora had shown him three of the plates and he'd been told they would all be embossed with a tree. He'd even been told about the cauldron's construction. Nora said she laced the plates together using leather thongs. He should have looked more closely at the plates and made sure they were the right ones.

'I'm sorry,' said Jack. 'I didn't expect there'd be any other cauldron plates in there. I'll go back and have another look.'

'Not now you won't. The Camp Prefect will be on his way back any minute now the briefing's over.'

'What shall I do?' he asked mournfully.

'The soldiers won't be back in their barracks for ages. You can go over there and get the third one back. Just remember it'll be really dull and dirty and have a hawthorn, oak or willow tree embossed on the front.'

'I'd rather fly over to the barracks, if you don't mind. These stones are killing my feet; they're really hard to walk on.'

'Ready?' Camelin asked.

'Yes,' sighed Jack.

Seconds later he shook the woollen blanket off his back. It dropped and covered the two bronze plates. They were soon flying towards the barracks at the far end of the camp. Each of the long buildings had a covered veranda where, earlier, the soldiers had been cooking their breakfast. They landed and touched foreheads once more. Jack was glad he'd got used to the strange sensation as his body transformed. After the blinding flash he stood naked again. Thankfully no one was about. Camelin looked longingly at the veranda.

'While you're inside I might just go and check out that covered area to see if there's anything left to eat.'

Jack couldn't believe Camelin was willing to risk being seen for the sake of a few scraps of bacon which might, or might not, have been left.

'Oh Camelin, I need you to keep a watch and warn me if anyone comes!'

'I can do that from the veranda. if I see anything I'll do the raven-owl call.'

'Well just be careful, don't go getting caught,' Jack whispered before he dashed over to the door.

He stepped inside a neat, tidy room with rows of identical beds. He took a thin sheet off the first one and wrapped it around himself. There didn't seem to be many places to look apart from the floor, which had been swept clean. At the far end of the room was another door; Jack made his way over to it. He cautiously pushed it open a fraction and peeped through the crack. It was full of equipment. There were helmets, shields, spears, several different kinds of armour, long and short swords, everything you could possibly need if you were a soldier in the Roman army. Jack wished he could have tried the helmets and armour on but there wasn't time.

Underneath one of the windows he saw the soldiers' packs. This was where he needed to search. Unfortunately they all looked the same now the equipment had been put away. The first three Jack looked in didn't have anything other than rations inside. The sheet was getting in his way and kept slipping down his arms. He'd seen a pile of red tunics on a table and swapped the sheet for one of these. The tunic came down to his ankles but it was better than the sheet.

The next pack he searched was the one he was looking for. He nearly cried out with joy when he saw the missing cauldron plate. It was much heavier and thicker than the ones from the Prefect's office. Camelin was right, it was tarnished and quite dirty. Embossed into the middle was an oak tree and there were holes down each side. He'd not be able to transform again while he had the plate; it would be far too heavy for him to lift in his beak. He'd have to stay like this and hope he wasn't seen as he made his way back through the camp to the Prefect's office.

Camelin was waiting by the door. Jack could see his beak was shiny with grease and presumed he'd rooted around in at least one of the frying pans.

'Is this it?'

'That's the one,' Camelin croaked and hopped around Jack to show how pleased he was.

'We'd better get back to the Prefect's office so we can see when he goes out again,' said Jack impatiently. 'The sooner I can get back in there the better.'

'That tunic's a bit bright.'

'I know, but if I keep in the shadows I should be alright. I'll swap it for the brown blanket when we get back to the offices.'

Camelin flew ahead to see if anyone was around. Jack followed as best he could, keeping close to the buildings to avoid being seen. At the same time he tried to pick out a route that didn't involve stepping on the gravel. He was almost in the centre of the camp when something sharp prodded him in the back. He stopped and turned around. A soldier with a drawn sword shouted at him. Jack couldn't understand what he said. Two more soldiers appeared. There was nothing else Jack could do but stand very still. It wasn't long before Maximus came hurrying around the corner accompanied by two guards.

Maximus pointed and shouted loudly; Jack didn't move. He realised the danger he was in. He'd stolen the tunic and the plate was in his hand. He'd not had time to do anything else with it. He couldn't run and escape. There was a sword pointing at his chest and soldiers were appearing from everywhere; he was completely surrounded. The two guards next to Maximus each grabbed one of Jack's arms, held him firmly and suspended him above the ground. He kicked out with his swinging legs but to no avail. The guards followed Maximus with their captive.

Once they were outside the Camp Prefect's office Maximus snatched the plate from Jack and examined it closely. He shouted more orders to the soldiers before disappearing into his office.

The soldiers laughed as Jack struggled again. He wondered if Camelin could see or hear what was happening. Should he call out? Would the soldiers understand him if he spoke? He decided he ought to warn Camelin and summoned up his loudest voice.

'Fly!' he yelled. 'I'm caught!'

The soldiers laughed even harder but Jack felt happier when he saw Camelin disappear over the wall into a nearby tree. He'd heard the warning.

Maximus strode out of his office and the soldiers immediately fell silent. He began shouting angrily again and looked intently at Jack as if waiting for an answer.

'I don't understand,' Jack said and shook his head.

Maximus threw his arms in the air and spoke gruffly to the soldiers. Jack knew he was in a lot of trouble. The Camp Prefect looked furious. Jack was taken around the back of the offices into a quadrangle. Another soldier appeared with a set of leg irons and he was pushed to the ground and shackled to a post. His arms and body ached from the rough treatment. He pulled at the irons. The bands weren't tight but there was no way he'd be able to wriggle his feet free. Even if he did escape would be impossible. One of the soldiers had remained in the quadrangle standing guard.

The sun beat down on Jack's head. There wasn't any shade and the cobbles were hot and uncomfortable to sit on. Luckily the tunic was big enough to pull over his head and gave him some protection from the sun. He had no idea what to do next. He could hear the whole camp being searched. What would happen when the soldiers found what they were looking for? Somehow Jack didn't think Maximus was going to release him. What would Nora tell his Dad and Grandad if he never got home again? He tried to put these thoughts out of his head but there wasn't much else to think about, until he wanted a drink. By now the sun was directly overhead and all Jack could think about was a glass of cool water. He racked his brain to remember any Latin words that might help him. Then it struck him, *aqua* meant water. He shouted over to the guard.

'Aqua, please.'

The guard completely ignored him. If they weren't going to give him any food or water he was probably going to suffer the same fate as Camelin.

Jack's throat was dry. It was pointless shouting to the guard again; he'd just be wasting his breath. The heat from the sun was making him sleepy but the noise around the fort, as the soldiers continued their search, made it impossible to sleep. A group of four soldiers entered the quadrangle with drawn swords. Jack gasped. He thought they'd come for him but they hurried past and searched the undergrowth by the buildings.

Jack was trying to be brave but fear of the unknown was getting the better of him. He wondered if Camelin had gone back through the window in time; he didn't want to be stranded in the past. To have come this far and fail at the first hurdle was almost too much for Jack to contemplate. He felt he'd let everyone down. He wished he could tell Camelin how sorry he was.

The search moved on.

Once the other soldiers had gone the guard moved into the shade and leaned against the wall. It was then that something hit Jack on the head. Not anything hard this time, something light, which seemed to have come from a great height. There by his feet was a stick. He poked his head out of the tunic and looked around.

'Psssst,' came a familiar voice from the tiled roof of the building opposite to where Jack was sitting.

Jack was so pleased to see Camelin he almost shouted his name out loud.

'What's happening?' he whispered back. 'I can't understand what they're saying.'

'They're looking for your clothes! Maximus has got Drusus in his office now demanding to know why he didn't bring him all three plates.'

'What did he say?'

'He said the oak tree was his family insignia and since

the plates were worthless he thought he'd keep it, but the good news is that all three plates are in one place now.'

'What's going to happen to me?'

'You're safe until tomorrow. Maximus told the guard you've got to stay out here without food or water until the morning, but don't worry. We've got a plan. I'll get you out of here at dusk.'

The guard stirred. When Jack looked back at the roof Camelin was gone. He pulled the tunic back over his head again. He wondered what Camelin had meant when he'd said *we've got a plan*. He'd no idea how long it was until dusk but Camelin had given him hope. All he had to do was sit it out until the sun went down. He closed his eyes; it might be a long wait.

Two soldiers shook Jack awake. One lifted him to his feet, the other undid the leg irons. He was grabbed once more underneath each arm and marched towards the Camp Prefect's office.

As soon as Jack entered the room he saw the three cauldron plates laid out on the table. Drusus stood to attention in front of Maximus with a fixed expression. Jack assumed from the look on the Prefect's face that he was still annoyed. Maximus banged his fist on the table making the plates rattle. He pointed at the plates and shouted at Jack. Each time he asked Jack a question he thumped the desk. Maximus picked up the plate embossed with the oak tree and held it in front of Jack's face. Jack thought he knew what he was being asked but had no way of answering. He didn't say a word. His silence seemed to annoy Maximus even more. The two guards restraining Jack were given more orders. Maximus was still shouting as Jack was marched out of the room and returned to the quadrangle where he was shackled again.

As the light began to fade the guard came over and checked Jack's irons. Two guards arrived in the quadrangle. The soldier who'd been on duty spoke briefly with them, then left. The night guard had obviously arrived. Jack could smell food and hear the sound of cooking; everyone in the camp must be sitting down to eat. He was very thirsty and he hoped Camelin wouldn't be long. Jack watched the rooftops as the sky darkened. The guards were laughing and chatting. Jack thought they were playing a game but by now it was hard to see across to the other side of the quadrangle.

Camelin appeared from around the corner of the office building. He covered the distance between Jack and the wall in a few hops.

'I'm numb all over,' Jack told him.

'No time to talk. Come on, let's get you out of those irons.'

Jack bent over and touched Camelin's forehead. There was a blinding flash, which lit up the whole quadrangle.

'Come on, we've got to get out of here,' urged Camelin. 'Now, before they come over.'

Jack looked at the soldiers. They were rubbing their eyes. He tried to take off but his body wouldn't respond. The soldiers were on their feet. He hopped to the end of the building; Camelin followed looking concerned.

'I can't fly! I've got cramp in my muscles from sitting on the cobbles so long.'

They hid behind three large barrels and listened to the soldiers arguing about what could have caused such a bright light.

'It's Fulgora, Goddess of lightning. She's angry. It's

always a bad omen to have lightning and no rain.'

'That was sorcery, nothing to do with Fulgora, but I agree it's a bad omen. Sorcery, you mark my words.'

They were too busy trying to decide who was right to notice Jack had gone.

'I need water,' croaked Jack. His throat was so parched he could hardly speak.

'Do you think you can fly now?'

'I think so.'

'Follow me. I've got supper waiting and plenty to drink too.'

Together they flew across the rooftops and out over the wall. Jack's body ached. He felt weak and faint.

'Have we got far to go?'

'No, over here,' replied Camelin as he began to descend.

Jack followed. They landed behind one of the large round houses on the outskirts of the fortress. Jack could hear faint clucking sounds coming from a coop and smelt cooking coming from inside the house. His stomach growled.

'Over here,' croaked Camelin.

Jack followed him over to a pen which smelt strongly of pig. There by the fence were two troughs, one full of water and the other food. Jack was so thirsty he hopped onto the top of the trough and was about to scoop up a beakful of muddy water.

'Not there!' Camelin cried. 'Over here.'

Much to Jack's relief he saw a bucket of fresh water. He drank his fill then drank some more.

'I thought I was going to die of thirst,' he gasped.

'When we've eaten I'll tell you about our plan.'

'I'm starving,' said Jack as his empty stomach growled again.

This time Camelin led him back to the trough.

'Pigswill!' exclaimed Jack.

'It's all we've got, unless you want to go digging for worms!'

THAT WHICH WAS LOST

Jack closed his eyes before plunging his beak into the trough of swill. He knew he had to eat.

'It's not that bad,' said Camelin when he saw Jack pulling his face.

'It's not that good either.'

'When you've finished I'll tell you what we've decided to do.'

'Who's we?'

'Me and Medric.'

'Medric?'

'Didn't I tell you? We've got some inside help.'

'You didn't.'

'Well, you know Gerda's mate who went missing?'

'Yes, but what's that got to do with us getting the cauldron plates back?'

'Gerda's mate's here.'

'Here!'

'Soldiers captured him and brought him to Maximus a few weeks before they started burning the groves. They'd probably have eaten him but Maximus wanted him to guard the shrine.'

'I don't understand. Why would Maximus need a goose as a guard when he's got a fort full of soldiers?'

'A goose is special; it honks loudly if it's disturbed. Nora once told me that a flock of geese saved Rome from being attacked. Medric used to be Nora's watchgoose before the soldiers took him. That's why Gerda does it now.'

'I still don't see how it helps us.'

'Maximus has his own reasons for not using soldiers to guard the shrine; it's where he keeps his stash. Only Medric knows where it is and he's not going to raise the alarm when we're inside the shrine.'

'That's great but it's the cauldron plates we need, not a stash of gold.'

'I'm coming to that but you keep interrupting me. While you were in the quadrangle I went back on the office roof so I could find out what was happening.

That's when I heard what Drusus had to say. Maximus wasn't pleased; he gave him a double guard duty for keeping the plate. When Drusus left it all went quiet and I had to drop down onto one of those barrels so I could see inside the window. Maximus took the basket with all the metal things inside and tipped them out. Then he sorted everything into piles. There were brooch pins, daggers and some more plates in there. He laid all the plates out on the table, matched our three together and tossed the rest back in the basket.'

'Is that when he sent for me again?'

'Yes, but I didn't know you spoke Latin?'

'I don't.'

'Well the guard told Maximus you'd asked for water.'

'I did. I know a few Latin words but I can't speak it and I couldn't understand what Maximus was saying.'

'Well, Maximus said that a night without food or water should improve your memory since he knew you could understand his questions and chose not to answer.'

'Thanks for getting me out of there. I dread to think what he'd have done in the morning.'

'When you'd gone he spoke to centurion Titus Antonius again. He asked him about the plates and about me. Maximus thinks they must be really important if someone sent a thief into the camp to steal them. He told Titus Antonius he'd keep them safe until he found out who you were, how you got into the fort without being seen and why you stole the plate.'

'That means we'll never get them back.'

'Naw, just the opposite.'

'I don't understand.'

'Guess where he's put them?'

'I've no idea.'

'In the shrine! He's got a hidey-hole and Medric knows where it is. He saw Maximus put something large and heavy into it. Now that we know where the plates are the rest's going to be easy.'

Camelin started hopping around. He looked disappointed when Jack didn't join in.

'What's the matter?'

Jack sighed.

'I'm worried what might happen if I get caught again. They'll search the whole camp once they find I'm missing.'

'Come on then. If we go back now we can be on our way home before they miss you.'

They flew back to the roof of the Camp Prefect's office. Camelin looked down into the shrine area. Before he could call Medric they both heard one of the guards from the quadrangle cry out. They looked to see Titus Antonius running into the quadrangle. It was Drusus who stood next to the post.

'The prisoner has gone!'

'Escaped?' asked Titus Antonius.

'Gone,' replied Drusus in disbelief. 'The irons and tunic are still here but he's not.'

'Sorcery, I said it was sorcery!' the other soldier next to Titus Antonius cried. 'We must report this to the Camp Prefect at once.'

'I'll make the report. Make sure nothing is disturbed. Maximus needs to see this for himself or we'll get the blame,' Titus Antonius informed them, but before he had chance to leave the quadrangle the silence of the night was shattered. The horn sounded five times from the top of the northern gatehouse.

There was a stir of excitement throughout the camp.

'A rider approaching,' Titus Antonius announced. 'I must go and see what's happening at the gate first before I go to the Prefect and report the prisoner's escape. You two must stand guard here until I return.'

Drusus stood a little way from the post after the centurion left the quadrangle. He didn't look happy.

'It must be something important,' whispered Camelin.

They listened intently. It wasn't long before they heard hoof beats pounding down the main street. The rider pulled the horse up outside the offices, jumped off and banged loudly on the Camp Prefect's door.

'An urgent message for Quintus Flavius Maximus from the Commander of the Fourteenth Legion,' the soldier shouted. When he didn't get an answer he banged even louder on the door.

In the distance they could hear Titus Antonius shouting orders. The commotion from the fort continued.

'Gaius Rufus Octavian,' the rider announced and saluted when Maximus eventually opened the door. 'I have a message for you from our commander. Mona is taken, the Druids are slain, their groves destroyed.'

Camelin and Jack exchanged looks. They were both aware from history what had happened but to hear the news, delivered like this, was quite a shock.

'Excellent,' Maximus said joyfully.

'I also have an urgent order from the Commander,' continued Octavian. 'We have been recalled to march to Londinium as soon as possible. Boudicca, Queen of the Iceni, has raised an army. Camulodunum has been destroyed.'

'You'd better come inside and tell me all you know.'

The soldier tethered his horse to the nearest post and went inside with Maximus.

'That's not good news for Medric,' explained Camelin. 'If the legion is moving out they'll kill and eat him before they go.'

'We'd better warn him.'

'It won't be necessary. I've already told him we'll help him escape, you know, in return for helping us. As soon as we're in the shrine and you've transformed open the gate. Before he goes he'll show you where Maximus hid the plates.

'Couldn't he have flown out of there before?'

'Medric's a big bird. He needs a long run up to take off and gain height. There just isn't room to do that in the shrine. He needs the main street. He'll try and escape once you've let him out.'

'What if they see him?'

'They'll shoot him. He's lucky there's no moon tonight. Lets hope they'll all be busy once the news about marching out spreads.'

'The soldier mentioned Camulodunum. Was that Colchester?' Jack asked.

'It was. Boudicca's army destroyed London and St Albans too. They were heading this way before they finally stopped her. Her tribe, the Iceni, really put the wind up the Romans you know.'

'Do you think it's safe to go down into the shrine? I'd like to get this over with as quickly as we can.'

'You're right. Medric will be waiting for us.'

'Once I've got the plates I can throw them in the spring can't I?'

'That's the plan,' croaked Camelin. 'Ready?'

Jack nodded, but as they were about to fly off the roof they heard louder knocking on the Camp Prefect's door.

'It's Titus Antonius!' exclaimed Camelin. 'It won't be long before Maximus knows you've escaped.'

'Not now centurion,' Maximus shouted when he finally opened the door.

'I wouldn't have disturbed you if it wasn't important,' the centurion replied.

'Be quick,' snapped Maximus.

'The prisoner has disappeared.'

'Disappeared! How?'

'I don't know Prefect. The tunic is empty and the leg irons are still closed.'

Maximus, still dressed in full armour with his

sword and dagger, pushed past Titus Antonius and marched around the corner towards the quadrangle.

'Search the camp,' he ordered. 'He has to be here somewhere.'

'It's now or never,' said Camelin.

They flew down into the shrine. A large white goose, bigger than Gerda, waddled over to them.

'Shield your eyes,' warned Camelin.

Medric stood still and obediently put his head under his wing. The flash of light momentarily lit up the whole courtyard. Jack went straight over to the tall gate and lifted up the wooden bar. He opened it enough for Medric to make his escape.

'He says if you go behind the shrine and look near the ground there's a loose stone. Behind the stone is a hole. Maximus keeps all his valuables in there, wrapped in a cloth. Medric says he's put the cauldron plates in there with his gold.'

Jack made his way around the shrine as he'd been instructed. He found the loose stone, pulled it out and put his hand inside the hole.

'I've got them!' exclaimed Jack triumphantly as he pulled the plates out.

He started to make his way around the shrine so he could throw the plates in the water when Maximus stepped out in front of him.

'Camelin!' Jack yelled as he dodged past Maximus who'd immediately begun shouting. 'What's he saying?'

'He says he's got you this time and now he's going to deal with you himself once he gets his hands on you,' Camelin explained. 'Don't let him catch you. He says he's going to kill you.'

The second voice distracted Maximus. He looked around to see who'd spoken. Jack ran around the back of the shrine again.

'The gate's open. Make a run for it,' yelled Camelin. 'We can throw the plates in the river when we get outside the fort.'

Jack knew if he left the safety of the shrine he'd never make it out of the camp. He had to get back around to the front of the shrine; he had to throw the plates into the water. Maximus was quicker than Jack anticipated. As he turned Jack felt a strong hand grab the back of his neck. He heard Maximus draw his sword. The grip on Jack's neck tightened. Maximus forced Jack onto his knees before the shrine. He pushed his head into the water. Jack struggled. He felt the water surge up his nose. He struggled again and managed to raise his head. Jack saw Camelin swooping towards the

Prefect. Once more Maximus thrust Jack's head back under the water. Then he heard Maximus cry out in pain; Camelin must have used his claws but Maximus didn't release his grip. Jack had to do something quick or it would be too late.

'Jennet!' he shouted as loudly as he could into the water with the last of his breath.

Seconds later Jack felt the water begin to bubble. A long-armed, green-skinned nymph appeared and rose past Jack's eyes, her face shrouded in a tangle of dark green hair. Maximus must have seen her too. He let go of Jack's neck and leapt back from the water's edge. Jack gasped for breath. He could see the look of horror on the Prefect's face as he wiped the water from his eyes. Maximus opened his mouth but not a sound came out. Jack's whole body was shaking. He coughed and spluttered as he tried to clear the water from his lungs. Maximus seemed unable to move. Jack quickly thrust the plates into Jennet's outstretched hand. For a moment everything went quiet. Then the nymph screeched loudly and dropped the plates into the water. She stretched out her long arms and grabbed Maximus and pulled him into the spring. Once his legs disappeared the whole spring erupted in a mass of bubbles.

'Quick!' said Camelin. 'Let's get out of here.'

Medric burst out of the doorway and started to run towards to the end of the main street. Once he was there the street would be long enough for him to take off and clear the wall. Jack and Camelin touched foreheads, the light once again lighting up the whole shrine. As they flew up onto the roof they saw bubbles rising again from the spring. There was another loud screech as Maximus was ejected from the water. He landed with a thud on the ground, spluttering and coughing, wearing only his tunic. His magnificent armour and weapons were gone. He'd been stripped of every shiny bit of metal he possessed. Maximus grabbed the package that contained his treasure and shook it into the spring. All his golden torcs, brooches and belts clattered into the water.

'Take it!' he screamed. 'Take it all Appias, mighty Goddess of the spring, and leave me alone.'

Jack could see that Maximus was shaking, though he didn't know if was from fear or anger. He finally spun around and burst out of the open gate.

'Guards!' he screamed as he left the shrine. 'The prisoner's escaped. Find him. He was here just now. He can't be far away, and kill that goose, it's out there somewhere, kill the boy, kill anything that's flying, I've been attacked.'

Soldiers came running from all directions. As Jack and Camelin flew away they could see the soldier's shocked expressions as they came to a halt in front of Maximus dressed only in his dripping wet tunic. They could still hear Maximus ordering the archers to shoot as they flew out of the camp. Medric was still only half way down the main street, running as fast as he could to get airborne.

'Go on, go on!' Jack shouted as Medric began to gain height.

The archers were ready with their bows. They loosed a volley of arrows as he laboured to clear the wall.

'Did he make it?' asked Jack.

'I don't know. I can't see him,' Camelin replied. 'Come on, head for the window. That was too close for comfort.'

As they flew towards Glasruhen they kept scanning the sky for Medric.

'I tried to make Maximus let go,' explained Camelin, 'but he wouldn't, even though I had my claws in his neck and Medric bit his leg.'

'It's OK. Really. It's over now and the plates are safe.'

'Did you see what Jennet did to the Prefect?' chuckled Camelin.

'It was no more than he deserved.'

'How much are we going to tell Elan and Nora when we get back?'

'We ought to tell them everything.'

'Even about Maximus trying to drown you!' exclaimed Camelin.

'If we don't tell them they're bound to find out from Jennet anyway.'

As Glasruhen hill came into sight Jack could see the glow from the smouldering remains of the Grove. The smell of burnt wood hung heavily in the air. 'Do you think Medric's alright?' Jack asked.

'I don't know. I hope so,' Camelin replied. 'It won't be long now. Are you ready to fly back through the window?'

'Ready,' replied Jack.

They circled around the hill, separated and took up their positions above each gateway at the opposite ends of the hill fort.

'Ready?' Camelin shouted.

'Let's fly,' Jack shouted back.

Just as they'd practiced time and time again they started their ascent, increased their speed as they flew towards the window and at the last minute they turned their bodies and shot past each other. There was a loud crack. Jack felt his body jolt; something heavy knocked him into a spin. He lost control and flapped his wings rapidly as he fought to regain his balance. His body went hurtling through the air. He tried to cry out but he couldn't find his voice. The jolt had winded him. Jack hit the ground hard as he crash landed.

'So sorry, so sorry,' cackled Medric as he waddled quickly over to where Jack lay. 'Are you alright?'

Jack felt shaken and very surprised to see Medric.

'You made it!' he exclaimed.

'Is anything broken?' Medric fussed. 'I'm so sorry I flew into you.'

'I think I'm OK, but where's Camelin? Did we come through the window?'

'There's no window here,' cackled Medric. 'We're at the top of the hill fort.'

Jack's heart sank; the collision must have knocked them off course. They must have missed the window in time. They'd have to try again.

'Camelin,' he called.

'Jack,' a familiar voice replied, 'Where are you? Are you alright?'

'Elan!' Jack exclaimed. 'I'm over here. Are we home, are we really home?'

'You're home,' she replied.

'We did it, we did it,' croaked Camelin triumphantly as he landed on Nora's shoulder. 'We found the plates and Jack got them into the spring; now all we have to do is get them back from Jennet. We'll be able to remake the cauldron, reopen the portal and go back into Annwn.'

'All in good time,' said Nora as she smiled at them both. 'Thank goodness you're home safe and sound.'

Medric looked confused.

'Were you expecting us?' he asked.

'I was expecting two ravens but a goose is a bonus! You've been gone rather a long time you know.'

They sat on top of Glasruhen Hill and watched the sun rise. Nora explained to Medric how long he'd been gone and what had happened since he'd been captured.

'Is Gerda still with you?' he asked.

'Oh yes,' replied Nora.

'Will she remember me?' he whispered.

'She never gave up hope of seeing you again. She's going to be a very happy goose when she gets up this morning and finds you're home.'

'We were so worried about you,' Elan said to Jack. 'We thought you'd only be gone for a few seconds but you've been gone for hours.'

'Are we ready to go home now?' asked Nora.

'For breakfast?' Jack and Camelin said together.

'For breakfast,' she confirmed. 'Then you can tell us everything that happened.'

'It was alright wasn't it?' asked Elan. 'Nothing bad happened to either of you?'

Jack and Camelin both laughed.

'We had to eat pigswill,' replied Jack. 'I think that was probably the worst thing.'

As they flew back to Ewell House Camelin suddenly did a triple loop the loop and started to laugh.

'You did it, Jack! You really did it; everything's going to be alright now. I knew you were *The One* right from the beginning.'

Jack laughed too. Neither of them had believed he could possibly be *The One* but he was glad he was. They'd had the most incredible adventure. He smiled as he remembered the last line of the prophecy:

That which was lost is found again.

The cauldron could be made again now that the plates were in the safe keeping of the Water Nymphs. He knew Nora and Elan would be upset when they learned how dangerous their journey into the past had been, but none of that mattered now they were home safe. He ought to be tired, but instead he felt elated. He knew he was far too excited to sleep. He couldn't wait to see everyone again, especially Orin.

Jack saw the trees rustle their leaves. A message was on its way to Arrana. Once the Dryads woke her she'd know they'd been successful. Jack wondered if he'd be allowed to go into Annwn and collect the Hamadryad acorns. It was too late to help the Gnori in Newton Gill but Glasruhen Forest was going to be saved. There'd be a new Hamadryad and Arrana would be able to pass on her knowledge.

He wondered how many leaves Nora would need from the Crochan tree to make the elixir? Did it mean she'd live forever once the elixir had been made again? Elan promised he'd be able to see her as she really was once she'd renewed her strength in Annwn. Did she need to drink the elixir too? She'd said she was one of the Fair Folk; he couldn't wait to see her. He knew she wasn't going to look like Jennet but he hoped she wasn't going to be as tall as Arrana. Maybe she'd be like one of the statues in Nora's garden.

Camelin swooped past Jack and interrupted his thoughts.

'Race you,' he croaked loudly.

They flew together at speed swerving and weaving through the trees. Jack's eyes filled with tears. Was it the wind in his face, relief to be home or the happiness he felt as he flew with Camelin towards Ewell House? He wasn't sure. His life changed the day the golden acorn bounced off his head. It would never be the same again, but he knew he wouldn't want it any other way.

ACKNOWLEDGEMENTS

I'd like to thank
Dad, Molly and Geoffrey for sharing the
journey, their editorial skills, help
and encouragement,
Ron for his honesty, support and faith in me,
Colin for his tutorage
and constructive criticism,
Tom, Jess, Judy, Lin and Joan, who kindly
read the first draft, and Bill, for reading the
completed book to his grandchildren,
Daniel and Jack.